"I'm sure as hell not the father of that baby."

Tyler's voice was cold and level. "Listen, Ruth, I never touched Jodie Hiltz. I'd hardly know the girl if I saw her on the street."

Ruth glanced up at him, aching to believe him. But Jodie's words were carved into her memory: *"He's so handsome without his clothes...he has a birthmark on his left hip...shaped like a map of Texas...."*

Ruth moaned softly. She remembered the sweet pleasure of the previous night when she and Tyler had made love, laughed and teased.

"Show me Amarillo," he'd whispered.

Ruth forced herself back to the present. She looked hopelessly at Tyler. "Jodie wasn't lying. Please take me home. I have to start packing."

Special thanks and acknowledgment to Margot Dalton for her contribution to the Crystal Creek series.

Special thanks and acknowledgment to Sutton Press Inc. for its contribution to the concept for the Crystal Creek series.

Published April 1993

ISBN 0-373-82514-5

COWBOYS AND CABERNET

Cowboys and Cabernet

Margot Dalton

Harlequin Books

TORONTO • NEW YORK • LONDON
AMSTERDAM • PARIS • SYDNEY • HAMBURG
STOCKHOLM • ATHENS • TOKYO • MILAN
MADRID • WARSAW • BUDAPEST • AUCKLAND

Dear Reader,

Welcome to Crystal Creek! In the heart of Texas Hill Country, the McKinneys have been ranching, living and loving for generations, but the future promises changes none of these good folks could ever imagine!

Crystal Creek itself is the product of many imaginations, but the stories began to take shape when some of your favorite authors— Barbara Kaye, Margot Dalton, Bethany Campbell, Cara West, Kathy Clark and Sharon Brondos—all got together with me just outside of Austin to explore the Hill Country, and to dream up the kinds of romances such a setting would provide. For several days, we roamed the countryside, where generous Texans opened their historic homes to us, and gave us insights into their lives. We ate barbecue, we visited an ostrich farm and we mapped out our plans to give you the linked stories you love, with a true Texas flavor and all the elements you've come to expect in your romance reading: compelling, contemporary characters caught in conflicts that reflect today's dilemmas.

Margot Dalton's fascination with the burgeoning Texas wine industry finds expression in this captivating tale of Tyler McKinney, the eldest McKinney offspring, and Ruth Holden, a Californian with a string of impressive credentials in wine making to her name, and a measured, analytical, thoughtful approach to growing grapes that puts our poor frustrated cowboy right off his feed!

And next month, watch for *Amarillo by Morning,* the story of Cal, Tyler's younger brother. An entrepreneurial young Texas bootmaker in search of an endorsement gets way more than she bargains for when she is bombarded by the formidable charms of rodeo rider Cal McKinney....

C'mon down to Crystal Creek—home of sultry Texas drawls, smooth Texas charm and tall, sexy Texans!

Marsha Zinberg
Coordinator, Crystal Creek

A Note from the Author

When Harlequin editors first approached me about writing these books, I was really nervous. I'd never even been to Texas…how could I write books about the place? But when my husband and I finally traveled to Austin for a research trip, I was amazed and delighted to find that I felt right at home. The countryside is truly big and beautiful—just like the hearts of the people. And Texas ranchers are every bit as colorful, rugged and lovable as their counterparts on the Canadian prairies where I grew up. They have the same hospitality and generosity of spirit, and that deep love for the land and its traditions that unites farmers and ranchers all over the world.

Now, when anybody mentions the place, I just smile and say, "Yeah, I love Texas. I'm even learning to speak the language."

Margot Dalton

Cast of Characters

AT THE DOUBLE C RANCH

John Travis (J.T.) McKinney	Rancher, owner of the Double C, his family's ranch. A man who knows his own mind.
Cynthia Page McKinney	J.T.'s wife. An ex-Bostonian bank executive learning to do things the Texas way.
Tyler McKinney	J.T.'s eldest son, a graduate of Rice University. Now he wants to grow grapes in his daddy's pasture.
Cal McKinney	J.T.'s second son, an irresistible and irrepressible rodeo cowboy.
Lynn McKinney	J.T.'s only daughter. She bucks the trend by raising Thoroughbreds in quarterhorse country.
Hank Travis	J.T.'s ancient grandfather. Old Hank has seen and done it all.
Ruth Holden	Californian vintner, daughter of Dan Holden, J.T.'s old army buddy. Ruth is visiting the Double C to help Tyler plan his vineyard.
Lettie Mae Reese	Cook. } Together they know all
Virginia Parks	Housekeeper. the household secrets.
Ken Slattery	Foreman at the Double C.

AT THE CIRCLE T RANCH

Carolyn Randolph Townsend	J.T.'s sister-in-law and neighbor.
Beverly Townsend	Carolyn's daughter and a former Miss Texas.
Lori Porter	Carolyn's cousin. Lori lives at the Circle T and keeps the ranch accounts.

AT THE LONGHORN

Dottie Jones	Owner of the Longhorn Motel and Coffee Shop.
Nora Jones	Dottie's son's ex-wife.
Martin Avery	Mayor of Crystal Creek.
Bubba and Mary Gibson	Old friends of J.T.'s.
Nate Purdy	The McKinneys' family physician.
Vernon Trent	Real-estate agent.
Wayne Jackson	Sheriff.
Jodie Hiltz	Teenage part-timer at the pharmacy. She harbors a secret that will scandalize the town.

CHAPTER ONE

THE WINTER CLOUDS rolled into California's Napa
Valley during January, dark and heavy, brooding on
the craggy hilltops and drowning the sheltered valley
in mist and rain. The fields that had so recently been
alive with color and motion now lay dormant, their
acres and acres of grapevines resting neat and bare in
long trellised rows, stripped of leaves and fruit,
awaiting the new growing season.

By late afternoon the light thinned and faded, then
slipped away behind piled masses of clouds. Night fell
early, a dank smothering blackness that rolled across
the hills in a solid ominous mass, blocking the moon
and stars.

Don Holden moved restlessly across his dining room
and pulled the drapes aside, peering out into the
darkness. He looked at his watch and frowned, then
glanced through the rain-splattered window again, his
face drawn with concern.

He was a slender, handsome man in his midfifties
with dark graying hair, mild brown eyes and a carefully trimmed beard. He wore casual brown corduroy
slacks, a soft flannel shirt and a tan cardigan with

suede elbow patches, and looked like a college professor or a respected artist or sculptor.

In actual fact, though, Don Holden was a businessman, a self-made entrepreneur with one of the most successful privately owned vineyards and wineries in the Napa Valley. He was firm in business dealings, incisive, knowledgeable and tough, well-known throughout the region for his rugged independence and his uncanny instincts for the wine-making business.

But tonight, in the privacy of his own dining room, Don Holden presented a somewhat less confident demeanor than his business colleagues were accustomed to seeing. In fact, the man's expression was positively timid when he turned away from the window and glanced through the wide Spanish archway leading to the kitchen, then peered anxiously out again into the rainy darkness.

Somewhere nearby a door opened suddenly, admitting a gust of damp air and a cool breath of freshness. Don's shoulders sagged with relief and he crossed the room quickly, smiling at the damp person who stood dripping in the entrance hall.

The newcomer stripped off a hooded oilskin cape to reveal a slim body in high rubber boots, jeans, denim jacket and faded Oakland A's baseball cap.

"For God's sake, get those muddy boots off, girl," Don said, trying to make his voice gruff, though he couldn't quite hide the fond smile that tugged at his lips beneath his neat beard. "Look at you. You're dripping all over the place."

His daughter pulled off the boots and set them casually on a rubber tray beside the door, then removed her baseball cap to reveal a head of tumbled short brown hair and a face of gamine prettiness. Flushed with cold, dressed in casual clothes, Ruth Holden looked more like a thirteen-year-old than a woman of almost thirty, Don told himself. Her skin was creamy and perfect, just a trace of summer tan remaining, and her eyes were golden brown, warm with affection as she smiled at her father.

"Oh, quit fussing," Ruth said mildly. "Here I am slaving away all day in the wet and cold, and do I get any appreciation for it? Not a bit."

"You love it," Don said, unmoved, leaning in the doorway and watching her. "You'd rather spend the day out there pruning and taking cuttings than doing anything else in the world. You know you're just doing it for pure enjoyment. It's still too early for pruning."

Ruth chuckled and pulled off her denim jacket to reveal a blue plaid shirt buttoned warmly over a white turtleneck. "How come you're so cranky, Dad?" she asked mildly. "You're growling just like an old bear."

Don rolled his eyes and threw a brief eloquent glance over his shoulder, then held out his watch.

Ruth peered at the time and gasped. She covered her mouth with a slim, dirt-smeared hand and gazed at the man in the doorway, her eyes wide and startled.

"Oh, God, I'm sorry," she murmured contritely. "I honestly had no idea it was getting so late. Is she really mad?" Ruth lowered her voice, glancing down the hallway just as her father had moments before.

Don nodded. "The atmosphere is getting quite tense," he reported solemnly.

"Oh, my. I'll just run real quick and wash." Ruth held up her cold muddy hands for his inspection. "If she comes in, tell her I'll be back in a flash."

"Don't dawdle, then."

Ruth nodded and hurried off down the hallway while Don moved back into the dining room, grinning privately.

"Well, is she *finally* home?"

Don sobered hastily and turned to nod at the heavy gray-haired woman who stood in the archway glaring at him. "Yes, Mrs. Ward. She just came in. She's washing up."

"Well, about *time*, I must say. Some people have no consideration at all for some *other* poor people who have to work all day in the kitchen, trying to make a decent meal that's practically burned to a crisp now because somebody *else* decides it's just not *important* to come to meals on time."

Mrs. Ward stood with hands on hips and feet firmly planted, delivering herself of this heavily emphasized and confusing statement with her steely eyes fixed on her employer's face.

Don nodded again. "I'm sorry, Mrs. Ward. I know it's inconsiderate of us. We'll both try to do better in the future."

There was a charged silence in the room while the big woman lingered angrily in the archway.

"I'm really sorry," Don repeated with a note of pleading in his voice.

The housekeeper continued to glare at him until she was apparently satisfied that he'd groveled sufficiently. Then she gave a curt nod and vanished down the hallway, her silver head glinting under lighted wall sconces, her ample rear churning indignantly beneath dark green polyester slacks.

Ruth edged hesitantly into the room, still in her jeans and plaid shirt, wearing a pair of casual leather moccasins. But her short hair was brushed till it shone, and she'd taken the time to dab on a bit of lipstick.

"Is she mad?" Ruth whispered.

"Of course," Don said matter-of-factly. "She says dinner is burned to a crisp."

"Oh, for goodness' sake. I'm about twenty minutes late, that's all." Ruth glared rebelliously down the hallway at the closed kitchen door. "We really shouldn't let her push us around like this, Dad."

"You're right. We really shouldn't." Don Holden and his daughter glanced at each other, then exchanged identical grins and rueful chuckles as they seated themselves at the gleaming oak table.

Mrs. Ward had been their housekeeper for the past fourteen years, and the Holdens were still just as terrified of her as they'd been at the start. She lived in a cottage a couple of miles down the road, on a tiny mixed farm of uncertain status with a timid, silent little Mexican who might or might not be her husband. Local gossips speculated endlessly about the mysterious couple, and frequently tried to extract information from the Holdens about their housekeeper.

In fact, Ruth and Don Holden had never even progressed to a first-name basis with this intimidating woman, and they had certainly never learned any intimate details of her private life. She arrived at work every morning on a stately old BMW motorcycle, a beautifully maintained 650 Boxer Twin that glistened like fine jewelry in the morning sun. Mrs. Ward rode, solemn and erect, on this startling conveyance, her steel-framed glasses glittering beneath the face shield on her helmet, her knitting and recipe books tucked away in the leather carrier bags.

She shopped carefully for groceries, worked efficiently all day, kept the big house spotless and served meals so varied and delectable that the Holden table was the envy of the valley.

"But," as Ruth was occasionally heard to comment wistfully, "she's not really all that *warm*."

Don smiled, remembering, and watched as Mrs. Ward entered with the Wedgwood soup tureen. She set it down heavily in the center of the table, giving Ruth a glance of pointed disapproval, and lifted the lid to send fragrant clouds of steam wafting around the room.

"Probably it's stone cold and *far* too thick by now,"
Mrs. Ward said with grim emphasis, addressing a spot
somewhere just beyond Ruth's shoulder. "It was *perfect* about a half hour ago."

"But it smells wonderful, Mrs. Ward," Ruth said
humbly. "And it must be hot. Just look at all that
steam rising from it."

Mrs. Ward waved the steam away with a heavy,
reddened hand and marched out of the room, her
shoulders stiff with annoyance.

Ruth glanced after her cautiously, then held out her
bowl for Don to fill with the big china ladle. He
watched his daughter eating the hot soup, his face
troubled as he lifted a silver spoon and dipped into his
own bowl.

Don Holden knew that Ruth had suffered through
the years from the lack of a mother figure in her life.
Don's wife, Thelma, had died when Ruth was just
five, and Don had been so devastated by the loss, and
so absorbed in restoring the tumbledown old winery
and raising his young daughter that he'd never managed to build another serious relationship.

Sometimes he regretted that omission and wished
that he'd provided a woman for Ruth during her
growing up. He'd been wrenched with sympathy, years
ago, when he noticed how his quiet teenage daughter
tried to build a relationship with their forbidding
housekeeper, hanging around in the kitchen while
Mrs. Ward worked, and even on occasion shyly confiding in her. But then as now, Mrs. Ward had been as

full of warmth as a mountain glacier, and just about as inviting.

Don frowned, watching while the housekeeper marched in with two heaped platters of Caesar salad, redolent with garlic and richly studded with croutons and anchovies.

Don looked hungrily at this delicious sight, and found himself, as always, beginning to forgive Mrs. Ward for her bad temper.

"Wonderful. Just wonderful." Don smiled up at her. "What's the main course, Mrs. Ward?"

"It's burned to a crisp," she said coldly. "Dry as old leather."

"Yes, but what is it?"

"Baked salmon stuffed with wild rice, mushrooms and chestnuts," she said over her shoulder as she returned to the kitchen.

Ruth sighed in bliss and dug into her salad with greater intensity.

"Baked salmon," Don repeated thoughtfully when his salad plate was empty. "What do you think, Ruthie? A nice Chardonnay?"

Ruth nodded abstractedly, chewing appreciatively on the last of the anchovies. "Probably," she said at last, swallowing and looking up at her father. "Do we have one up here?"

"Well now, we just might," Don said mysteriously. He got up and hurried over to the big antique sideboard where he took out two wine goblets and a bottle from a lower cabinet.

"Oh, my," Ruth murmured behind him as Mrs. Ward entered with the fish course. The salmon rested in a creamy golden coating of perfect hollandaise, tender and flaky, exquisitely pink, delicately toasted around the edges and oozing a delectable rice filling.

"Ruined," Mrs. Ward announced, her face grim. "Completely ruined."

Ruth and Don both nodded solemnly, watching in respectful silence as the woman swept out of the room. Then they exchanged a glance and burst into laughter that they stifled hastily, casting nervous glances at the hallway.

"Burned to a crisp," Ruth said in a fair imitation of Mrs. Ward's haughty tone.

"Dry as old leather," Don agreed, crossing the room and glancing at the tender pink fish. "Try the Chardonnay," he added, handing his daughter a goblet brimming with clear pale wine.

She accepted it and sipped obediently, then nodded. "That's nice," she said. "Which one is it, Dad?"

Her father looked down at her in disbelief, moving around to seat himself at the opposite end of the table. "Ruthie, I can't believe you don't recognize this."

"Why? Should I?"

"It's our new Chardonnay. The one we've been waiting to sample. Johann said it was ready yesterday, and I thought I'd surprise you with it."

"Oh." Ruth sipped at the wine again, then tried to smile. "Well, I guess we were right, Dad. It's really a lot better than the last one, isn't it?"

Don continued to gaze at the slender young woman, his eyes darkening with concern. "Ruth," he said gently, "is everything all right?"

"What do you mean? Oh, Dad, can you spoon up a little more of that sauce for me? Just there on the edge, please, and some more rice..."

"I mean," Don said, filling her plate carefully, "that you just don't seem like yourself lately. You seem kind of... depressed," he finished awkwardly. "Not my cheerful optimistic girl at all."

Ruth avoided his eyes, concentrating on the plate of food in front of her. "It's probably the weather," she said. "You know how blue I always get in the winter, with all these clouds and rain and no real work to do outside. It just makes me crazy, Dad, waiting and waiting for spring to come so the world can start again."

"I know, but this year things seem different, somehow," Don persisted gently. "Is it something to do with Harlan?"

Ruth's cheeks tinted delicately and she flashed a glance at her father, then looked quickly down at her plate again. "Harlan is no longer part of my life," she said without expression.

"Yes?" Don looked with sudden alertness at his daughter's glossy head. "Since when?"

"Since forever, I guess," Ruth said with a bleak smile. "I mean, that relationship was doomed from the beginning. But it was officially laid to rest last night."

"I see." Don hesitated, sipping the delicious pale liquid. "By whose choice?"

"Oh, mine, absolutely," Ruth said. "Harlan would have been very content to marry me, move us both into a nice house with a three-car garage and have two-point-one children. He says he's ready for... quote... that particular stage in one's life."

"And you're not?"

"Not with *him*," Ruth said helplessly.

"Poor Harlan." Don shook his head, though if the truth were told, he wasn't really all that devastated by this piece of news.

"Dad, he's so *boring*," Ruth said with a hint of desperation creeping into her voice. "I mean, he and his friends are so horribly predictable. They all say the same things, do the same things, buy the same things, and I swear to God they have the very same conversations every time they get together. They talk about their golf games, their stock portfolios and their new cars, and then they sit around and gossip about each other. It's just deadly."

Don nodded, his face carefully noncommittal. "Maybe," he said, setting down the wine goblet and toying with the heavily engraved handle of his butter knife, "you just need a holiday."

"A holiday? Where would I go?"

Don cleared his throat. "Well, how about Texas?"

"*Texas?*" Ruth stared at her father as if he'd suddenly taken leave of his senses. "What would I do in Texas?"

"Well, for instance, you could pay a little visit to the McKinneys, spend some time on the ranch and see how they're—"

"Why would I want to do that?" Ruth interrupted. "I've never even liked the McKinneys all that much. They're your friends, Dad, not mine. And now J.T. has this new little fluff ball of a child bride..."

"She's thirty-five years old," Don said mildly. "And she's an investment banker. Hardly a *fluff ball*, Ruthie."

"Well, I just hope you don't get any ideas," Ruth said, glancing at him severely.

"About what?"

"About following the example of your old friend J.T. McKinney and bringing home some woman my own age to be my stepmother."

"Not likely," Don told her with a wolfish grin. "Bear in mind that you're almost thirty, my girl. I'd want somebody a lot younger and fresher than *that*, if I were to get involved again."

Ruth chuckled and her face lightened a little. "Isn't this salmon just the most wonderful thing you've ever tasted? By the way, Dad," she added, reaching for the salt, "why did you suddenly start thinking about visiting the McKinneys?"

Don cleared his throat again and tried to look casual. "Well," he began, "actually, J.T. called last night, and we talked for quite a while."

"Really? You didn't tell me."

"I didn't see you. It was after midnight when you got home, and then this morning you were already up and out in the yards before I left for Sacramento."

"I just felt so restless," Ruth confessed. "After last night, all I wanted this morning was to get out there and work with the vines for a while."

"Even in the rain?"

"Even in the rain," Ruth said. "Besides, if I waited for it to stop raining," she added bitterly, "I'd be in the house for a month. I'd have to take up knitting or something."

"Knitting is a fine womanly art," Don said cheerfully, toasting her with his wineglass.

Ruth gave him a lopsided grin, her delicate face animated by a flash of the old sparkle. "Yeah, *right,*" she said with amiable contempt, sipping her wine.

Don smiled back at her, encouraged by this welcome change of mood.

"About J.T.," his daughter prompted. "What did you two discuss last night?"

"Well, let me see. Apparently his honeymoon is progressing well, the staff and family are all finally adjusting to his new wife, young Cal is still deeply involved in rodeo, Lynn's shocked the whole countryside by getting interested in Thoroughbreds rather than quarter horses, and Tyler's still thinking about opening a winery on the Double C."

Ruth choked and took a hasty gulp from her water glass, then stared at her father in stunned amazement.

"Your mouth is hanging open," Don told her gently.

Ruth closed her mouth and continued to gaze at him, her clear brown eyes wide with shock.

Don smiled and foraged thoughtfully among the scattered remains of fish and rice on his plate, looking for mushrooms.

"I don't believe it," Ruth said finally. "You're making it up."

"Why wouldn't you believe it? This is not a completely new idea, you know. Texas has been developing a wine-making industry for years."

"Chateau Bubba," she said scornfully.

"Come on, Ruth. You know perfectly well that Texas Cabernet—"

"Has been served at state dinners at the White House," Ruth interrupted wearily. "I know, I know. It just seems so...rotten, somehow."

"Rotten?" Don gave his daughter a curious glance. "Why?"

Ruth shifted restlessly in her chair, gazing out the dark, rain-smeared window. "I don't know," she said at last. "I mean, Texas already has everything, right? They have oil, gas, beef, grain, textiles...every primary industry you can think of. Why do they have to horn in on *our* thing? Wine making is practically all we have out here."

"Ruth, the domestic wine market is expanding at a tremendous, unheard-of rate. There's room for everyone, you know. We're certainly not going to suffer from the competition.''

''I know,'' Ruth said, her eyes dark with rebellion. ''But it still doesn't seem right to me. People shouldn't go into the wine industry just to make a whole lot of money. They should do it because they *love* it.''

''That's a pretty idealistic attitude.''

''Well, how are the McKinneys planning to go about this? Just buy the best equipment, pay all the best people to come work for them and then, every time there's a problem, throw a whole wad of money at it?''

''That seems to be the Texas style, all right,'' Don said with a grin.

''Maybe so, but it sure won't work in this business. You'd better tell your friends that, before they get in too deep.''

''Why don't you tell them?''

''Me?'' Ruth asked blankly.

''That's what I was thinking. Why don't you just fly out there for a little visit, see how advanced their plans are and what advice you can give them about the business?''

''Did J.T. ask for me to come?''

Don hesitated, recalling his old friend's troubled voice on the phone. ''Not exactly,'' he confessed. ''Actually, I invited Tyler to come and stay here with us for a few weeks, have a look at our operation.''

Ruth shook her head. ''That's crazy, Dad. There's nothing to look at at this time of year but a whole row of casks. And he'd get awful weary,'' she added with a fond teasing smile, "of listening to that boring lecture you give the tour groups six times a week."

"It *is* boring, isn't it?" Don said cheerfully. "But the tourists seem to enjoy it."

"Oh, pooh. They just enjoy the wine tasting. They'll suffer through any dry old lecture to get their hands on those free samples."

Ruth was silent a moment, obviously deep in thought. Her father waited for her to speak as he cleaned his plate with care.

"What's the climate like in Texas?" she asked finally.

"Which part? Texas ranges from tropical seacoast and eastern woodlands to grassy plains and western desert. Take your pick."

"I mean where the McKinneys live. Near Austin, isn't it? I can hardly remember anything about the ranch, it's been so long since I was there."

Don nodded. "The Hill Country. It's a nice area. Close to a region four, I'd say."

Ruth looked at her father in surprise. "Really? They have a heat summation that high?"

"Oh, I'd think so. There's a lot of hot sunny days in Central Texas."

Ruth frowned in concentration. "If they're region four," she said slowly, "then with some hybrid plants along with vinifera they could choose between table wines or dessert wines, right? That degree of sugar content gives them a lot of options."

Don nodded again. "A good portion of the Texas industry seems to be centered farther west around Lubbock, where it's hard to assign a heat summation. But their wineries show a lot of flexibility, and Austin actually has a slightly more moderate climate. Certainly they have less danger of hail than over at Lubbock."

Ruth nodded again, her brown eyes sparkling with interest. "Worse and worse," she said. "That means the whole thing is actually feasible. What does J.T. think about this little project? Somehow I can't imagine him involved with anything but horses and cows."

"Well, he's not wild about it," Don said honestly. "In fact, he sounds quite reluctant. I guess his wife was too, at first, but apparently Tyler's won her over and now they're both pushing poor J.T. to get the project off the ground."

Ruth grinned. "For the sake of your old friendship, I guess the kindest thing would be to give J.T. some support, right? One of us could go out there in a semiprofessional capacity, throw all kinds of cold water on the whole proposal and then just come back home."

"I think J.T. might be very grateful for that," Don said with a solemn twinkle.

"So, why don't *you* go?" Ruth asked.

"I don't need a holiday," Don said, topping up his wineglass. "I'm not the one who's breaking up with boyfriends and grumbling about the weather all day long. Besides," he added, "I have my tour groups six times a week."

"I could lead the tour groups."

"Certainly not. You don't take it seriously enough."

"Wine making? Come on, Dad. Nobody takes this business more seriously than I do."

"No, I meant tourism," Don said with a grin. "You don't have the proper level of respect for the importance of the tourist, my girl."

"Well, I can't argue with that," Ruth confessed. She was silent a moment, resting her elbow on the table, chin cupped thoughtfully in one hand. "Maybe I will," she said at last.

"Go to Texas?"

"Just to see what they're planning, and give your old friend some backup. Texas cowboys really shouldn't try to make wine, Dad. I think I'll just go out there and tell them so. Let the dragon lady know that I'm too full for dessert, okay?"

With a sudden rush of energy Ruth bounded from her chair and whirled across the room to drop a kiss on the top of her father's head, then vanished down the hallway in a blur of faded denim and blue plaid, leaving Don gazing after her in bemused silence.

While the rain hissed softly against the tall, leaded-glass windows, Don Holden sat alone in the quiet dining room and sipped his wine, wondering ruefully if he'd done his old friend any favor by suggesting this little holiday.

THE HOLDEN HOUSE was built in the manner of a traditional Spanish hacienda, a low pillared square surrounding a central courtyard. The decor was cool and rustic, with dark polished wood floors, clean plastered walls and bright splashes of color in the woven Indian rugs and wall hangings.

Ruth's rooms were tucked away in a quiet corner of the house—a bedroom, bath and small sitting room with glass doors opening onto the courtyard. She wandered into the sitting room and shut the door carefully, her burst of energy already fading, replaced by a flood of doubt and a fresh wave of the lassitude and depression that had dogged her so much of the time lately.

For a moment Ruth stood restlessly by the windows and gazed out at the flowing darkness, then looked back into the room as if seeking comfort. But for once the gracious furnishings, the carefully chosen watercolor prints on the walls and the beautiful Navaho rugs did nothing to lighten her mood.

She went over to punch a disk into her player, and the cool liquid sounds of classical guitar spilled through the quiet rooms. Ruth adjusted the volume, then looked around with a questioning air.

"Hagar," she called, sinking down to lie full-length on her small couch. "Hagar, where are you? I need you, sweetie."

Pleasantly muscle-weary from her long day of physical labor in the cold and rain, she propped her moccasined feet on the opposite arm of the couch and adjusted the pillows behind her head, then smiled as a huge orange Persian cat came padding out from the bedroom, yawning voluptuously.

Hagar was a big fluffy Viking of a cat with a wild russet cloud of fur that rayed out all around him in bright splendor. Ruth adored him, loved the regal air and noble carriage that hid an unusually gentle and loving soul.

Mrs. Ward, however, hated Ruth's cat with cold passion because of the silky orange fur that he deposited everywhere. Frequently the housekeeper muttered dark veiled threats about Hagar's personal safety, driving Ruth almost wild with protective outrage and causing even more conflict and tension between the two women.

"You know what, Hagar?" Ruth said, smiling down fondly into Hagar's brilliant green eyes as he sat by the couch. "You really are a Viking, aren't you? I should make you a little tiny hat with a pair of those Viking horns on it, shouldn't I? That would really suit you."

Hagar yawned again and leaped lightly onto Ruth's stomach, pausing to turn around deliberately a few times and knead Ruth's shirt with his gentle blunted claws before sinking in a huge orange mass on her abdomen and resting his chin on folded paws.

Ruth sighed in gratitude, stroking the comforting furry warmth of her cat and brooding about the way she felt these days. Even this beautiful suite of rooms, which had always been the place she loved more than anywhere else on earth, didn't seem able to soothe her anymore. She felt so restless and agitated all the time, full of nagging doubts and strange nameless yearnings.

Partly this was because of the deteriorating relationship with Harlan, followed by its inevitable demise. Not that Ruth really expected to miss Harlan very much, but the breakup still tended to accentuate her solitude, and the terrifying swiftness with which her life was passing by.

Most of Ruth's college friends already had growing children, mortgages, houses full of furniture and settled suburban lives. Ruth, on the other hand, still lived in the same place she'd spent her whole life, except for the year she'd been in Paris working on her master's thesis. Her earlier studies had been at Davis University, so close to the Holden winery that she was able to come home every weekend.

She sighed again. Hagar glanced up at her, licked her hand with urgent sympathy and subsided once more, purring like a plump energetic dynamo as if hopeful that the sound might be soothing to his mistress. Ruth stroked his soft fur with a gentle absent hand, gazing at the ceiling and thinking about the McKinneys.

She didn't really like J.T. McKinney, never had, though she was fair enough to recognize this as a completely unreasonable emotion. When her father's old friend came to visit, striding through the quiet rooms of their house with his tanned handsome face, his rolling cowboy gait, his beautiful handmade riding boots and jaunty Stetson hat, Ruth always felt a small surge of resentment.

In J.T.'s presence, her own beloved father seemed to shrink mysteriously, to diminish somehow until he looked pallid and small. Ruth, who adored her father, felt a defensive flood of concern for Don whenever his colorful friend came to the West Coast, bringing gifts and laughter and rip-roaring stories of Texas past and present.

And now J.T. was planning to go into the winemaking business, to usurp the one area where her father held undisputed mastery. And with all that family money at his disposal, Ruth thought bitterly, he'd probably make a success of it, too.

She frowned, trying to recall what she knew about J.T.'s son Tyler, who apparently was the driving force behind this winery idea.

Like her, Tyler still lived with his father, fully absorbed in the family business, and Ruth was fairly certain that he'd never married. In fact, none of the McKinney children had managed to find partners yet. J.T. and Don frequently commiserated with each other about their backward offspring.

But Tyler McKinney hadn't seemed all that backward on the one occasion she could recall meeting him, Ruth thought with a brief wry grin.

That had been about nineteen years ago, the summer she was eleven and Tyler was fifteen. Don Holden had accepted an invitation to spend a two-week summer vacation at the McKinneys' Texas ranch, and Ruth had been allowed to take along her friend, a precocious thirteen-year-old with the unlikely name of Mimsy Muldoon. Mimsy's parents operated a small winery just down the valley, and she and Ruth were passionate best friends for several years.

Ruth could still remember the pain of that summer, caused in large part by the burning envy she felt for the McKinney children with their warm happy family, and especially the gentle soft-spoken mother who loved them so much and treated them with such tenderness.

But worst of all had been Tyler's attitude. A lanky brash adolescent, he'd been obviously charmed by golden-haired Mimsy, who had a ripely mature young body and a flirtatious manner beyond her years. Ruth had spent a lot of miserable afternoons watching the two of them frolic in the family swimming pool.

She remembered her suffering and embarrassment as she hid her own gangly undeveloped body under baggy T-shirts, huddled with her book in a poolside chair while handsome, dark-haired Tyler flirted with her best friend. Grinning boldly, he ducked Mimsy and chased her across the pool and pretended to be terrified of her swimming prowess.

With a sudden blinding flash of total recall, Ruth saw Tyler pulling his muscular young body out onto the concrete ledge, standing arrogantly with feet apart as he laughed down at Mimsy, throwing his dark head back to send sparkling droplets arching into the hot Texas sun in a shower of rainbows.

"Jerk!" Ruth had muttered under her breath, glaring up at him from behind the pages of her book.

Ruth smiled now at the memory and looked down at Hagar, whose emerald eyes were closing in bliss as Ruth stroked his silky ears.

"You know, Tyler McKinney really was a jerk, Hagar," Ruth told her cat solemnly. "I wonder if he's changed at all."

Hagar yawned in drowsy contentment, revealing his sharp white teeth and the pink interior of his mouth. Ruth felt her spirits begin to rise a little. She gazed at her closet doors with thoughtful speculation, wondering what the weather was like in Central Texas these days and how many clothes she should pack.

CHAPTER TWO

WINTER SUNSHINE, as pale and sparkling as good champagne, spilled over the rolling hills and valleys of Central Texas. The cool afternoon light sparkled on the bustling city of Austin, glinted on lines of brisk-moving traffic and brightened the windows of downtown high-rise office buildings.

Inside Austin's Mueller Airport Tyler McKinney shifted restlessly in a hard vinyl chair and glanced up at the arrivals board, checking on the business shuttle flight from Abilene. The plane was already a half hour late and the arrival time had apparently been shifted back again. Tyler muffled a groan, aching with frustration and impatience.

Of course, he told himself, trying hard to look on the bright side, it was probably better that the flight was delayed. This way, he wouldn't have to search for ways to entertain the woman until it was safe to take her home.

"Don't you *dare* turn up here with her before four o'clock," Cynthia had warned him darkly, her beautiful face comically stern under the navy-blue bandanna that she'd tied over her hair. "If you do, Tyler

McKinney, I swear I'll skin you and set you out for the coyotes to finish off.''

"My, my! Such gruesome violence," Tyler had teased her wickedly. "And from a Boston blueblood, at that."

"Oh, shut up," Cynthia muttered, swatting his arm with a wallpaper roll and whirling off down the cluttered hallway.

Tyler grinned, remembering.

All the women were in an uproar over the renovations currently under way at the Double C. And, being women, they wanted to have it all. They wanted the place redecorated, but they also wanted to impress the visitor from California with how elegant and smooth-running the household was.

"But, darling," J.T. had protested mildly over his breakfast coffee, "it just can't be helped, can it? She's bound to notice that things aren't exactly neat as a pin around here these days."

"I know that," Cynthia said. "But if Tyler can hold her off till four o'clock this afternoon, at least the painters will be gone and we can lift some of the drop sheets in the lower rooms, get the paint cans out of the hallway and the ladders put away...."

Tyler grinned again. He couldn't deny that it was entertaining to see his usually poised stepmother getting a little flustered. For some reason it mattered terribly to Cynthia, this hastily planned visit from Ruth Holden, who was the daughter of one of her husband's oldest friends. There seemed to be something mysteriously female about Cynthia's anxiety, some kind of need to prove herself as mistress of the place....

An expressionless, disembodied voice, announcing that the flight from Abilene would be slightly delayed, interrupted Tyler's thoughts.

He groaned again and shifted his broad shoulders wearily, wondering if the plane had even left Abilene yet. If it hadn't left, wouldn't they know? And if it had, shouldn't they know when it was going to arrive? Abilene, for God's sake, was only a few minutes away by air.

Maybe the plane had been hijacked. Tyler chuckled suddenly, his quirky imagination supplying him with an image of a hard-bitten Texas farmer, calf halter in one hand and pitchfork in the other, holding the crew at bay and demanding to be flown to Fort Worth for the Fat Stock Show.

When he laughed, his tanned sculpted face lightened and his dark eyes sparkled warmly. Tyler McKinney was a tall man in his midthirties with a lean muscular frame, dressed in jeans, riding boots and tweed sport jacket over a casual open-necked white shirt. His pearl-gray Stetson lay on the seat across from him, and his crisp dark hair kept falling down across his forehead no matter how many times he brushed it back.

A small child wriggled quietly in the seat next to Tyler, a boy about three years old with a manly clipped haircut that was neatly parted and slicked back with a wet comb. The little fellow, waiting with his mother and baby sister in a stroller, was trying hard to be good, but Tyler could see that the long delay was starting to get to him as well.

The child gripped the metal chair arms with his small hands and slid way down on his spine, legs stiffly extended, seeing how low he could go without falling off the chair. His mother, who was busy with the baby, whispered to him sharply and he sat erect, peeking up at Tyler with cautious interest. Tyler grinned down at the child, slipped him a couple of peppermints from a roll in his jacket pocket, then returned to his thoughts.

His face darkened as he brooded over the impending arrival and what his responsibilities were going to be toward this visiting scientist. "You'll pretty well have to take care of her," his father had told him casually. "The girls are busy with all this damn decorating, so they won't have much time to entertain her."

"Me?" Tyler said blankly. "What am *I* going to do with her?"

"Well, talk about wine making, of course," J.T. told his son impatiently. "You're the one who wants to start this business, aren't you? And she's an expert. She's a qualified chemist with a list of college degrees as long as your arm."

"Oh, great," Tyler had muttered rebelliously, feeling about eight years old. "That's just what I need, to spend a week listening to some California scientist with thick legs and a mustache, lecturing me about temperature variations and pH levels."

"I haven't seen Ruth Holden for quite a few years," J.T. said with an amiable grin. "But near as I recall, she didn't have thick legs *or* a mustache."

"I'll bet," Tyler said grimly. "I'll just bet."

He didn't really know why he'd formed such a negative mental image of the woman. Maybe it was his recollection of that one time he'd seen her, years ago. He remembered her as a mousy quiet child with a skinny awkward body and teeth covered in ugly braces.

Of course, she'd really suffered badly in comparison with her friend. Tyler smiled, remembering the ripe body of that other girl, the silly blond one. Misty? Molly? Whatever her name was, she'd certainly made an impact on his raging young hormones.

No wonder little Ruth Holden, sulking in a chair behind a book, had seemed so homely and unappealing. Tyler could just visualize the kind of woman she'd turned into. He pictured her with thick ankles and a severe look, her colorless hair hanging lank and unwashed around her ears. She'd be wearing thick glasses and carrying a clipboard at all times, and she'd probably be dressed in a white lab coat over a baggy gray flannel skirt.

This image had grown so real to him during the past few days, ever since he heard about the woman's impending visit, that now, as Tyler glanced frequently into the arrivals area, he expected to see her come marching up the ramp, clipboard and all.

But the lounge was mostly empty, except for a few long-suffering people who were still waiting for the flight from Abilene.

Tyler became aware of a small movement beside him, a sudden charged air of expectancy.

The little boy was gazing up at him with wide eyes, holding out his hand. A tiny object rested on the small damp palm, and Tyler bent closer to look. It was a futuristic warrior figure, beautifully detailed, complete with small swords and laser guns.

Tyler nodded solemnly and smiled down into the sparkling blue eyes, understanding that the figurine was just being displayed for his enjoyment, not offered as a gift.

"That's real nice," he murmured to the child, who grinned happily.

Tyler smiled back and dug into his jacket pocket again, taking out his keys and snapping a small object off the key ring. It was a tiny leather saddle, no bigger than the end of his thumb and intricately crafted with miniature swinging stirrups and a little horn and cantle. He placed the saddle on his hard callused palm and held it out for the child's inspection.

The boy gasped and stared at this enchanting object, then looked up at Tyler again, holding his breath and putting two fingers automatically into his mouth.

"Take it," Tyler whispered. "You can have it."

His seatmate gazed at him with astonishment and growing wonder. A small hand crept out cautiously and touched one of the little stirrups in an agony of longing.

"Michael!" the harried young mother said abruptly, turning away from her crying baby in the stroller. "What are you doing?"

"It's all right, ma'am," Tyler assured her with his most engaging grin. "I told him he could have it."

The woman glanced uncertainly at the tall, handsome rancher, then at her little boy, who was now holding the miniature saddle, his face pale with tension.

"Well, all right," she said reluctantly. "Michael, say thank-you."

"Sanks," the child whispered, drumming his feet on the chair and gazing ecstatically at the tiny object in his hand. He balanced the saddle on one small finger and set the stirrups swinging gently, his pink face rapt with happiness.

"You're welcome, cowboy," Tyler said cheerfully. The woman smiled, then gathered her children and hurried toward a short cheerful man in a crumpled suit who stood waiting by the entry gate.

While Tyler watched, the young father gathered the baby into his arms, kissed his wife and caressed the shining head of the little boy, who was joyously hugging his legs. The man bent to hear what his son was saying, then knelt and studied the tiny saddle that was held up for his inspection. He listened, smiled briefly over the child's head at Tyler and turned back to his family.

Tyler smiled automatically in return, feeling a familiar vague sorrow as he watched this small tableau.

Nobody would ever know how much Tyler McKinney longed for children of his own, how deeply he yearned for the love of a small son like that little fair-haired child. This emotion was something Tyler hid from everybody, even his family and closest friends, most of whom considered him ambitious, cold and clearheaded, probably even a little ruthless.

But Tyler knew himself better, knew that he had great depths of tenderness to give the right woman, though he'd never managed to find the one he dreamed of. Dark or fair, short or tall—her looks didn't really matter—but she'd have a sweet voice and gentle hands and a tender caring manner similar to his mother's. Tyler knew this was an old-fashioned picture, and that women just weren't like that nowadays. But still, he longed to find a woman who fulfilled his fantasies, who'd give him love and support and some little children to hold.

But his soul mate never seemed to come along, or else he'd just never found time to search for her. Tyler had been so busy during his college years, driven by his need to excel both scholastically and athletically. Then there'd been the absorbing interest of his new position as a full partner in the ranch, trying to use his training in business to develop methods of making the huge unwieldy operation more efficient and profitable.

And then, as he was trying to contend with the economic slide that followed the sudden crash in oil prices and threatened to drag the whole state of Texas into poverty, Tyler suffered the dreadful agony of his mother's death.

The past five years in his life hadn't been a real good time to think about building a relationship, Tyler reflected bitterly. In fact, there'd hardly been time to think about himself at all. Mostly he'd just passed those years putting one foot in front of the other, getting from day to day as best he could, hoping for some kind of light at the end of the tunnel.

Lately, Tyler had begun to hope that he'd found that light. His idea of building a winery on the Double C had thoroughly captivated him, and the more he researched the concept, the more excited he got. Miraculously, he'd even managed somehow to get Cynthia on his side, and now she was also exerting her considerable influence over his father.

But this damned Holden woman could throw a monkey wrench into the whole works, Tyler thought miserably. J.T. McKinney had tremendous respect for his old friend Don Holden, and for the success Don had had with his wine-making business. He was sure to pay some attention to the man's daughter, possibly even to be swayed by her opinions. And if she was one of those carping, scientific doom-and-gloom types...

Tyler was so absorbed in his own gloomy thoughts that it took some time for him to remember that he and the woman with her children had been waiting for the same plane. He sprang to his feet, feeling embarrassed, and looked wildly around the receiving area.

But there was no woman anywhere who looked at all like Ruth Holden. Tyler moved uncertainly out into the lounge, hat in hand, wondering what could have happened to her.

Likely, he told himself with a wry grin, she was already in the washroom doing preliminary tests on pH levels in the Texas water.

While he was enjoying this uncharitable thought, he noticed a young woman near the luggage carousel who stood gazing at him with shy intensity. Tyler caught his breath and stared.

The woman was lovely. She wore a fitted suit of winter white with a cropped jacket and short skirt that showed off a slim, well-proportioned body and a pair of fantastic legs. Her brown hair, cut quite short, was casually windblown, and she had a beautiful complexion, creamy and warm, with the biggest, sweetest brown eyes he'd ever seen.

She paused uncertainly, a tan leather bag slung over her shoulder and another at her feet.

When Tyler gave her a startled grin of admiration she smiled back, an engaging nervous smile that tilted up on one side, causing a dimple to appear in her cheek. Tyler swallowed hard and found himself battling a crazy masculine urge to stride across the room, gather her into his arms and kiss that dimpled face.

To his astonishment, this lovely apparition lifted the bag at her feet and came toward him, extending a small hand. Tyler shook it, still surprised by her approach, and was further amazed by how hard and firm her hand was. The rest of her looked so deliciously soft, but she had a palm almost as callused as those of the Double C ranch hands.

"You must be Tyler," she said in a low husky voice. "You look just like your father."

Tyler, who heard this observation all the time, merely nodded and stared at her, his mind slowly absorbing the wonder of this situation.

"My God," he said at last. "You're not...you can't be..."

"I'm Ruth Holden. Sorry the flight was so late," the woman added cheerfully while Tyler stood gazing at her like a schoolboy. "They couldn't leave Abilene because they were waiting for some kind of delivery, and apparently nobody could find it. They kept running back and forth from the terminal to the...excuse me, Tyler, are you all right?"

Tyler gathered himself hastily in hand and bent to lift the case at her feet. "Sorry," he said, smiling down at her. "You're just not quite what I expected, Ruth. Where's the rest of your luggage?"

"This is it," she said, surprising him further. "I'm only staying a week or so," she added casually, "and Dad assured me that you people don't dress for dinner. Mostly I just brought some jeans and shirts. I hope that's all right."

"That's fine," Tyler said, still feeling dizzied by her smile. "That's just fine. Everybody wears jeans most all the time."

In fact, Cynthia had made a few attempts to initiate the habit of dressing for dinner at the ranch, but the suggestion had been met with general indifference from the rest of the family, and such caustic scorn from old Hank that she'd backed off, at least for the moment.

"So, what did you expect?" Ruth asked, walking beside him to the entrance door.

"Beg pardon?" Tyler fitted his Stetson on his head and held the door for her, moving behind her into the pale sunshine.

"You said I wasn't what you expected. I wondered how you'd pictured me."

Tyler hesitated, his tanned cheeks flushing a little as he remembered the dowdy woman he'd visualized. "Just...different," he said lamely. "More like a scientist, I guess."

Ruth chuckled. "Well, it's been a long time since we saw each other, and back then," she added, giving him a cheerful yet pointed glance, "I'm not sure you even knew what I looked like. You spent the whole time drooling over my friend."

Tyler grinned. "Yeah," he said, reminiscing fondly. "What was her name? Milly?"

"Mimsy," Ruth said dryly. "Mimsy Muldoon."

Tyler chuckled and gazed with narrowed eyes across the parking lot, trying to bring his dazzled mind back to earth and remember where he'd left the car. "Mimsy," he echoed. "Whatever happened to that girl?"

"Oh, Mimsy came to a bad end," Ruth said, walking beside him. "She married an older man for his money, and now she lives a captive existence in Bel Air with a dozen fur coats and two Porsches and diamonds the size of hazelnuts."

"But no real happiness," Tyler said solemnly.

"No real happiness," Ruth agreed. "Poor thing," she added soulfully, sparkling a glance up at Tyler that made him burst into laughter.

They paused beside the car and he opened the trunk to put her suitcase inside, fighting another powerful and irrational urge to take this delectable woman into his arms and kiss her, right there in broad daylight.

"Wow," Ruth said thoughtfully, gazing at the gleaming Cadillac. "Is this what cowboys drive around in down here?"

"They made me bring it," Tyler said. "Mostly to impress you, I guess. Usually I just drive one of the pickup trucks."

"Well, that would have been more my choice, too," Ruth said, her tomboy expression belying the stylish elegance of her suit. "I've spent most of my life riding around in pickup trucks."

Tyler hesitated, wondering what to do. The prospect of filling in an hour or so with this visitor didn't seem nearly as awful as it had just a short time ago, but he couldn't decide where to take her.

"Are you hungry, Ruth?" he asked.

Ruth shook her head. "They served lunch on the plane, and it was really good. Besides, the lady in the next seat gave me all her peanuts."

Tyler nodded, moving slowly around to let her in the car. Ruth glanced up at him. "You seem thoughtful," she said. "Is something the matter?"

"I'm not supposed to take you home yet," Tyler confessed, pausing with his hand on the passenger door. "The women said they'd kill me if we arrived before four o'clock."

"Kill you? That seems a little harsh."

Tyler grinned. "Yeah, well, they're a harsh bunch, those women."

"But I don't understand. Why can't you go home?"

"They're doing a whole lot of renovations out at the house. It's a real mess these days, and they don't want you to get there till they've had time to tidy away some of the painting stuff."

Ruth smiled. "I see. Lucky the plane was late." She glanced at her watch. "How long does it take to get to Crystal Creek, Tyler?"

Tyler grinned back at her. "Depends who's driving. For my brother, Cal, about half an hour. For most everybody else in the world, forty-five minutes or so."

"Well, it's just after two o'clock now," Ruth said. "How about if we drive out there and have a cup of coffee somewhere in Crystal Creek before we go to the house? Is there a restaurant in the town?"

"You bet. It's called the Longhorn, and it hasn't changed one bit the past half century. Its owner, Dottie, serves the best doughnuts in Texas."

"Great." Ruth smiled up at him, then drew back in surprise as his hand brushed her shoulder.

"What's this?" Tyler asked, holding up a bit of rusty fluff.

Ruth peered at his tanned fingers, then smiled awkwardly. "It's cat hair," she confessed. "I hugged my cat this morning when I said goodbye, and that's how he rewards me."

Tyler let the bit of silky fluff drift away on the afternoon breeze and found himself envying the damned cat who had so recently been in her arms. "You like your cat?" he asked, holding the door open and helping her inside, then leaning in to look down at her.

"I love him," Ruth said, smiling and gazing up with wide brown eyes dazzled by the sunlight. "I miss him already."

She waited silently in the car as Tyler came around and unlocked the driver's door. He folded his long body behind the wheel and turned to smile at her, feeling almost weak with pleasure at her nearness, the delicate fragrance of her perfume and the sweetness of her face, enclosed next to him within the intimate luxury of the big car.

"You know, I'm really worried about him," Ruth said in an abstracted tone, gazing out at the crowded parking lot.

Tyler turned the key in the ignition, puzzling briefly over this statement until he realized that she was still talking about her cat. "Why?" he asked, resting an arm along the back of the seat and backing expertly into the slow-moving lines of traffic.

"Our housekeeper is just so awful," Ruth said. "She's always threatening poor Hagar with all kinds of horrible things, like putting him in the clothes dryer and turning it on. I don't what she'll do to him when I'm not there to protect him."

"She sounds pretty awful, all right," Tyler said, fascinated by a vivid image of the cat in the dryer.

Ruth told him about Mrs. Ward, with her bossy forcefulness and grumbling accusations, her motorcycle and her knitting and the mysterious little man she lived with.

By the time she finished he was shouting with laughter. Ruth, too, had begun to smile again, her worries apparently forgotten for the moment as they left the city behind them and the quiet Texas countryside began spinning past the windows.

RUTH GRIPPED her hands tightly in her lap and looked out at the rolling hills and valleys dotted with grazing livestock, brightened by the occasional glimpse of a deer flashing though the brush.

"What kind of trees are those?" she asked.

"Mesquite. Probably the most genuine native vegetation we have around here. It grows a long pod that fills up with beans, and the cattle love 'em. The branches get big enough that the wood's sometimes used for furniture, and old-timers say the roots can grow sixty feet long, looking for water. It's a great wood for barbecues, too.''

Fascinated, Ruth peered out at the tangled thickets. ''I think there's mesquite in Southern California,'' she said. ''But I don't recall any of it growing up where we live. Of course, the land is pretty thoroughly cultivated.''

They fell silent again, and Ruth stole a cautious glance at her escort.

She didn't really know what to think about Tyler McKinney. He was certainly as handsome as she remembered, with all of his father's easy cowboy charm and sculpted good looks. But she noticed something else about this man. There was a hard, modern edge to J.T.'s elder son, a firm set to his jaw and a crisp look about him that spoke of a coolheaded businessman, somebody who certainly didn't suffer fools gladly.

Normally, Ruth wasn't attracted at all by that kind of man, the type who exuded power and confidence and an easy arrogant control of all situations. But Tyler McKinney seemed different somehow, hard to put a label on.

Just when Ruth thought she had him figured out and was ready to dismiss him, she'd catch a disturbing sparkle deep in his brown eyes, a flash of gentleness and winsome humor that was both surprising and unsettling. And when he threw back his head and gave one of those hearty, infectious laughs, Ruth found herself smiling all over in response, as warmed and delighted by his company as any fluttery, teenage girl.

"Well, how do you like it so far?" he asked cheerfully when she turned to gaze out the window again. "Is it like you remembered?"

"I really don't remember much of anything from that visit," Ruth confessed, "except you and Mimsy playing all day in the pool, and Cal bringing a live rattlesnake into the house."

Tyler roared with laughter. "God, I'd forgotten that snake. Didn't my mama have fits? I thought she'd die on the spot."

When he realized what he'd said, Tyler fell abruptly silent. His face paled beneath the tan and he gripped the wheel silently, his jaw knotted with anguish.

Ruth reached over and touched his arm gently. "We were so sorry when we heard about your mother, Tyler," she said in a soft voice. "I know that it was terribly hard for all of you."

Especially Tyler, she recalled. Don Holden had confided to his daughter that in his opinion, Tyler had suffered more than any of the McKinney children from the loss of his mother, though he seemed least able to express his pain.

Tyler turned to his passenger and tried to smile. "It was all a long time ago," he said lightly. "And now there's a new woman redecorating my mama's house. Life goes on, I guess."

"It must feel so strange," Ruth commented shyly.

"What's that?"

"Having a stepmother close to your own age. Isn't it hard to adjust to?"

"Lots of things are hard to adjust to," Tyler said with his eyes fixed on the winding road ahead of him. "But that's part of life, too, isn't it? When you come right down to it, life is just a long series of adjustments."

"I guess so." Disturbed by the air of tension in the car, Ruth steered the conversation back into safer channels. "You know," she commented, "I think this could probably be wine-making country, after all. It actually reminds me of some of the provinces in the south of France. But they're a lot more heavily populated, of course."

Tyler looked around, his taut features relaxing. "Really? When were you in France, Ruth?"

"I spent a year in Paris doing the thesis for my master's degree."

"Yeah? What was your topic?"

"Carbonation methods in French sparkling wines," she said casually, peering out at an unusual limestone formation capping a small hill.

"Wow," Tyler said. "Pretty heavy stuff." He was silent a moment. "I guess," he ventured finally, "that you're a real expert on all this, aren't you, Ruth? Wine making, I mean?"

"Pretty much," she said. "Whatever 'expert' means. The field is expanding so rapidly and changing so fast that the things you learn today are practically obsolete by tomorrow.''

''Well, thanks. That's real encouraging to us beginners,'' Tyler told her with a wry grin.

Ruth smiled back at him. ''Sorry. It's just that wine making is like computer technology these days. You really hesitate to call yourself an expert. Every time I read a trade publication, I run across new things that I'd like to go away and take courses in.''

''Where did you go to college?''

''Davis, in California,'' Ruth said. ''They have one of the most extensive wine-making research and teaching facilities in the world.''

''I sure envy you that education, Ruth. I don't know how much my business degree is going to help me with the details of something like this.''

''Education is okay,'' Ruth said thoughtfully. ''But what's really important is the hands-on experience. I grew up in the winery, hanging around listening to my father talk with the other workers, smelling and tasting the wine, watching all the different processes from harvesting to bottling. I think that's how you really learn wine making.''

''So, what about me, Ruth? Is it too late for me to learn?''

''Of course it isn't. Not if you want to learn badly enough. After all, my father never set foot in a winery until he was an adult, and now he's one of the very best.''

Ruth gazed out at the remote brush-covered hills, feeling a sudden painful flood of homesickness for the neat vineyards of the Napa Valley, for the salt tang of the Pacific Ocean breezes blowing over the hills and the comfortable rooms of their house, with her father and Hagar and the orderly sprawl of the brick winery nearby.

Tyler seemed to catch some of this mood, because he gave her a glance of quick sympathy.

"You really love it, don't you?" he asked, looking intently down the winding road as a loaded cattle truck swayed past them.

"What do you mean?"

"This whole business," Tyler said. "Wine making, I mean. When you talk about it, your face gets all passionate and your eyes have that faraway look, just like my sister, Lynn, when she talks about horses."

Ruth smiled awkwardly. "I guess we can't help what matters to us. You're right, I do love the business. I love everything about it, from the vines growing in the fields to the wine bottled in rows in the cellar. It's such a satisfying process."

"Like I said, Lynn feels that way about every horse on the ranch," Tyler mused, "and Cal loves his rodeo. Both of them are passionate about what they do."

"What about you?" Ruth asked, glancing over at him. "Are you passionate about anything, Tyler?"

Apparently unsettled by the sudden serious turn of the conversation, Tyler turned and gave her a flashing grin. "Well, sure I am," he said. "I'm passionate about making money. I just love seeing my books in the black. And if wine making is going to accomplish that particular goal, then you can bet I'm going to love the business just as much as you do."

Ruth felt a sharp stab of disappointment. She looked for a moment at his clean-cut profile, then turned to gaze out the window again, fighting the urge to say something brusque and tactless.

If Tyler McKinney wanted to open a winery on the ranch and make a lot of money, that was his business. Ruth was only here to advise him on feasibility, as a courtesy to her father. She'd test the soil, check the climate and water conditions, examine Tyler's site for drainage and exposure potential. Then she'd look at his plans, give him her honest opinion and return to California.

And she'd forget about how his dark eyes sparkled when he laughed, or the engaging way he tilted one eyebrow and turned to look at her with a warm teasing grin. Those things might make her heart flutter, but Ruth Holden certainly wasn't the kind of woman to be taken in by a handsome face and a charming smile.

There was no doubt that this man looked good. In fact, he was strongly appealing to her on a purely physical basis. But when the chips were down he was just another greedy Texas opportunist, looking to make a quick fortune from something that she cared deeply about, and Ruth could hardly wait to get away from him.

CHAPTER THREE

WITHIN the cool shadowed depths of the Longhorn, afternoon coffee time was in full swing. The place was crowded as usual. Most of the regulars were already there, including the people from offices like Martin Avery, a busy lawyer, and Vernon Trent, a real estate agent.

A few local ranchers were present as well, in town for supplies and gossip. Tyler noticed Bubba Gibson and Brock Munroe sitting around with hats pushed back and booted feet extended, shouting and wrangling cheerfully with veterinarian Manny Hernandez and Sheriff Wayne Jackson.

They seemed to be arguing over the intricacies of setting up a football pool for the Super Bowl, which was coming up on the weekend. Apparently one group favored a richer payoff while the opposing faction wanted more opportunities for each entrant to win.

Tyler grinned privately, thinking that the coffeeshop crowd fought about the same thing every single year and never came to any firm conclusion.

When he entered with Ruth, the men fell abruptly silent for a moment, staring and nodding at her with bluff respect. A few even touched hats and caps while

Bubba, with his usual showmanship, swept the Stetson from his shaggy gray head and placed it soulfully over his chest as he greeted the newcomers.

Texas men just hadn't moved into the modern world, Tyler thought, gesturing toward the nearest booth, then smiling at Dottie and ordering coffee and doughnuts for two. These men still made a firm distinction between "ladies" and "gals," and what was more, their instincts were remarkably consistent.

When someone like Ruth Holden appeared, they greeted her with respectful deference. But if Bubba's current flame, Billie Jo Dumont, came sashaying into the coffee shop, she'd be met with lewd jokes and slaps on the rear. And these men would probably be outraged if anyone suggested they were doing anything out of line.

While Tyler was pondering the socialization of the Texas male, his companion was gazing around with parted lips and wide eyes, clearly enchanted by the Longhorn and its genuine fifties ambience. Tyler stole a glance at her, and felt another surge of impatience with himself.

Why had he made that stupid remark about caring for nothing but money?

They'd been getting along so well up to that point, but he'd sensed a chill as soon as he uttered the words. He could almost feel her disappointment in the way she'd turned aside and deliberately excluded him, gazing out the window with concentrated attention as if he were simply a hired cabdriver, not worthy of her further attention.

Tyler had been enjoying her company so much, and now he regretted the rift between them. He almost considered apologizing for his words, but a kind of stubborn annoyance kept him from doing so.

For one thing, it was true, what he'd said.

He *did* like making money and seeing the books balance, and what was so terrible about that? Tyler's sister reacted the same way as Ruth. She loved her horses passionately and was always outraged if somebody suggested actually making money by selling a horse for profit. But it was the people who earned the money who made it possible for the horses to exist at all, to be kept on the ranch even at a loss to the company.

And besides, Tyler did love something with real passion. He loved the Double C, the ranch that had been home to him all his life. Sometimes in the darkness of his bed he'd stare at the ceiling and tremble, even feel hot, embarrassing tears stinging in his eyes at the thought of losing the place.

What if finances ever got so bad they'd have to give up the rolling ten thousand acres that were the heritage of the McKinney family? His children, and Cal's and Lynn's, would never ride across the green hills or fish in the river, or feel the warm Texas wind in their hair....

But he wasn't about to share something so deeply private with a woman he'd just met and didn't even know. After all, such emotions were difficult for Tyler to express even to the people who were nearer and dearer to him than anybody on earth.

He shifted restlessly on the worn vinyl of the booth seat, wondering if a woman like Ruth Holden expected that kind of openness in a man.

Maybe she did. Probably she hung around with sensitive guys in silk shirts and neck chains, who studied their horoscopes every day and were in touch with their feelings.

"Hey, Tyler, whadda ya think?" Wayne Jackson called across the room. "Ten bucks a square, an' the winner gets a case of whiskey?"

"Two bits a square," Tyler called back firmly, "and the winner gets a free beer. The problem with you guys," he added, grinning at Ruth, "is that y'all are just so damn greedy."

Ruth's cheeks colored faintly when he said this and she met his eyes with a startled look, then glanced quickly away, wondering if the man had somehow read her mind.

Not likely, she thought. Tyler McKinney didn't have enough sensitivity to read any woman's mind. He was probably like a lot of people, always quick to criticize something in others that was actually one of his own worst flaws.

She dismissed the thought and returned to her examination of the coffee shop with its red-checked cloths, its chalkboard and big vinyl menus and miniature jukeboxes on each table.

"Care for a tune?" Tyler asked, flipping though the numbered pages and squinting at the various musical offerings while a pleasant young woman delivered their coffee and pastries.

"No thanks," Ruth said automatically. She smiled up at the waitress and wondered who'd chosen the song currently playing, a noisy wailing number in which some errant husband was apparently pleading with his wife to open the door and let him in.

While they were eating Ruth gazed curiously at the other patrons of the coffee shop, mostly bluff hearty men with hats and boots. But there were a few women, too, secretaries enjoying afternoon coffee breaks and young ranch wives in town for a day's shopping with their babies.

Two women sat in a booth near the back, and Ruth grew interested in them when she realized that the younger of the pair was studying her and Tyler with unwavering attention.

She was actually just a girl, Ruth realized, probably in her late teens. She had a pale pretty face, carefully made up, and a cloud of dark curly hair. Her eyes were her most arresting feature, large and shining and such a light blue that they were almost transparent, giving her a remote, ethereal look. The young body was ripe and full-breasted, probably destined to become hefty with advancing years. But Ruth didn't realize until the girl shifted in the booth that her pink gingham shirt was actually a maternity smock, curving neatly over a small swollen abdomen.

The girl had a strangely passionate, concentrated look about her, an avid expression that was unsettling in its intensity. She seemed sly and secretive when she met Ruth's glance, like some small predatory animal peering out from behind dense cover, pondering whether to attack or escape.

The woman with her was entirely different, tall, plain and rawboned, with a gruff sensible manner and large work-worn hands. Her hair was mostly gray, hacked off carelessly around her ears, and she wore a man's shirt and jeans. Still, there was a mysterious similarity between the two, a likeness in bone structure and features that told Ruth they were probably mother and daughter.

While Ruth watched, the two women finished their fries and paid the bill, then gathered up handbags and parcels and walked toward the door. They passed close to Ruth and Tyler, and the younger one gave them another look of such intensity that Ruth was startled, even a little troubled.

"Tyler," she whispered when the two had gone by, "who are those women?"

Tyler peered at the departing pair, frowning as he searched his memory. "I think their name's Hill, something like that," he said finally. "There was a big family of them, about eight kids, living in a little shack on the outskirts of town. Their daddy wasn't good for much, just drinking and odd jobs. He got killed on the road a few years back, run over by an oil truck when he was walking home one night, and she moved the kids over to Lampasas. I think she's working for a turkey farmer up there.''

"And the girl? Is that her daughter?"

Tyler nodded. "Must be the oldest girl. She's all grown-up now. I remember her as a scrawny kid with a bunch of little brothers and sisters trailing after her. Come to think of it," he added thoughtfully, "somebody told me she was back in Crystal Creek, working for Ralph Wall over at the drugstore. I forgot about it till you asked.''

"She looks like she's pregnant.''

"Looks like," Tyler said with a grin. "Why? What's so interesting about those two?''

Ruth hesitated, wondering whether to tell him about the girl's fixed scrutiny and the disturbing light in her eyes while she watched them.

"Oh, nothing," she said finally. "You're right about one thing," she added, trying to sound cheerful. "These are just the most wonderful doughnuts in the whole world.''

"I told you," Tyler said. "Dottie makes 'em fresh every morning. Well, are you ready to leave, Ruth? It's probably safe to go home now, and I want to show you my plans for the vineyard.''

Ruth nodded automatically and gulped the last of her coffee, then waited while Tyler paid the bill and escorted her toward the door with its cheery curtain of red gingham.

She shivered when he took her elbow and pressed close behind her, disturbed by his nearness and the feel of his body against hers. No matter how she felt about Tyler McKinney, Ruth told herself again, there was certainly no denying the man's physical appeal. She'd have to be careful to...

But she didn't have a chance to finish the thought. When she and Tyler emerged onto the street in the slanting afternoon sunlight, the mother and daughter from the restaurant were standing just a few doors down, looking in the window of a clothing store while the older woman held forth on the exorbitant prices of children's clothes these days.

The young girl looked at them and quickly fumbled with something that looked like a camera, then turned away with deliberate composure, rummaging in her big patchwork handbag and answering a question from her mother.

Ruth paused nervously and glanced up at Tyler to see if he'd noticed. But he was laughing and chatting with a young cowboy who'd slowed his pickup truck on the street to call out a greeting, and had apparently missed the whole incident.

Still feeling unsettled and troubled, Ruth walked beside Tyler in silence and allowed him to help her into the waiting Cadillac, while the pregnant girl in the pink smock stood on the sidewalk, watching their departure with those smoldering pale blue eyes.

"JODIE HILTZ, what in the world do you think you're doin'?"

"My name is Jacqueline," the dark-haired girl said, strolling along the street and gazing dreamily at her reflection in the store windows. "Jacqueline Hill-croft."

"Like hell it is," Marg Hiltz said coldly. "Your name is plain Jodie Hiltz, and you'd better stop put-tin' on all these phony airs, girl. They'll bring you nothin' but grief."

Jodie ignored her mother. She smiled to herself as she patted her small bulging abdomen, then frowned angrily when a teenage boy with headphones and a skateboard careered past her, almost jostling her from the sidewalk.

"You took a picture of them people," Marg said after an awkward silence.

Jodie remained silent, reaching up to pat her dark curls, tucking a strand of hair thoughtfully behind her ear.

"Didn't you?" her mother persisted.

"A baby has a right to know what his daddy looks like," Jodie said in a soft voice. "He'll say, 'Mama, what did my daddy look like when I was born?' And I'll show him the picture and say—"

"You'll do nothin' of the sort!" Marg stopped in midstride and reached out a big hand to grip her daughter's arm, leaning forward to glare at the girl. "And what's more," the older woman added, glanc-ing furtively over her shoulder and dropping her voice to a harsh whisper, "you better stop sayin' things like that, Jodie Hiltz. You're fixin' to get the whole family into trouble, talkin' such nonsense.''

"I'm not talking nonsense,'' Jodie said calmly, shaking her mother's hand away and resuming her march up the street.

"Tyler McKinney is not that baby's father, and you know it,'' Marg muttered furiously. "I got no idea who *is* its father, but it's damn sure not one of the McKinneys! You're just crazy, girl.''

Jodie gave her mother a placid secretive smile. "I know what I know,'' she said.

"You know *nothin',*'' Marg said forcefully. "An' if you got any brains at all, you'll come back to Lampasas with me an' help with the other kids, and forget this nonsense.''

"I'm staying right here. I want my little baby to grow up close to his daddy,'' Jodie said with imperturbable calm. Marg shook her head helplessly, glancing at her oldest child and wondering what on earth ailed the girl... besides being pregnant, of course.

The fact of Jodie's pregnancy was something that Marg dismissed quite casually. These things happened. In fact, Jodie had happened to her at just about the same age, though these days Marg certainly looked older than her years.

Raising eight kids with no money could do that to you, Marg thought philosophically. But she wasn't complaining. The kids were healthy and if truth be told, life was really a whole lot better since Joe was gone. Now she could save a bit, and the kids could have a few nice things in return for all that hard work.

The prospect of another mouth to feed didn't worry Marg. If Jodie would just quit her silliness and move back home they could make do when the baby came along, just as they always had. It would even be nice, Marg thought wistfully, having a sweet new little one around the house again. She'd always loved babies.

But Jodie was getting to be a real worry. Just last year she'd quit high school a few courses short of her diploma and announced that she was moving back to Crystal Creek to get a job. Then had come this pregnancy, though Marg had had no idea her daughter even had a boyfriend. And suddenly, just a month or so ago, she'd confided to her mother that Tyler McKinney, of all people, was the child's father.

Marg didn't know what to make of it. She couldn't bring herself to believe the girl's story, and yet there was Jodie's calm unshakable conviction, and the clear absence of any other male in her daughter's life, at least none that Marg could see on her visits to Crystal Creek.

They paused by the bus depot and Marg squinted at the sun. "There's another bus leaves in a couple hours," she said hopefully, "an' Tommy promised he'd look after the chores for me tonight. I could just go on over to your place for a while, Jodie, have a mug of coffee an' see what your—"

"No," Jodie said quietly. "You better catch the early bus, Mama. Tommy's awful young to be looking after the chores all on his own."

Marg looked at this pretty daughter she'd never really understood, even when she was just a little bit of a thing.

"You don't want me at your place, do you, Jodie?" she asked sadly. "You been there for months, livin' on your own, an' you never let me step inside. I call that real mean."

"A person is entitled to their privacy," Jodie said with her usual air of impenetrable calm. "I don't let anybody into my place, Mama. Except Tyler," she added with a small faraway smile. "Anytime Tyler likes, he can come into my place."

"Tyler McKinney has never once set foot in that shack of yours," Marg said, her voice rising. "An' you *know* it, Jodie."

"He'll come," Jodie said dreamily. "When his son is born, he'll come and bring me flowers."

"More likely he'll bring you a summons for tellin' lies about him." Marg hesitated, gazing unhappily at her daughter's pale withdrawn face, searching for words to bring the girl back to reality. But the bus was pulling in, its dusty sides glinting in the fading afternoon light, and there was no more time.

Reluctantly Marg climbed on board, handed her ticket to the driver and found a seat by the window where she could see Jodie. But the girl didn't even linger for a parting wave, just turned and headed briskly up the street without a backward glance.

Marg settled back against the soiled upholstery with a troubled sigh and closed her eyes, hoping to snatch a few minutes of welcome sleep before she got home.

JODIE HEARD the rumbling growl behind her as the bus pulled out and lurched around the corner, heading for Lampasas. She felt a surge of relief, though her pretty face remained impassive. It was getting increasingly awkward when her mother visited, with all her stupid questions and warnings.

Her mother didn't know anything. How could Marg Hiltz give advice about Jodie's life? Only Jodie knew.

And Tyler...

Jodie's pale eyes glistened and she began to quicken her steps, ducking through a gap in the ragged hedge and running around behind the drugstore. In the vacant lot at the rear of the store was an old building, originally a stable, then a garage and storage area. Recently, hoping to attract an employee who would stay a while, the drugstore owner had converted this ramshackle building to a small self-contained living area with an old couch that doubled as a bed, a sink, toilet and hot plate, and an old bar fridge beneath the makeshift counter.

With a glow of proprietary pride, Jodie took the key from her big colorful handbag and let herself inside the old building, then switched on the naked light bulb that hung from the ceiling.

She glanced around with satisfaction at the small shuttered space where she lived. The single room was very neat, and attempts had been made to brighten the rough interior with plastic flowers, a couple of travel posters on one wall, a few stuffed animals on the lumpy ancient couch.

There was one window opposite the bright posters, heavily muffled with cheap drapes, and the other two walls were covered with pictures and newspaper clippings featuring Tyler McKinney. Most of the pictures were Polaroid snapshots, like the one that Jodie now took from her purse and tacked carefully on the peeling mildewed wall.

The photographs showed Tyler in a variety of candid poses, getting in and out of vehicles, striding along the street, sitting at the cattle auction, riding his horse on the ranch, even whirling through the steps of a square dance. It was obvious in all the pictures that he hadn't realized he was being photographed, though the images showed a degree of rudimentary skill in the matters of framing, timing and composition.

But the success of the pictures was clearly accidental; it was obvious Jodie wasn't concerned with technical issues. She stepped back and gazed at the new picture with cold narrowed eyes, then, removing it from the wall, she went to a drawer, took out a pair of scissors and cut away the image of the slim woman in the white suit who stood next to Tyler on the street.

With quick savage strokes Jodie slashed the woman's face and body to ribbons and tossed the scraps of paper in the wastebasket. Then she moved slowly back across the room and replaced the photograph, her pale eyes dreamy with love, touching Tyler's face in the pictures and reading the yellowed newspaper clippings.

Some of the clippings were originals, cut from recent issues of the local paper and describing the comings and goings of the McKinney family, their prizes at the stock show, the awards won by their quarter horses, J.T.'s recent wedding.

Others were older, photocopied from past issues of newspapers at the library, going all the way back to Tyler's days as a high school athlete and his brilliant college career.

Jodie's special favorite was a clipping that dated from about the same time Tyler McKinney had first held her in his arms, three years ago at a community square dance. They'd been doing a circle dance called Sadie Hawkins, where all the men danced in a ring looking out and the women circled them in the opposite direction, facing the men. When the music stopped, you grabbed the man directly in front of you and he was your partner for the next dance.

Fifteen-year-old Jodie had found herself opposite tall handsome Tyler McKinney, and he had come laughing into her arms and swept her across the floor as light as thistledown.

Jodie could still remember the dreamy joy of that night, the marvelous feeling of being in Tyler's strong arms and drifting through the steps of the dance like a princess.

"Your daddy's just the most wonderful man," Jodie whispered to the small bulge of her abdomen, caressing it gently. "Just the most wonderful." As if he could understand her words, the baby stirred and moved beneath her fingers. Jodie smiled, suddenly radiant with happiness.

She'd first felt this quickening only a week ago. It had come exactly when her mother said it would, just about halfway through the fifth month when the worst of the morning sickness was finally over. Now the baby moved every day, reminding Jodie of the sweet precious burden she carried and how Tyler would want her to take care of their child.

Still smiling, she went to the tiny fridge, took out a carton of milk and poured herself a glass. Jodie sank onto the old couch and drank the cold liquid with deep childlike gulps while Tyler's handsome face smiled warm approval at her from the crowded walls.

AT ABOUT the same time that Ruth Holden and Tyler McKinney were enjoying coffee and doughnuts at the Longhorn, jealously watched by Jodie Hiltz, another coffee break was under way in the big kitchen of the Double C ranch house.

"Gawd," Lettie Mae Reese sighed, sinking heavily into a chair and smiling across the table at Virginia Parks. "What a day."

Virginia nodded agreement, then gazed into the distance with a worried frown. "Lettie Mae, did somebody think to clear all those paint cans and newspapers out of the front closet? I forgot to check if—"

"They're gone," the cook said comfortably, stirring cream into her coffee with weary satisfaction. "Just relax, girl. We got it all done as best we could, and not a minute too soon, I'd say."

"You impertinent child," Virginia said comfortably. "Almost ten years younger than I am, and you're still calling me 'girl.' Show some respect."

Lettie Mae grinned and shoved a plate of sliced fruitcake across the table toward the housekeeper. "Seven years younger," she said. "And I'll call you anything I like, missy. Especially when you got paint smudges on your nose."

Virginia gave her friend a rueful grin and rubbed at her small shapely nose. She was an attractive woman of sixty, pleasantly plump, with vivid blue eyes in a sweet gentle face and shining gray hair that she wore in a casual pageboy.

With her fair prettiness, Virginia presented a sharp contrast to thin energetic Lettie Mae. The ranch cook was an arresting woman with a lean alert face, rich brown skin and graying black hair that sprang from her head with the same kind of electric vitality that characterized everything she did.

"Lordy," the cook muttered, munching on a piece of cake and taking a thirsty gulp of coffee, "I never saw such a hullabaloo in all my days. What was J.T. thinking of, inviting the girl to visit in the middle of all this mess? Miss C.'s just having fits."

Virginia gave the other woman a brief grin. "Not too long ago you'd have been loving the idea of giving her fits, Lettie Mae."

Lettie Mae's vivid face clouded slightly. "I know," she confessed. "I was awful to her. We all were, Ginny. Funny how things change, isn't it? When the lady first came, I'd have enjoyed seeing her all worried and flustered like this. Now it just seems to tear at my heart a little bit."

Virginia nodded and looked wistfully at the rich sliced cake. "I know I shouldn't," she said, her face puckered with guilt, "but..."

"But you always do, so stop being silly," Lettie Mae said cheerfully. "You worked hard today, hauling all those wallpaper rolls around and keeping the tray filled up."

"The dining room looks nice, though, doesn't it?" Virginia said. "I really didn't like that paper at all when Miss C. first showed it to us, but I have to admit it's perfect with the new furniture."

"She's one classy lady, that one," Lettie Mae said. "She knows what she wants, and she's got a real good feel for things like that. This old house is going to be a sight for sore eyes when she gets done."

Virginia's pretty face clouded and she sipped moodily at her black coffee. "But it won't even be the same house, Lettie Mae. It'll be so different in a month or so that Miss Pauline wouldn't recognize it if she came back.''

"Ginny, Miss Pauline is never coming back," Lettie Mae said gently. "And life is moving on, and we should move on with it."

Virginia was silent, munching on her cake.

Lettie Mae stared out the window, her dark face suddenly moody. "But I surely do hate all this ruckus," she said abruptly. "It's real bad for Miss C. right now."

"Why right now, especially?"

Lettie Mae looked at her fellow employee with pity. "Because," she said, "the lady is wanting a baby. And anybody knows that all this fluster is just no way to go about getting a baby."

"A *baby!*" Virginia stared at the other woman, aghast. "But . . . she's . . . she must be . . ."

"She must be about thirty-five," Lettie Mae said firmly. "Not too old at all. And J.T.'s just fifty-five. That man's got lots of miles left in him."

Virginia shook her head. "I don't believe it. What gave you this crazy idea?"

Lettie Mae snorted. "Crazy? Didn't you see her face when your niece was here with that baby? When Miss C. held him, anybody with eyes in their head could see she was dying for a baby. And then she was looking through those knitting books of yours, asking you about all the little baby patterns. . . ."

Virginia shook her head. "She was just being nice. She's always interested in what we're doing. It's just...part of her nature."

"Oh, this has something to do with nature, all right," Lettie Mae said, leaning back expansively. "But not that kind."

Virginia shook her head again. "It's just too many changes," she said helplessly. "All this redecorating, and now Tyler's talking about building some kind of wine-making place, and Lynn's getting so much into racehorses, and poor Cal doesn't know *what* he's doing, so he'll probably wind up coming home and being underfoot again, and now if J.T.'s starting another whole family..."

"They'll need more help," Lettie Mae said cheerfully. "Probably they'll put us out to pasture and hire some younger girls to take over. It'll likely take about ten of 'em, Ginny," she added with a grin, "just to do what we're doing."

Virginia looked curiously at her friend. "How do you feel about that?"

"About being put out to pasture?" Lettie Mae shrugged. "I don't mind. I'd move into Austin and buy a nice little house close to my sister's place, and have a big garden of my own and play bingo whenever I felt like it. That doesn't sound like such a terrible idea after working almost forty years."

Virginia was silent, gazing into the depths of her coffee mug while Lettie Mae rambled on.

"Lucky for us that J.T.'s paid us so well all these years," Lettie Mae said, "and we never had to pay for room and board, neither. We've both saved enough to buy places of our own and not be beholden to anybody. With that money in the bank and the little bit that comes from Social Services when the time comes, I can have a pretty nice life. I feel real lucky that I've had such a generous boss."

Lettie Mae became aware that her friend wasn't responding, and gave her a sudden intent look. "Ginny, where do you plan to go when you leave here?"

Virginia shifted uncomfortably. "Well, I haven't really thought about it much," she lied. "I guess I wouldn't want to move into the city, though. Most of my family's still around Crystal Creek. I'd sure miss the kids if I moved away."

Lettie Mae sniffed and reached a long arm for the coffeepot on the counter, her expressive dark face showing her opinion of Virginia's restless brood of nieces and nephews.

Virginia Parks had grown up in Crystal Creek and she and Lettie Mae had come to the Double C with their mistress, Pauline Randolph, more than thirty-five years ago when Pauline and J.T. were married. Virginia's young husband had been killed in a horse-training accident while they were still at the Circle T Ranch, and Virginia had never remarried, so the children of her numerous brothers and sisters became like her own, demanding much of her vast store of love and tenderness.

And, Virginia thought gloomily, quite a lot of her money, too, in recent years, what with wedding gifts and college tuition and car loans that never seemed to get paid back.

Avoiding Lettie Mae's thoughtful gaze, she got slowly to her feet and turned toward the door. "I think I'll just run down to my room and freshen up a bit," she said. "Call me when they get here, Lettie Mae."

"Sure thing," the cook said affectionately, relaxing in her chair and giving the housekeeper a wave of her coffee mug.

Virginia trudged down the hallway past her own cozy room, letting herself quietly into the bathroom that she shared with Lettie Mae. All these years the big roomy Double C ranch house had been home to Virginia Parks, and there was a time when she wouldn't have been able to imagine living anywhere else.

But now everything was changing with such bewildering speed. Since the day their mistress died, life had begun a kind of dizzying spiral, spinning down and burning up before Virginia's shocked and frightened eyes.

First there had been the trouble with her nephew Gerald, and the hefty lawyer's fee, paid by Virginia, that had narrowly averted a prison term. Then Jennifer thought she wanted to be a ballerina, and the training had been so expensive that Auntie Virginia had to help out, and soon afterward Matthew had the motorcycle accident, and then J.T. brought home this new bride with all her new ideas....

Virginia left the bathroom and wandered into her cheerful bed-sitting-room. Still absorbed in her thoughts, she rubbed her back wearily and sank into the old padded rocker by the window, gazing out at the garden that was sere and bleak on this January afternoon.

The scene matched her mood as she thought about how the children's various crises had seriously depleted her comfortable bank account. As Lettie Mae had said, their savings were their security. J.T. made no bones about that issue.

"I don't believe in pensions," he told his employees. "I believe in paying people a real generous wage and letting them look after their future security out of that if they've got a mind to."

And he was certainly generous. Virginia had no doubt that Lettie Mae, who earned the same wage as the housekeeper, had a sizable nest egg tucked away after all these years. Certainly she'd have enough to buy her "nice little house" and enjoy a life of welcome leisure.

But Virginia's nest egg had been sadly eroded. And the final blow had been her foolish investment in Vanguard Mines.

"Don't touch it," J.T. warned his cook and housekeeper after Virginia's brother visited them and brought out the glossy prospectus. "Don't even think about it. You'll lose your shirts, girls."

And Lettie Mae had wisely left her money in savings. But Virginia had secretly disregarded J.T.'s advice and taken the plunge, because her brother was so convincing and she was seduced by the wonderful promise of replacing her lost nest egg in just one or two dividend periods.

Of course, J.T. had been right. The company went bust and the shares dropped so low they weren't worth the value of the paper. And a few months ago, when she started thinking seriously about a retirement move away from the Double C, Virginia had realized to her horror that she barely had enough money in her bank account to pay for rent and food for a single year, let alone a whole lifetime.

She huddled in the chair and covered her face with her hands, trying not to cry. But she was overwhelmed with self-pity and regret.

If only the future didn't look so frightening and unsure. If only she hadn't listened to her brother and thrown away the last of her money. If only she didn't feel so tired all the time....

Virginia's face puckered with unhappiness. She leaned forward in the rocker, rummaged in the bottom drawer of her dresser and drew out a pile of letters, all shapes and sizes, on every kind of writing paper from fancy vellum to smoothed-out brown wrapping paper.

She took a deep breath and glanced at the first letter.

"Dear Blue-Eyed Gal," it began, "I seen your letter in the *Claro Courier* and you sound like a real cute little chickie. Just the perfect gal for me as I am also sixty-plus but still a lusty young cockerel if I do say so myself. I was thinking..."

Virginia read a few more lines, her face turning pink with embarrassment.

"Lusty young cockerel!" she muttered scornfully. "More like a randy old buzzard is what *you* are, mister."

She turned to the next letter, which was entirely in poem form, though some of the lines suffered badly from a desperate effort to preserve the rhyme.

Dear Blue-Eyed Gal,
   You sound so sweet,
   And very neat,
   The girl to sweep me off my feet,
   So I must repeat
   That we should meet
   Maybe on the street
   If you like beets...

Virginia was briefly intrigued, wondering how the unknown letter writer planned to work beets into his love poem. But as quickly as it flared her interest died again, washed away by an overwhelming wave of misery at her situation and the desperate measures she'd been forced to adopt.

She tossed the poem aside and moved on to another letter, which was laboriously hand-printed and had obviously been copied word for word from some ancient book on letter-writing etiquette.

The writer would be pleased if your return correspondence would be received at the above address by the earliest possible

"Virginia!" Lettie Mae called from the hallway. "Come quick! They're here, and you should see how pretty she is!"

Hastily Virginia bundled the messy pile of letters and shoved them out of sight in the bottom drawer, wondering when she would ever get time to read them, what with all that was going on at the ranch. Then she smoothed her dress over her hips, touched her hair and hurried out through the kitchen.

Lettie Mae was concealed behind a graceful fold of drapery in the newly decorated dining room, staring with concentrated interest at the curving front drive where Tyler and a slender woman in a white suit stood gazing into an adjoining field.

Tyler gestured expansively, waving a long arm and talking with animation while the woman nodded thoughtfully and said little.

Ruth Holden really was beautiful, Virginia thought, leaning close to Lettie Mae while they both peered shamelessly at the young couple. The California visitor had a slender graceful body and a shy pretty air about her.

Tyler turned and started toward the house, drawing Ruth along with him. Virginia forgot her own troubles for a moment, smiling at the proud way Tyler held the girl's arm and escorted her up the walk.

Like a lusty young cockerel, she told herself wryly,
enjoying the spring in his step and the glow in his dark
eyes while the girl walked along beside him, as dainty
and beautiful as a pale white rose.

CHAPTER FOUR

RUTH PULLED a tan cashmere sweater over her head, settled it hastily against her shirt collar and smoothed the waistband of her slacks. She paused, looking around at the cozy interior of the Double C guest house, which reminded her pleasantly of her own rooms at home.

The colors were the same, with dark wood, creamy-colored plaster and Navaho rugs, and the big fireplace was neatly stacked with cedar logs and kindling. Ruth gazed wistfully at the generous brick hearth, thinking how nice it would be to spend the evening here curled up with a book, have a sandwich on a plate and not be required to join the family for dinner.

In spite of years of college and a good deal of traveling, Ruth was essentially a solitary person who was shy about meeting new people, often nervous and mildly tongue-tied in unfamiliar social settings. And Tyler had casually assured her that the whole family would be present at dinner, except for Cal, of course, who was still away on the rodeo circuit.

Ruth sighed, ran an anxious hand through her hair and let herself out of the guest house, hurrying across the shadowy terrace toward the kitchen where a lighted window beamed into the darkness.

She knocked tentatively on the door, waited shivering in the evening chill and was admitted by the energetic Lettie Mae whom Tyler had introduced as the cook.

"My Lord," Lettie Mae said comfortably, "look at you shaking in that cold night air. You don't need to knock, Miss Ruth. Just come on in."

Ruth smiled automatically and followed the cook into the bright warmth of the ranch kitchen, where a man and woman sat finishing their meal at the big oak table.

"Virginia Parks," the woman said with a gentle smile in response to Ruth's sudden look of panic. "I know it's a lot of names to remember all at once, Miss Ruth."

Ruth smiled her gratitude and took pains to memorize the name, then shifted her glance to the other person seated at the table. This leathery, bright-eyed old man had to be the great-grandfather Tyler had spoken of with such fondness.

"Hank Travis," Virginia said. "Mr. Hank, this is Ruth Holden. You remember J.T.'s friend, Don Holden? This is his daughter, come for a little visit."

"The California boy who makes wine?" Hank said, swiveling in his chair and fixing Ruth with a penetrating gaze.

Ruth nodded, struck by the quick intelligence in those ancient eyes and the man's sparkling sardonic expression.

"Well, how's your daddy, girl?" the old man asked. "I don't believe we've seen him 'round here for a few years, have we?"

"He's fine," Ruth said diffidently. "He's been really busy with an expansion at the winery, and—"

"Who'd've thought that no-account little slip of a boy could perduce such a good-lookin' daughter?" Hank interrupted her, deliberately using a piece of bread to mop up the pool of rich gravy on his plate and giving her a wolfish grin. "How 'bout it, girls?" he asked Lettie Mae and Virginia. "Ain't you surprised?"

Ruth stiffened, outraged that her father was being attacked in his absence by yet another of these arrogant cowboys. Even when they were a hundred years old, they apparently never lost the maddening air of smug superiority that allowed them to make fun of everybody else.

But before she could express her indignation Ruth caught a broad wink from Lettie Mae, who was standing by the counter behind the old man. Ruth held her tongue and forced herself to smile, gazing steadily into that ancient face.

He was teasing her. Hank Travis might be immensely old, but he was still perceptive enough to spot a weakness almost instantly, and mischievous enough to needle the tender area a bit.

"My father's not big but he's actually pretty tough," Ruth said in a casual voice. "You know, he once beat J.T. in a boxing match when they were young, knocked him out cold in the third round, I believe. Of course," she added thoughtfully, "poor J.T., he grew up in Texas and probably never learned a lot about manly things like self-defense."

She met Hank's eyes and found him gazing at her in startled silence for a moment, his old head stiffly erect. Then he burst into laughter, choking and slapping his bony knee while Virginia patted him anxiously on the back.

"You're all right, missy," he said to Ruth when he could speak again. "You're just fine. Have they fed you yet?"

Ruth looked around anxiously from Lettie Mae to Virginia. "I wasn't sure... I lay down in the guest house for a little nap and when I woke up I couldn't remember if Tyler said seven or seven-thirty, so I thought I'd better—"

"It's seven," Virginia said gently. "But you've got lots of time, Miss Ruth. Why don't you sit and have a cup of coffee with us before dinner? We're just finishing. Mr. Hank doesn't like to wait that long to eat with the family, so the three of us usually have an early meal here in the kitchen."

She patted the chair beside her with such a welcoming smile that Ruth felt her heart begin to warm in gratitude. The atmosphere here in the ranch kitchen was so different from her home, where Mrs. Ward guarded the domestic areas like a tigress in her lair and became fiercely sullen and bad-tempered if anybody dared to trespass.

Ruth seated herself next to Virginia and looked up at Lettie Mae with an appreciative smile when a steaming mug of coffee appeared in front of her.

"I'd offer you a glass of wine," Lettie Mae said, "but I'm scared to, you being such an expert and all. What if it's the wrong kind?"

Ruth shook her head. "There's no such thing as the wrong wine. Whatever you like is the right wine to serve, Lettie Mae. All those rules about white wine with poultry and so on, it's really just nonsense. We drink whatever we're in the mood for."

"Well, this is what we're serving tonight," Lettie Mae said with a sly grin, holding up a bottle. "Miss C. thought you just might like it."

Ruth took the bottle and was charmed to discover that it was a new Zinfandel from the Holden winery. Ruth hadn't even met this new wife of J.T.'s, but she was finding the woman more impressive all the time.

"So," Virginia asked solemnly, "is this wine all right for our main course?"

"Well, let's see." Ruth examined the bottle with a studious frown, entering into the game with them. "What meat dish are you serving?"

"Venison medallions in brown sauce," Lettie Mae said.

"Wonderful. I think the Zinfandel is an excellent choice for venison," Ruth assured them.

Hank snorted rudely and attacked the piece of apple pie that Virginia had cut for him. "In *there*," he said, waving his hand toward the elegant dining room, "it's venison medallions in brown sauce. Out here in the kitchen, it's deer 'n' gravy."

Ruth chuckled. "You know, you're absolutely right, Mr. Travis. It's always seemed to me that the main difference in things is just what people call them, nothing else."

"Damn right," Hank said placidly. "An' if you call me Mr. Travis one more time, I swear I'll never talk to you again, missy. The name's Hank."

"Hank," Ruth echoed obediently, watching in fascination as the old man demolished his hefty wedge of warm apple pie.

"So, you're an expert on wine, are you?" Hank asked, wiping his mouth on a linen napkin and holding out his coffee mug for a refill.

"I guess I am. I've been studying for years and years, so I must be."

"I never heard of such damn fool nonsense," Hank said comfortably. "Goin' away to school to learn about *wine*, for God's sake."

Ruth was getting used to his manner, and found herself tickled rather than offended by his brusque observations. "You just wouldn't believe the things people go to school to learn these days," she said solemnly. "I have a friend who's getting a master's degree in fly tying."

"*Fishin'* flies?" Hank asked in disbelief.

Ruth nodded, avoiding his eyes, while the old man stared at her in deep suspicion.

"You're joshin' me," he said finally. "You're a real bad girl."

Lettie Mae beamed at Ruth and said in delight, "I think maybe you've met your match here, Mr. Hank."

Ruth grinned back at her and Virginia. She felt so happy and warm in the big gleaming kitchen that she hated the thought of leaving. But Lettie Mae glanced at her watch, nodded briskly and hurried across to stir a pot of soup bubbling on the stove.

"It's time," she announced. "Just through that door over there, Miss Ruth. They're coming in now, and the soup's on."

Ruth nodded reluctantly, getting to her feet with a last glance at Virginia's comfortable face. Virginia smiled encouragement, and Ruth moved slowly through the door into the gracious dining room.

Lots of people were entering, all of them talking and laughing at once, most wearing casual clothes and riding boots. A slim blond woman in tailored cream slacks and a taupe silk blouse appeared at Ruth's elbow, her brown eyes offering a welcome.

"Hello, Ruth. I'm Cynthia McKinney," she said, extending a slim firm hand. "Sorry I wasn't here to greet you when you arrived. I was busy scrubbing off paint stains when the two of you drove up, and then Tyler whisked you away so fast we didn't even get a glimpse of you."

Ruth smiled back, her shyness melting in the face of the woman's warmth and sincerity. Cynthia McKinney was a beautiful woman, poised, gracious and intelligent, though her finely drawn face showed some signs of fatigue.

"The room looks lovely," Ruth said softly, waving her hand at the elegant pale surroundings. "I really like that wallpaper."

"Do you?" Cynthia asked, squeezing her arm gratefully. "Well, bless you for saying so. I liked it when I picked it out, but I've looked at so many samples lately, I really don't know what I like anymore. It's all kind of spinning together in my head."

"I think it's perfect. You must have a real talent for decorating."

"I don't know about that. But *you* certainly have a talent for saying the right thing to a weary hostess," Cynthia said with a chuckle, giving Ruth's shoulders an impulsive hug. "Carolyn," she called, turning to the crowd in the room, "come meet our guest."

Another attractive golden-haired woman crossed the room, about ten years older and much more casually dressed than their hostess. In fact, this guest wore jeans, boots and a soft white cotton shirt that accentuated her warm tanned skin.

"Hello, Ruth," she said. "I'm Carolyn Townsend, Tyler's aunt. I'm happy to meet you," she added, taking Ruth's hand in a firm businesslike grip. "We've all been very fond of your daddy through the years."

Nothing the woman said could have pleased Ruth as much. She smiled, feeling herself relaxing more and more, warming to this laughing group of cheerful unpretentious people.

The two younger women, just back from a day of horseback riding, were Tyler's sister, Lynn, a small shapely girl with auburn hair tied back with a red bandanna, and Carolyn's daughter, Beverly, who was a tall striking young woman with a beauty-queen smile.

J.T. McKinney greeted Ruth cordially, looking as handsome as ever but a little tired.

The past few months had probably been difficult for J.T. and his new wife, Ruth thought. They were obviously deeply in love, but that couldn't solve all the problems of adjustment and adaptation that had to take place when two people chose to blend their lives. Especially if one of them had an existing family, Ruth reminded herself, thinking ruefully of her warning to her own father about his bringing some dizzy young bride into the household.

J.T. was talking quietly to a tall sandy-haired man with a craggy face, likely the ranch foreman Tyler had spoken of. J.T. confirmed this by introducing the man, named Ken Slattery, and everyone sat at the table.

Ruth glanced around nervously, wondering where Tyler could be, and was surprised at the surge of relief she felt when he hurried through the door and slid into a chair beside her, bringing a breath of cool outdoor air with him.

"Two of the new Brangus bulls started fighting down in the big corral just a few minutes ago," he told his father and Ken. "We had to get them apart before one of them broke a leg."

J.T. tensed and looked sharply at his son. "Any problems?"

Tyler shook his head, smiled down at Ruth and unfolded a napkin onto his blue jeans. "A couple of the boys helped me move the big feller into the round corral. But we should maybe run a few yearlings in there to keep him settled down a bit, Ken. He's just plumb on the fight."

Ken nodded. "I'll tend to it right after we eat," he said. "They're a lot of dollars on the hoof, those big ol' boys. We sure wouldn't want one of 'em going down."

"We sure wouldn't," J.T. echoed with a sudden grim edge to his voice.

Carolyn launched into a discussion of a new bull she'd recently purchased, and Tyler smiled at Ruth.

"How's it going? Are you getting introduced to everybody?" he asked softly, bending so close that she could smell the clean scent of his after-shave.

Ruth swallowed her mouthful of soup hastily and nodded. "Pretty well," she murmured. "I'm trying hard to remember all the names, and I've only had one fight so far."

"You've had a fight?" Tyler halted with his spoon halfway to his mouth and gazed at her, his dark eyes full of interest. "Who with?"

"Your grandpa," Ruth said with a grin. "He criticized my father so I told him that Dad once knocked J.T. out cold in a boxing match, and implied that all Texas men were wimps. Then he made fun of my education, and I said..."

Tyler chuckled. "Oh, Ruth, you're just gonna fit right in. Grandpa loves you already, or he wouldn't get into that kind of sparring match with you."

"Really?"

"Really. If he thinks people are no-account types, he just ignores them."

"It must be so nice," Ruth commented wistfully, "to be old enough that you can be rude and get away with it. I'd just love that, being able to ignore people that were boring or nasty."

Tyler laughed again, and J.T. glanced over, smiling at his son's amusement. "So, Ruth," he said amiably, "has this boy been talking your ear off with all his plans for his damned winery?"

Ruth glanced at her host and paused. "Well," she said carefully, breaking open a crusty roll on her plate and buttering it as she spoke, "he certainly seems excited about the project."

"And what do you think?" J.T. asked. "Is it feasible?"

This was her chance, in front of witnesses, to throw cold water on the whole project right at the outset. But something made Ruth hesitate.

Perhaps it was the way Tyler, sitting next to her, tensed suddenly and gripped the handle of his soup-spoon so hard that his knuckles turned white. Or the sudden interest in the blue eyes of Carolyn Townsend, who leaned forward waiting for Ruth's reply. Or the quick glance that passed between J.T. McKinney and his wife, and the strange intent look on J.T.'s handsome face as he turned back to study his guest.

"It's hard to tell," Ruth said finally. "A lot of things have to be considered before a determination can be made about feasibility, J.T."

"But just off the top of your head," J.T. persisted. "What's your gut instinct, Ruth?"

Again that taut silence fell around the table. Ruth was beginning to sense strong undercurrents here, and a powerful feeling that perhaps this wine-making project was more than just a casual impulse, another money-making fling for the McKinney family.

Maybe the economic situation on these big Texas ranches was more strained than it appeared. What if the family really needed to diversify in order to survive? In that case, Tyler's expressed desire to make money and balance the books seemed a lot less odious and greedy than it had just a few hours ago, and Ruth found herself reluctant to dismiss his plans in a casual manner.

"Well," she began slowly, "my gut instinct tells me that the basic idea is probably feasible. The climate is ideal, for one thing. I spent a day at the university before I left, checking temperature tables for this area, and it looks really favorable."

"Our climate?" Beverly Townsend asked in disbelief. "For making *wine?*"

Ruth nodded, looking at the younger girl's flawlessly beautiful face. "Wine chemists have a complex method of classifying climate zones according to the heat summation. Simply put, that means the total cumulative number of days above fifty degrees from April through October."

"God knows we get lots of days like that," Carolyn said with a laugh.

"Enough to make this area a probable region four," Ruth said. "And the higher the heat summation, the more sugar content in the mature grapes. And a higher sugar content, like what's found in a region four climate, gives the wine maker a lot of flexibility in what type of wine he chooses to specialize in. That's usually a powerful economic advantage."

The group around the table gazed at her in fascination. Ruth fell silent, embarrassed by the attention she was receiving, while Cynthia rescued her by telling a funny story about purchasing wine at the local store.

Tyler squeezed Ruth's shoulders under cover of the general laughter and bent close to her, his dark eyes shining. "Thanks, Ruth," he whispered. "That was great! With your support, I'm halfway there already."

Ruth nodded, feeling her cheeks warm uncomfortably at his impulsive hug and the feel of his strong muscular arm around her.

She returned to her soup, puzzling over her own confusion, wondering what was happening. Her emotions, usually so carefully controlled, were all in turmoil, and her firm opinions seemed to be wavering and shifting before her eyes, growing hazy and drifting away like wisps of smoke on a seductive breath of warm Texas wind.

TYLER PAUSED inside the guest house, looking down at Ruth, who smiled back nervously and moved across the room to stand beside the big fireplace.

Tyler followed her and leaned one arm on the mantel, kicking absently at a heavy log on the floor near his boot. "Are you sure you don't want to go into town with the girls, Ruth?" he asked. "They haven't left yet. I think I could still catch them. And you'd like Zack's. It's a real old-time cowboy honky-tonk."

Ruth shook her head. "I don't think so, Tyler. I'm really tired," she said with a brief smile of apology. "This day seems like it's already been about a week long. I'm used to leading a pretty quiet life, you know."

Tyler nodded, looking at her in thoughtful silence.

"But you can go, can't you?" Ruth said, shifting uncomfortably beneath his penetrating dark gaze. "I mean," she added with a smile. "It's okay with me to be left alone, Tyler. I like being alone."

"Except for your cat."

"Yes," she said, with another wistful little smile that tugged powerfully at his heart. "I really miss my cat. I'd give anything to have him here tonight."

"What does he do that's so comforting?"

"He sleeps on my stomach," Ruth confessed. "In a big warm furry ball. It's the most wonderful feeling."

With most other women Tyler would probably have risked an off-color remark at this point, but he looked into Ruth's candid eyes and found himself at a loss for words.

"You know, I really like your family," she told him shyly. "They seem so wonderful, all of them. And the staff, too," she added.

"The staff?"

"I mean Ken and Lettie Mae and Virginia, all of them. The whole atmosphere at the ranch seems so...democratic, somehow. Like everybody's just one big happy family."

"Well," Tyler said cheerfully, "we've always been pretty democratic. In fact, it's a bit of little-known family history, but the Travis men actually voted against the Confederacy and went over to Kentucky to fight with the Union troops."

Ruth gazed at him, fascinated. "Really?"

"Really," Tyler said solemnly. "So it's not all that surprising that we choose to treat the staff like human beings, is it?"

Ruth flushed. "I didn't mean that," she said. "It's not just a matter of . . . class and power, that kind of thing."

Tyler watched as she knit her delicate brows, searching for words to express herself.

"They all seem to be so close to your family, and genuinely care about them. But our housekeeper, Mrs. Ward," Ruth said haltingly, "it's not as if she considers herself inferior to us. It's more like she uses her position as a shield, to make sure that no closeness ever develops. You know?"

Tyler nodded. "Why strive for equality with her employer?" he said cheerfully. "That would be such a comedown for her."

Ruth chuckled, obviously delighted by his understanding. Tyler gazed down at her. Again he fought the irrational urge, wearily familiar by now, to gather her into his arms and cover her face with kisses.

But when she saw his warm intent gaze, her expression grew cautious and she looked down hastily at her feet, smoothing the bright rug with the toe of her shoe.

"That was real nice of you, Ruth," Tyler said huskily, "telling my daddy that our climate is suited to wine making. I sure can use that kind of support."

"Why?" she asked, looking up at him with wide thoughtful eyes. "Why is the whole thing so important to you, Tyler? It's not just the money, is it?"

"Of course it's the money," he said, shifting awkwardly under her questioning gaze. "But I don't want to get rich and buy a gold-plated Ferrari, if that's what you mean. Things are getting real tight in the beef industry these days, Ruth. We need to find alternative sources of income."

"Just you? I mean, are the problems just here at the Double C, or is everyone in the same boat?"

"Oh, everyone's in the same boat," Tyler said grimly, "and it's getting pretty damn leaky. People are trying everything they can think of just to survive. Rare breeds of cattle, hunting lodges, dude ranches, exotic livestock, bed-and-breakfast operations... you name it, somebody's doing it to keep their ranch alive."

"And how many are trying wine making?"

"Some. There's already a few wineries right around Austin, and more over by Lubbock. I've been to all of them."

"Are they mostly producing dessert wines? Muscat, sherry, port, those kinds?"

Tyler shrugged. "I don't know. I didn't pay a lot of attention to that kind of stuff. I'm just interested in how the books balance."

Ruth stared at him in disbelief. "Tyler, you have to decide what kind of wine you intend to make. It's vital to your whole operation."

He set his jaw stubbornly. "That can all come later. The way I look at it, if you're going to be a rancher, it doesn't matter if you're raising Hereford or Brangus," he added with a shrug of his broad shoulders. "You still need to fence the land and find out what feed costs and beef sells for."

"But it's just not the same as..." Ruth paused, her face pink with distress, and then took herself in hand, trying to smile. "We'll talk about it tomorrow," she said. "Okay?"

"Okay," Tyler said, charmed again by the sweetness of her face when she smiled. She was clearly tired, and he felt a powerful longing to take care of her in a physical sense—an urge that was, surprisingly enough, almost nonsexual. He wanted to slip off her shoes, rub her feet, remove that heavy sweater and massage her back until she fell into a deep gentle sleep.

"Care for a back rub?" he asked her softly.

She stared at him in alarm. "I don't...I don't think so."

"All right, then. Anything else I can do?"

"No, thank you, I'm just fine. What time is breakfast?"

"Seven-thirty, or whenever you wander in. Or they'll feed you in the kitchen if you like. The ladies seem to adore you already, so I don't think you'll have any trouble finding something to eat."

"But I'd like to spend the day with you," Ruth said, "looking at the sites you're considering. Maybe you could give me a wake-up call if I oversleep, all right?"

"I'd love to," Tyler said promptly. "I'll come around at the crack of dawn and throw pebbles at your window. You know, I really appreciate this, Ruth,'' he added, the teasing note dropping from his voice.

He hesitated, still yearning for some kind of physical closeness with her, finding it strangely difficult to tear himself away. Somehow the little guest house seemed like a cozy golden haven.

"I'll see you tomorrow," Tyler said huskily, touching her arm and turning away before his resolve could begin to weaken once more. "Sleep well, Ruth."

JODIE CROUCHED in the dense tangle of honeysuckle vines beneath the window of the guest house, flattening herself against the wall when Tyler came out and closed the door quietly behind him.

She held her breath and gazed intently from her screen of branches, watching his tall erect form stride away toward the lighted house. Then she exhaled softly and edged up cautiously to peer through a tiny crack in the curtains.

The woman was undressing, taking her clothes off with weary slowness but still pausing to fold them neatly and put them away in the drawers of the big rosewood armoire next to the bed.

Naked except for bra and panties, she stopped to yawn and stretch, then turned and padded toward the adjoining bathroom. Jodie peered critically at the woman's slim pale body, relieved to see that though her hips were slimmer than Jodie's, her breasts were much smaller as well.

Jodie smiled secretly, touching her swelling young bosom beneath the dark fabric of her nylon jacket. She knew that Tyler loved her breasts, and that he wouldn't have any interest in this scrawny, short-haired woman, whoever she was.

Still, Jodie glared through the window at the closed bathroom door, a worried frown creasing her face when she remembered how Tyler had lingered by the fireplace and gazed fixedly at the woman, talking to her in low tones that Jodie couldn't overhear, try as she might.

But they were just talking. He never even touched her, and he left right away. Jodie relaxed once more and turned to gaze at the looming bulk of the big ranch house, wondering where Tyler had gone.

Months of careful surveillance had made her familiar with his habits, but he wasn't always predictable. He might be down at one of the workers' bungalows or having a late-night beer with Ken Slattery or visiting the family of one of the ranch hands. Or he could be in J.T.'s study, talking quietly about business matters with his father.

Sometimes he joined Lynn and Cynthia in the upstairs sitting room watching television, or chatted in the kitchen with the cook and housekeeper while they fussed over him and plied him with cookies.

Jodie smiled, thinking dreamily about how handsome Tyler was and how much everybody loved him.

She decided not to track his movements tonight, since the moonlit yard was bright and she might be seen. She'd go straight to his room and wait for him.

Matching actions to thoughts, Jodie slipped like a blackened shadow along the stretch of hedge between the guest house and the main one, pausing at the base of the veranda.

Over by the old man's stone house one of the ranch dogs lifted his head and glanced at her lazily, but the dogs knew Jodie well and were still wolfing down the rich scraps of meat she'd brought for them as usual from the butcher shop in town.

It wasn't always easy, balancing the greasy bleeding package of meat on the handlebars of her bike on the long cold ride out from town, then carrying it under her jacket as she crept onto the ranch grounds. But it was worth the effort because the dogs always waited for her with tails wagging eagerly and made no sound after she fed them, no matter where she wandered on the property.

Jodie paused, breathing deeply, and patted the small bulge of her stomach. Then she began to climb rapidly and silently up the matted screen of Virginia creeper vines to the safety of the second-floor balcony.

Once on secure footing, she held her breath and crept the length of the balcony, pausing to gaze in windows as she went.

Lynn's room was empty, of course. Jodie had seen the two laughing women leaving for town in Beverly's little car and felt a brief surge of envy, thinking about their lives. They never had a whole slew of whining little brothers and sisters to care for. They didn't have to work in a grubby old drugstore thirty hours a week, and live in a single room and be treated like dirt.

"But neither will I," Jodie whispered to herself, gazing at Lynn's empty room, so warm and beautiful and full of riding trophies and prize ribbons. "As soon as our baby is born, Tyler will marry me and I'll live right here with the McKinneys and have all kinds of pretty clothes and a shiny Cadillac convertible to drive around in."

She sighed in bliss and edged past the master bedroom, which was empty as well. Jodie felt a pang of regret, because she liked watching J.T. and his lovely blond wife, especially when they kissed and fondled and made love. It was fun to pretend that the two people in the massive bed were her and Tyler, running this big ranch and loving each other in the privacy of their bedroom at night.

But she couldn't wait for J.T. and his wife, because she had to be in position before Tyler came back. Almost faint with excitement and anticipation, Jodie crouched low and slipped past the remaining windows to the one at the end that looked into Tyler's room.

The room was lighted, and Jodie's heart began to pound wildly. She pushed aside a trailing fall of vines and edged into a cavity among the heavy branches, fitting her body in place with the ease of long practice. Then she lifted her head, peeped in a lower corner of the window and caught her breath.

Tyler stood in the middle of the room stripping his clothes off and tossing them onto a worn leather armchair. Light glistened on the knotted muscles of his arms and shone on the soft mat of curly hair that covered his chest, running in a dark line all the way down his hard flat abdomen.

Jodie sighed in pleasure, watching avidly as he flipped the fastening on his tooled leather belt and unzipped his jeans, pulling them down and kicking them aside, then bending to hang them over the back of the chair. He tugged off his socks and stood erect, his powerful legs braced, his undershorts bulging with the familiar rich maleness that made Jodie feel weak and faint with desire.

She moaned softly and rocked on her heels, almost overcome as the man in the lighted room dropped to the floor and began to do a rapid series of push-ups. Jodie wet her lips and gazed at his long powerful body, his rippling biceps and the lock of dark hair that kept falling over his forehead.

"That's your daddy," she whispered to the baby that kicked lazily within her. "See him? That's your daddy. Isn't he just wonderful?"

Oblivious to cramped legs and nighttime chill, Jodie crouched in the shadows and peered through the lighted panes of glass. Far below, the dogs sniffed the ground looking for any missed pieces of their late-night treat, and an owl in the trees by the river sounded its melancholy three-note call in the pale moonlight.

CHAPTER FIVE

RUTH LOUNGED in the saddle, enjoying the feel of the thin winter sunshine on her back. She slipped her riding gloves into her pocket, loosened the cotton bandanna around her neck and undid the top buttons on her denim jacket, smiling dreamily as her horse picked his way down the steep rock-strewn hillside.

Just ahead of her, Tyler's tall bay gelding switched its tail and skittered sideways when its metal-shod hoof dislodged a couple of smaller stones that went clattering down the slope. Tyler shifted and adjusted in the saddle with careless ease, his tall body swaying and straightening like part of the animal that he rode.

Tyler had removed his jacket earlier and tied it in a neat roll behind the cantle. He wore a faded plaid shirt that strained across his back and rested easily on his broad flat shoulders. Ruth liked to gaze at those big shoulders, the easy grace of him in the saddle and the hard-muscled leanness of his waist circled by the wide, tooled leather belt.

Abruptly she frowned and tried to gather her wayward thoughts, a process that seemed to be getting more difficult with each passing day.

Ruth had been at the ranch for almost a week, which was the entire length of time she'd originally planned to stay. But she didn't feel that she'd made any progress at all. She and Tyler were still no closer to a conclusion on the future of the Double C winery than the day she stepped off the plane in Austin.

Ruth shook her head, gazing at his dark hair beneath the brim of the gray Stetson. The mind inside that handsome head was so stubborn and so rigidly determined that Ruth despaired of getting Tyler McKinney to change his opinion about anything.

Cynthia had complained fondly to Ruth that J.T. was exactly the same. Ruth, however, saw a fundamental difference between Tyler and his father, because coupled with Tyler's stubbornness was a driving ambition and a kind of buoyant energy that was truly alarming.

For instance, she'd learned to her horror that Tyler actually intended to start his vineyard this spring, within a couple of months. To Ruth, who would have preferred two or three years of careful research and planning, this prospect was not only terrifying but appalling. He knew almost nothing about soil conditions, hybrid plants, water levels, winery equipment or even the type of wine he intended to produce, and yet he was prepared to rush out and plant the grapes.

"Might as well get the vines started, right?" he'd say serenely. "They take three years to mature, so by the time we work through all these other little details, there'll be some grapes ready to pick."

"*Little details,*" Ruth would echo, aghast. "Tyler, these things are absolutely, positively..."

But he'd already be off on another tangent, questioning her about bottling methods, or market prices and common stocks, and she'd find herself shaking her head in despair.

Tyler interrupted her thoughts now by glancing back over his shoulder, his tanned face deeply shadowed beneath the brim of his hat.

"How about this, Ruth?" he asked, waving a hand at the field beside them. "I think this has got everything you said we needed. Eastern exposure, drainage toward the river, a moderate slope and a good rich soil bed."

Ruth glanced dubiously at the area he indicated. "It looks pretty rocky, Tyler."

"We can clear the rocks. Get all the ranch hands' kids out here some weekend with a tractor and a stoneboat, pay 'em a couple dollars an hour and get the whole thing cleared in a few days."

Ruth gazed at him, fascinated by the man's irrepressible ability to overcome any problem with floods of positive thinking.

Tyler grinned. "Come on, Ruth, don't search so hard for negative stuff. Look on the bright side for once. This is a perfect spot to plant the grapes, and you know it."

"That's what you said about the first site, and it was a valley bottom so poorly drained that all your vines would have rotted the first winter."

Tyler shrugged. "Well, I've learned something since then. That's what you came here for, right, to teach me about the business? And I've been a real good pupil, haven't I?"

Ruth spread her hands wide in a gesture of despair. "Tyler, nobody could ever teach you *anything*. Not a thing. You're absolutely hopeless."

He grinned, then edged his horse closer to hers, his handsome face suddenly sober. Ruth tensed in the saddle and pretended to be interested in a lonely tumbledown little shack near the crest of the hillside. She squinted up at the weathered gray building, her heart thundering beneath the denim jacket.

This was beginning to happen all the time as she and Tyler spent long days together. His gaze was getting darker and more intent, the light in his eyes more meaningful.

And Ruth's treacherous body was aching to respond but at the same time her mind was screaming a warning. One of these days Tyler McKinney was going to take her in his arms, and unless she fled back to California before it was too late, Ruth was deeply afraid that a relationship with this man might prove to be her undoing.

Every time Ruth got involved with a man, the result seemed to be painful and embarrassing. None of them seemed to understand her passion for her job. She would always be disappointed and begin to draw back amid accusations and bitter arguments, eventually finding herself alone and somewhat relieved. In fact, after the recent disaster with Harlan, Ruth had pretty much given up on men. Wine making, she'd decided, was much more rewarding and certainly safer.

"Tyler, what's that funny little shack over there?" she asked, struggling to keep her voice light and casual.

Tyler turned away with an easy grin that told her he wasn't fooled by her pretense. "One of the horse wranglers built it years and years ago."

"How many years?" Ruth asked, sensing a story. To her surprise she was growing to love the colorful stories of old Texas, especially when the big sprawling ranch was a piece of living history that unfolded before her eyes each morning.

"Long before I was born," Tyler said. "It's been there ever since as I can remember."

"Why did he build it?"

Tyler lifted a long denim-clad leg over the pommel and slid easily to the ground, then turned to help Ruth down, his hands lingering on her waist as he set her on the ground.

"He was a loner," Tyler said, turning with Ruth at his side and leading the horses toward a little stand of rustling live oak trees near the path. "The legend was that he was educated at a college back east and came out to the frontier to be a horse wrangler when his girl jilted him. He didn't like living with the rough-and-tumble ranch hands, so he built that little shack up on the hill where he could see all the buildings and corrals, and he spent all his free time up there. I guess he used to have the place full of books and wood carvings that he whittled, but they all got lost and scattered when he died.''

Ruth was silent, her eyes shining as she pictured the solitary quiet man with his broken heart and his quiet cabin full of books.

''Can we go up and look at it?''

Tyler shook his head. ''Nothing to see. Just four walls and a couple of sagging old benches and tables. Cal and I used to play up there sometimes when we were kids, but I doubt that anybody's been inside the place for years. Maybe the odd polecat and rattlesnake.''

Ruth shivered and drew a little closer to Tyler, sinking down beside him on a broad flat rock at the edge of the grove.

Tyler put a long arm around her shoulders and drew her casually against him, smiling down at her. ''You still haven't told me what you think about this site, Ruth.''

''I'm afraid to,'' she confessed.

''Why?''

''Because,'' Ruth said helplessly, ''if I tell you it looks pretty good, you'll rush into town tomorrow and order the vines, and start planting them in a month or two.''

''Of course I will. What's wrong with that?''

''Tyler, we haven't even decided on what kind of vines to plant.''

"*You* haven't decided yet," Tyler said, unruffled. He cuddled her closer and bent to rub his cheek casually against her hair. "I told you, I'm starting with six or seven types of vinifera, like everybody else does. That's the variety that grows the best on this continent. All the wineries use it."

"Vinifera has a lot of advantages," Ruth said slowly. "But I still really think you should consider specializing in a few of the hybrids, Tyler. With this climate, a hybrid vine would give you much more control of the sugar content, and that's important to wine quality when you're just getting established."

Tyler shook his head stubbornly. "Hybrid vines are a lot more expensive, and slower-growing, too. And they're not as hardy. I'm not taking any risks with this project, Ruth. If I plant a half dozen types of vinifera, I can see which ones grow the best and concentrate on them."

Ruth frowned. This was a familiar argument, and one that she had little hope of winning. Still, her careful scientific mind recoiled at the man's impulsiveness, his cheerful willingness to rush ahead and fling himself headlong into such a complex project without long, cautious scrutiny and planning.

"What's the matter?" Tyler asked, leaning forward to peer at her face.

"It just scares me," Ruth said, trying to put her misgivings into words. "You're so... reckless."

"I'm not reckless. I'm just confident. That's the spirit that won the West," Tyler said placidly. "This is a rugged country, Ruthie. No place for cowards and sissies.''

''*Cowards* and *sissies?*'' Ruth echoed, glaring up at him.

But she couldn't stay angry with Tyler. His enthusiasm was so infectious, and his brash self-assurance always made her smile in spite of her fears. He caught the laughter in her wide eyes and smiled back at her fondly, bending his head to nuzzle her cheek in casual brotherly fashion.

Ruth pulled away and pretended to be deeply interested in the fastening at the cuff of her jacket. ''Tyler...'' she began.

''Yeah?'' Tyler squinted at the field beside them and then across the rolling hills into the hazy blue distance. ''You know, Ruth,'' he said thoughtfully, ''we could branch off the highway right there and run a road in at the base of the hill so the trucks can get in and out. That would be even better, because the traffic from the winery wouldn't cause a lot of noise and uproar over at the ranch.''

Ruth chuckled. ''It's a barren rocky field,'' she said aloud to nobody in particular. ''He hasn't even selected his vine stock. And he already sees long lines of trucks driving in and out, loaded with cases of wine.''

''A man has to plan ahead,'' Tyler told her serenely. ''I'm a real cautious kind of guy, you know. I like to consider everything.''

Ruth choked and raised her arms in despair, not trusting herself to respond. Instead she went back to the matter she'd been thinking of a few moments earlier. "Tyler, was Virginia ever married?"

"Sure," Tyler said, still gazing at the enchanting network of roads and vineyards that flourished in his mind's eye. "But it was a long time ago, before we were born. Her husband was a ranch hand at the Circle T. You know, where Carolyn lives now? We had dinner over there on Tuesday."

Ruth nodded.

"He was breaking a colt and it reared up and rolled over on him. He died instantly."

"Oh, that's awful," Ruth said, her delicate face turning pale. "Poor Virginia. And she never remarried?"

Tyler shook his head, bending to pick up a small flat rock and roll it absently between his fingers. "She came over to the Double C when my mama and daddy got married, and since then she's been pretty much wrapped up in the family. Of course," he added, "she's got a whole lot of nieces and nephews, and she sees them all the time. Why do you ask, Ruth?"

Ruth moved uneasily on the rock. "I've talked to her quite a bit since I came. She's so nice, Tyler. She's even offered to teach me to sew. I really like her."

Tyler nodded, holding the stone between his thumb and middle fingers as he pulled his arm back in experimental fashion. "She's a terrific lady, Virginia is. Lots of times she covered up for me when I did something I shouldn't, and kept me from getting into trouble. She never said a word, either."

"I think she's . . ." Ruth paused, staring at the man beside her. "Tyler, what are you doing?"

He grinned, a little abashed. "This is a perfect skippin' stone, Ruth. I'll take it with me, and when we get to the river I bet I can skip this stone twelve times."

"Twelve times!" she scoffed. "Nobody can skip a stone twelve times, Tyler McKinney. It's just not possible."

"Wanna bet?"

"What stakes?" Ruth asked, dropping her eyes so she wouldn't have to meet that mischievous gaze.

"Well, let's see. If I skip it twelve times, you have to kiss me."

"Certainly not," Ruth said with dignity.

"Why not?" he teased. "If you don't think it's possible, why would you hesitate?"

"Because I'd hate to risk something so terrible. About Virginia," she added hastily, to forestall whatever he might be about to say. "I'm really concerned about her, Tyler."

"Concerned? Why?"

"I think she's worried about the future."

Tyler turned to look at the woman beside him, his handsome face startled.

"What do you mean, the future?"

"You know," Ruth said awkwardly, "about where she's going to live, and how, after she finally leaves the ranch."

"Why would she leave the ranch?"

"She and Lettie Mae aren't young women anymore, Tyler," Ruth said gently. "They may have been around all your life, but they can't go on working here forever. They'll both have to retire sometime. What happens to them when they do?"

"Has Virginia told you she's worried?"

"Oh, no. Not in so many words. But a couple of things she's said have made me wonder if—"

Tyler shook his head firmly. "You must have misunderstood. Neither of those ladies has any worries about the future. Daddy's paid them a real good wage over the years, Ruth. And a while back, maybe five or six years, I even had the accountant discuss their investments with them just to make sure they were in good shape. Both of them can afford a pleasant retirement."

Ruth subsided, feeling relieved. "Well, that's good to hear. She's just so nice, Tyler, and so gentle and sweet. I'd hate to think of her being frightened or in uncomfortable circumstances."

Tyler smiled down at the slender woman beside him. "What a girl," he teased. "She worries about the housekeeper, worries about her father and her cat and the weather and what kind of wine I should make.... Ruthie, is there anything you *don't* worry about?"

Ruth opened her mouth to protest, but she was too late. He was already pulling her close to him, his dark face full of laughter as he bent toward her.

Ruth gasped and stiffened, then felt herself melt alarmingly as his hard lips found hers. Their kiss was tentative at first, growing more passionate as Ruth's body and mouth betrayed her completely by responding with fiery intensity.

She stirred in his embrace, folding herself against his broad chest, loving the feel of his arms around her and the seeking mouth that moved from her lips to her cheeks and eyelids and throat.

"Sweet little Ruth," he whispered huskily. "The minute I laid eyes on you, I wanted to kiss that dimple. Just like this."

His mouth roamed hungrily across her face, nuzzled the soft hair around her ears and the silky skin at her throat beneath the cotton bandanna, then drifted back to her lips again. His hands, too, began to move gently over her body, stroking her hips and thighs, creeping up beneath her jacket to cup her breasts.

Ruth shuddered and trembled on the brink of utter abandonment, an unfamiliar and disturbing emotion for her. Frightened by the pounding intensity of her reaction, she summoned all her resources so she could pull away from him. Then she turned aside in awkward silence, patting nervously at her hair and adjusting her shirt collar.

"We shouldn't do that, Tyler," she whispered finally.

"Why not?" he asked, his face still warm with emotion. "Why shouldn't we, Ruth? I told you, I've wanted to kiss you since I first saw you. And I don't think you hated it all that much, either."

Ruth shook her head. "We have business to attend to," she said. "You have some really important decisions to make, choices that could have far-reaching financial consequences for this whole ranching operation. And I'm here as your adviser. I think it's dangerous to complicate that relationship."

"I see," Tyler said, gazing down at her. His tone was sober but his dark eyes began to dance with mischief. "Business before pleasure. Is that it, Ruthie?"

"Something like that," she whispered, resolving fervently to place herself far, far away from this man before they could indulge in the kind of pleasure he was thinking of.

"Okay," he said, surprising her by leaning back and folding his hands casually behind his head, like a man with nothing on his mind but relaxing in the sun. "What's the next order of business, then, boss?"

"I think we should go to Lubbock," Ruth said promptly, grateful for the change of subject. "I'd like you to look at some of those functioning wineries, Tyler."

"I've seen most of them already."

"I know, but I'd like to take a closer look at their presses, and the kind of stemmers and crushers they use. Also, I think you should consider the possibility of leasing winery space over there for a few years while you start your vine stock."

"*Leasing?*" He stared at her in horror.

"Yes," Ruth said firmly. "It's done all the time in California, Tyler. You rent space in another winery, contract for the grapes and produce a few vintages while you're waiting to establish your own operation. It's a terrific way to learn the business, and it doesn't—''

Tyler was already shaking his head and Ruth felt a familiar sinking of her heart when she saw the set look of that handsome jaw.

"Tyler, why are you so obstinate? Why won't you even *consider* a new idea? You can't just reject it out of hand, without even thinking about it!"

"I've already thought about it," he said calmly. "I researched the concept of leasing months ago, Ruth. It's not done here nearly as much as it is in California, because the grapes just aren't available, for one thing, and neither is the winery space."

"But if it's possible at all, it's worth—''

"Ruth, I'm not going to lease space. Almost all the major estate wineries in Texas produce eighty to a hundred percent of their own grapes.''

"But you're not a major winery!" Ruth said in despair. "You don't even have a single vine planted yet, Tyler!''

"I will," he said placidly, getting up and reaching a casual hand to help Ruth to her feet. "And when I get started I'll have the biggest, shiniest, most efficient, most profitable operation in this half of Texas. Just wait and see, Ruthie.''

She stood slowly and gazed at the man in helpless silence, wondering whether he could be right.

Tyler McKinney's particular brand of confidence and determination had a way of making dreams into reality...and of brushing aside anyone who got in the way, Ruth thought with a little shiver.

"So when should we go to Lubbock?" he asked cheerfully. "Tomorrow?"

Ruth suppressed her troubled thoughts and paused to concentrate. "Not tomorrow," she said finally. "We have those appointments in Austin, remember? We're getting the results of the soil and water analysis, and talking to representatives from the grape-growers' association."

"Right," Tyler said cheerfully. "I forgot about all that boring scientific stuff. Sorry, Ruth," he added hastily when she glared at him and punched his arm with considerable force.

"All this stuff you find so *boring,*" she began stiffly, "is absolutely necessary, Tyler. I don't care if you decide to go with all vinifera plants, you still need to have some idea what kinds to select, and what areas of the ranch are best suited to them."

"Okay, no problem. Besides," he added with a grin, "I sure won't be bored when we go to Lubbock."

"Why?"

"Well, because it's a long trip, Ruthie. We'll have to stay over a couple of nights. I think that little field trip could prove to be real interesting."

Ruth flushed and turned away, concentrating on mounting her horse and settling herself in the padded seat of the big stock saddle.

"On second thought," she said after a long awkward silence, "maybe I shouldn't go to Lubbock. You can probably manage just as well on your own, Tyler, especially if I give you some notes on what to look for. You don't need me."

He swung his long leg over the cantle and drew himself erect in his saddle, turning to gaze at her with a hurt look. "Why wouldn't you go?"

"Well, for one thing," Ruth began, moving aside as he reined his tall horse close to hers, "you're not going to listen to a single thing I say, anyhow, so why bother taking me along as an adviser? And besides," she added, her face clouding, "that trip's going to keep me here for at least another week, Tyler, and I really should be getting home."

"Why? You told me there's nothing to do at home right now, that it's a real quiet time."

"That's true, but..." Ruth paused, looking troubled as she toyed with the heavy, braided leather rein. "I'm really worried about Hagar," she confessed finally, looking up and meeting Tyler's gaze, her brown eyes wide and troubled.

"Your cat?"

Ruth nodded. "He's all alone with Mrs. Ward all day long, and she's so..."

"Mrs. Ward's the housekeeper?" Tyler said. "The one who rides the motorcycle and puts cats in clothes dryers? Sorry, Ruth," he added hastily when he saw how her delicate face twisted with anguish.

Ruth shuddered. "She's just heartless, Tyler. And Hagar's such a sweetie, and so trusting. He loves everybody. He's just so vulnerable, all alone with her. I can't stand the thought of it."

"So," Tyler said calmly, "let's phone tonight and see how he is. Tell your daddy that you're concerned and get him to make sure the cat's kept safe. I can't have you leaving yet, Ruth. I need a lot more help before you go."

Ruth hesitated while both horses shifted restlessly on the rock-strewn path. She gazed up at Tyler, wondering how to respond.

Did he really value her advice, or was he just looking forward to the sexual possibilities of their upcoming trip? She trembled in the pale sunlight, haunted by a sudden burning vision of herself lying naked in this man's arms, alone with him in some quiet hidden place while the two of them allowed their passions free rein. . . .

"Ruth?"

Ruth shook herself and turned her horse around on the path, facing back toward the ranch. Tyler followed, watching her intently.

"I'm just wondering," Ruth said over her shoulder, "how much attention you'll really pay to my opinions on this little trip to Lubbock."

"Oh, I'll pay you all kinds of attention," Tyler assured her with a flashing grin. "*Constant* attention, Ruth."

"Tyler, I'm warning you—"

"I'll take a notebook," he continued, warming to the subject, "and write down every word you say. I'll listen to every little pearl of wisdom that drops from your lips. I'll memorize all the scientific data and answer skill-testing questions. Just promise you'll come with me, Ruth."

She threw him a skeptical glance over her shoulder, then turned aside to hide her smile. No matter what Tyler's motives might be, Ruth knew that he was speaking the truth. This man had a mind so quick and brilliant that he remembered everything she told him, and though he didn't seem to pay much attention to her suggestions, there were definitely times when she could tell from his conversation that he'd been thinking about something she'd told him earlier.

"Ruth?"

"All right, I'll go," she said wearily, spurring her horse into a canter to put some distance between them. But the smile on her face, hidden from his view, and the sudden warm glow in her eyes belied the crispness of her tone.

TYLER GAZED thoughtfully at the slim woman beside him as they rode back toward the ranch buildings. She was so appealing, this woman, and she looked lovelier every day. The more he got to know her, the more deeply he valued her sweetness and honesty, her intelligence and the feisty independence that made her stand up to him and defend her own views with such tenacity.

She was more than just a pretty face, much more. And yet he was powerfully drawn to her on a physical basis as well. She looked so delicious, like some rich and wonderful confection that promised to be the most completely, utterly satisfying thing you'd ever tasted.

Tyler's mind slipped ahead to the prospect of their trip to West Texas. His throat tightened and his mind spun dizzily when he thought about getting Ruth by herself, far away from family and responsibilities, free to respond to him without distractions.

She seemed so reserved and cool, with her reams of scientific data and her ladylike self-contained manner. But Tyler suspected that there was a lot more to this woman, a rich well of passion and spontaneity just waiting to be tapped by the right man.

In fact, Tyler was convinced that Ruth Holden, despite her severity and businesslike approach, was going to be all kinds of fun in bed.

He could hardly wait.

Tyler grinned as he rode beside her, fingering the smooth flat stone in his pocket and noting how firmly she'd reined her horse around and beaten a path back to the ranch.

No danger of passing near the river, losing their bet and having to kiss him again, not for this little woman. She wasn't taking any chances, because she'd liked it too much the first time. He could tell how much she'd liked it by the feel of her in his arms, the clinging warmth of her body and the urgent sweetness of her lips.

God, what a woman, Tyler thought, shifting awkwardly in the saddle, suddenly tense and aching with need. He squinted at the distant hills, battling another stormy wave of longing.

Their little trip to Lubbock, he told himself ruefully, wasn't coming a moment too soon.

JODIE HILTZ edged across the floor, crouching low to keep from being seen through the window. She raised herself on one knee and peered out, expelling her breath with noisy relief when she saw the two horses retreating along the path.

Slowly the girl straightened and gazed through the sagging window of the little cabin, frowning at the two riders as they emerged from the screen of oak trees, descended the hill and dropped out of sight.

She picked up an old corn broom leaning in the corner and plied it furiously on the rough slate floor of the cabin, sending dust flying in clouds around her head.

"Stupid woman," Jodie muttered aloud, her pretty face white with anger. "Hanging around him, throwing herself at him all the time when anybody can see he can't stand her. Why can't she just go back where she came from? I *hate* her."

Jodie had been busy inside the abandoned cabin, getting ready for Tyler to come and visit her. She hadn't even been aware of the two riders until they were almost at the doorstep, and for a brief heart-stopping moment she'd thought the woman was actually going to come up and look inside.

"But Tyler wouldn't let her," Jodie murmured, smiling with satisfaction. "Tyler always protects me, because he loves me. And you," she said to the swelling lump that was their baby. "He loves you, too."

She propped the broom back in the corner and surveyed the interior of the little cabin with narrowed eyes and a brief smile of pleasure.

Cal and Tyler McKinney probably wouldn't have recognized this as the abandoned building they'd played in when they were boys. In those days the cabin had been musty and strewn with animal droppings, old birds' nests and windblown dust. But over the past few months, Jodie had wrought a number of changes. She'd hauled water from the spring out back and cleaned and scrubbed, tacked heavy plastic across the gaping window, even brought tools and tightened the hinges so the door couldn't sag and let dust in.

Bright checked place mats adorned the old table, which was neatly set for two with plastic dishes, mismatched cutlery, even a jar of plastic flowers in the center. The food for their meal was still in the basket nearby—tins of baked beans, a loaf of bread, a plastic carton of coleslaw and a couple of apples.

Jodie surveyed the table setting with satisfaction, arching her swollen stomach and rubbing the small of her back in an unconscious gesture of weariness.

It wasn't easy, bringing all these things out so she and Tyler could have their secret dinners together. She could only come on days like this one, when she had the whole afternoon off. She had to balance the heavy basket on her bike all the way from town, but she was able to manage the awkward trip because she had been using a bicycle for transportation almost since she was old enough to walk.

The hard parts were hiding the bike in the weeds by the road, hefting the basket through the fence onto Carolyn Townsend's property and hiking almost a mile under its weight, then hauling the bulky container up the limestone cliffs until she could cross the barbed-wire fence onto McKinney land and reach this little cabin.

But the journey was well worth the effort because once she was in the cabin, Jodie could see the whole sprawling ranch house and yards, watch the comings and goings of all the McKinneys and everybody else on the property.

And she was never bothered up here. Nobody came near the cabin, and they never suspected Jodie's presence, never knew about the secret dinners that she and Tyler had up here, the love they shared all alone in the privacy of the snug little cabin on its windy hilltop....

Jodie sighed in anticipation and crossed the room to take some of the food out of the basket. She arranged it invitingly on the table and then hesitated, glancing at her watch.

Still just four o'clock. It wouldn't start getting dark for a while yet and she had to fill her time somehow, waiting for the magic nighttime with its blissful hours of sweetness and passion.

Her eyes glistened. She wandered over to the window again, watching idly as Tyler and Ruth rode into the ranch yard far below and were met by the foreman, Ken Slattery.

Jodie hurried to get her small binoculars from the basket, then returned to the window and trained them on the distant scene, frowning thoughtfully. The foreman seemed to have something important to tell Tyler. She could see how Tyler tensed and looked anxiously toward the house, then turned back to Ken as if to ask more questions. Meanwhile the woman sat silently on her horse, listening to the two men.

Jodie watched the scene, hating the woman who rode so close to Tyler and knew everything that was going on. Jodie felt shut out and alienated, the way she had a few minutes ago when Tyler and the woman got off their horses and vanished into the grove of live oak trees.

"It's not fair. He's the father of *my* baby," Jodie muttered angrily. "I should be the one down there with him, listening and knowing what's going on. It's just not fair."

But soon she'd be there, Jodie told herself soothingly. Soon Tyler would acknowledge her in front of all the world and take her home with him so their son could be born in dignity and luxury. Soon she'd be the

only woman who ever walked beside Tyler Mc-
Kinney, and that other pale thin woman would be
gone as if she'd never existed.

"If she hangs around much longer," Jodie muttered grimly, "I'll kill her. I'll just find some way to
kill her before she gets any closer to Tyler. She de-
serves to die, anyhow, the awful thing."

She continued to frown angrily as she returned to
the table, rearranging the place settings, putting the
flowers farther over on the table where Tyler would see
them the minute he came in.

CHAPTER SIX

"I REALLY LIKE what you've done with the living room, Cynthia," Ruth said, while Lynn nodded agreement from across the table. "Those drapes are just lovely, and so is the carpet. They match the new wallpaper perfectly."

Cynthia McKinney smiled gratefully at the two younger women over the littered remains of the dinner table, and poured old Hank, who had stayed to eat with the family, another cup of coffee. "Thanks, Ruth. It's always so scary, making a final choice. I start to have doubts almost immediately."

"Me too," Ruth said gloomily. "I wish I could be more like Tyler. I don't think he ever has any doubts about anything."

J.T. chuckled. "That's what Cynthia always says about me, Ruth. But we're not nearly as confident as we seem, are we, Grandpa?"

"Beg pardon?" the old man said, cupping a gnarled hand around his ear and frowning at his grandson.

"Texas men," J.T. said more loudly. "We're really gentle and sensitive, aren't we, Grandpa? We just pretend to be tough to impress the womenfolk."

Hank snorted rudely and reached for another praline from a tray on the sideboard, then glanced up in concern as Tyler entered the room.

The tension mounted while Tyler paused in the doorway and everyone around the table waited for him to speak.

"Well," Tyler said finally, coming over to drop a hand on Ruth's shoulder as he lowered his long body into the chair beside her, "I think he's going to be okay. He just needs a whole lot of rest and some good food. He's lost a couple lately and hasn't felt much like eating."

J.T. shook his head and moved restlessly in his chair. "Damn stupid kid!" he exploded. "What the *hell* does he think he's doing?"

"Cal's not a kid, Daddy," Lynn told her father gently. "He's a thirty-year-old man. He has every right to live his life as he chooses."

"Even if it means starving to death and crippling himself at this damned rodeo?"

"He's not crippled, Daddy," Tyler said calmly. "He has some bruised ribs and a compressed disk in his back that's giving him a lot of pain, and his left knee's gone weak on him again. It could have been worse. I guess the horse mashed him into the fence pretty good."

"Damn right it could have been worse," J.T. muttered. "If Ken hadn't gone up to Fort Worth and found him in that seedy hotel, he could have lain there for days without anybody looking after him at all."

Cynthia reached out and covered her husband's hand gently.

"Well, at least Ken brought him home," Tyler said. "And I'll lay odds that he won't stay in bed more than a day or two. He'll be riding bucking horses again before the month ends, Daddy."

"Not if I can help it," J.T. said.

Ruth cast a troubled glance at Tyler, who smiled and gave her a casual hug. "Don't let my little brother's problems upset you, Ruth," he said lightly. "Rodeo cowboys get lots of bumps and scrapes, and they always come out smiling. Cal's going to be just fine. He wants to meet you," he added.

"Me?" Ruth asked, startled.

"I told him you were just about the prettiest girl in the world. Cal's always got an eye for a pretty girl," Tyler added cheerfully, "but don't let him get to you or he'll break your heart. He's just a rolling stone, that boy. He'll never settle down."

J.T. nodded gloomily in agreement, staring into the dregs of his cup while Cynthia smiled at the others and poured more coffee all around.

"Tyler," Ruth murmured hesitantly, "I was going to call my—"

"Sure you were. I almost forgot." Tyler got to his feet and held Ruth's chair, smiling easily at his family. "Ruth wants to call home and tell her daddy she's staying a while longer. We'll use the phone in the study, all right?"

"That's fine." J.T. looked up, his handsome face warmed by a brief grin. "Say hello to your daddy for me, Ruth. Tell him he's lucky he had such a nice daughter instead of these no-account trouble-making sons."

Tyler grinned and led Ruth down the hall to the study. "Daddy can't stand Cal riding in the rodeos," he told her in an undertone. "Sometimes I think it's something he wanted to do himself when he was young, but he got married too soon to cut loose and follow the circuit."

Ruth shuddered. "I think it's awful. Taking such risks with your body, and leading a wild unsettled life like that..."

"Nothing wild and unsettled about you, Ruthie," Tyler said in a warm teasing voice. "Or is there? Could there possibly be a wild woman in there somewhere, just waiting to get out?"

Ruth ignored him, dialing the phone and waiting anxiously for her father to answer.

"Good evening, Holden residence."

"Dad! How are you?" Ruth waved at Tyler, who was turning to leave the room. "Don't go," she whispered over the mouthpiece. "He might want to talk to you."

"I'm just fine, dear. How's the weather in Texas? Have you tamed all those wild cowboys down there?"

"Speaking of wild cowboys, Cal just got here, Dad. He got hurt in a rodeo at Fort Worth, and the ranch foreman had to go up and bring him home."

Ruth went on to tell her father the news of the ranch and listen to details about the winery while Tyler stood nearby, smiling down at her. Don chuckled from time to time, causing Ruth to frown in thoughtful silence. There was something about her father's voice . . . something different. . . .

"Dad? Are you sure everything's all right?"

"Ruthie, everything's just great." Don paused a moment, then went on in a confidential tone. "I've met somebody, Ruth."

"Met somebody? What do you mean?" she asked blankly, clutching the telephone.

"A *woman*, you dummy. A very nice lady who teaches philosophy at the college. Definitely not a fluff ball, so you don't have to be concerned on my behalf. We've gone out a couple of times, and we get along just splendidly."

"Dad," Ruth said in despair, "how can you possibly have started a relationship already? I've only been gone a few days!"

Don laughed. "A lot can happen in a few days, Ruth," he said, sounding so boyishly happy that she felt chilled and excluded.

"I was calling to let you know that I might stay down here another week or so," Ruth began slowly, "but I can tell you don't mind."

"Not a bit," Don said heartlessly. "Stay as long as you like, dear. We're just fine up here."

"How about Hagar?"

"Hagar?" Don echoed blankly. "What about him?"

"Is he all right?"

"The big orange cat? Why wouldn't he be all right?"

"I mean," Ruth said, taking a deep breath, "have you seen him lately? Does he look okay?"

She waited through a long silence at the other end. "Dad?" she prompted finally.

"I'm trying to remember if I've seen him since you left."

Ruth felt a brief stirring of panic. "Dad, go and look, okay? Check my room and see if he's there."

She held the receiver and looked over at Tyler, trying to smile. "He's checking," she whispered. "He's gone to— Yes? Dad, did you see him?"

"He was lying in the middle of your bed," Don reported. "But when I looked into the room he dived underneath the dresser like a streak of orange lightning."

"Oh, no," Ruth moaned. "That means he's scared. He always hides under the dresser when he's scared of something. Dad, I should come back right away. I think I'll—"

Tyler moved over beside her and gently took the receiver from her hand. "Don? This is Tyler McKinney."

He waited, smiling while Don Holden greeted him, then went on. "Yeah, she's just fine. A little bossy, but a real nice girl. Don, do you think you could make sure that the damned cat's all right? Otherwise Ruth's going to pack up and go home, and I really need her down here a while longer."

Again he waited, grinning as he listened. "Sure thing," he said finally. "Thanks, Don."

Tyler handed the receiver to Ruth, who glared darkly at him as she concluded her conversation with her father.

Finally she hung up and marched out of the room while Tyler ambled behind her.

"So," he ventured, pausing near the foot of the stairs, "what's bothering you the most? Are you really worried about the cat, or are you just upset that your daddy's got a girlfriend? Or that he doesn't need you there every minute to keep the winery operating?"

"You think you're so smart," Ruth said, avoiding his glance. "You think you know everything about me, Tyler McKinney."

"I like to learn about things that interest me," Tyler said placidly. "And I find you very interesting, Ruth Holden."

"Well, if you must know, it's Hagar," she said, ignoring his last comment. "I'm certainly not so selfish that I'd want to deny my father the pleasure and companionship of a nice woman. And I know that he can run the place perfectly well without me. But I can't stand the thought of poor Hagar being alone and frightened. I really think I should go home, Tyler."

"Just stay till after we go to Lubbock," Tyler pleaded. "The cat will be all right, Ruth. Your daddy promised me he'd look after him. Please stay a few more days."

She paused reluctantly, one hand resting on the carved oak newel post.

"Please, Ruthie," Tyler repeated with his most charming smile.

"All right," she said at last. "Just a few more days."

"Great. Now come up and say hello to Cal."

Ruth hesitated. "I promised I'd go to Virginia's room right after dinner. She's going to show me how to cut out a sewing pattern."

"This won't take a minute. Come on, Ruth."

Ruth nodded and started to climb the stairs with Tyler close behind her. She glanced down at him, uncomfortably conscious of the warm appreciative scrutiny he was giving to her hips and thighs as she moved. But when she glared at him he just winked and arched an eyebrow with a meaningful grin that made her blush furiously.

At the top of the stairs Tyler took her arm and directed her into Cal's room, cluttered with rodeo trophies, scattered jeans and jackets, broad-brimmed hats and riding equipment. Ruth paused on the threshold, gazing shyly at the handsome young man who lay on the rumpled bed.

Cal McKinney was lean and rangy like his brother, and shared Tyler's sculpted good looks, though his coloring wasn't as dark. He was propped on a bank of pillows, wearing a faded navy-blue T-shirt, his face pale and drawn with pain.

"Cal, this is Ruth Holden."

"Hi, Ruth," Cal said with a smile, and Ruth caught a flash of the warm cowboy charm that probably gave this man a devastating appeal when he was on his feet and healthy. "I hear you're a world-class expert on wineries."

"I've studied quite a lot," Ruth murmured, wondering why these people felt such a need to exaggerate her qualifications. Of course, she told herself, Texans seemed to exaggerate everything, but they were so cheerful and good-natured about it that you had to smile anyhow.

"Well, Tyler's sure impressed with you. He says you really know your stuff."

"I wish he'd listen to me sometimes, then," Ruth said dryly, and Cal chuckled.

"Tyler's the most stubborn man in the whole world," he said cheerfully. "Changing his mind about anything is like trying to move the Colorado River a few miles to the west."

"I'm beginning to discover that, I'm afraid."

"Ruthie, that's just not true," Tyler protested, sounding hurt. "I listen to you all the time. I pay real close attention to everything you say."

"And then go ahead with your own plans regardless," she said tartly.

"Can I help it if my ideas are the best?"

Ruth stiffened, then caught the grin between the two brothers. She relaxed, smiling ruefully.

"I know that I'm being oversensitive," she told Cal. "But I'm so worried about this whole project, because I know it means a lot to the ranch, and I can't seem to get Tyler to consider things seriously."

"*Tyler?*" Cal asked in disbelief. "Tyler always takes everything far too seriously. I wasted most of my boyhood trying to get him to lighten up and have some fun."

Ruth hesitated, looking into Cal McKinney's brilliant hazel eyes. She was speaking to the younger brother, but she realized that the conversation was giving her a chance to say some things that she wanted Tyler to hear.

"It's not that he's careless or overcasual," she said earnestly. "It's just that he doesn't seem willing to consider all the possibilities. He really needs to... to explore every avenue and be sure he's aware of all the things that might go wrong."

"I don't see why," Tyler said, also addressing himself to Cal, who lay in the bed looking from one face to the other. "I'd rather concentrate on all the things that could go right. Is that so terrible?"

Cal grinned, shifting awkwardly on the pillows and wincing with pain. Tyler moved over quickly to help his brother sit straighter in the bed.

"Gawd," Cal drawled with a sparkling boyish grin, "I can't believe it. Tyler McKinney's gone and found a girl so careful and well organized that she makes *him* look wild and carefree. Who'd've thought it?''

Both brothers laughed and Ruth turned pink with annoyance. "Look, I'm not what you both seem to—" she began stiffly.

Tyler interrupted her by reaching out and cuddling her close to his side, looking over her head at Cal. "You quit teasing her," he told his brother. "She's just about the nicest girl in the world, Cal. She's smart and honest and reasonable, and she's got enough on her hands trying to get me to smarten up, let alone fighting with you besides."

Ruth nestled gratefully in his embrace for a moment, warmed by his nearness and by the surprising ring of sincerity in his words.

"Miss Ruth?" a voice called from the lower hallway. "Are you up there? I'm ready to start now."

Ruth drew herself away from Tyler hastily, avoiding the interested gazes of both brothers. "That's Virginia," she murmured. "I'd better go now. I asked her to let me know when she was... Cal, I really hope you feel better soon. If there's anything I can do..."

She stopped talking, smiled awkwardly at the two men and hurried from the room, conscious of their handsome amused faces watching her in silence as she left.

Cal gazed at the empty doorway for a moment, then turned to his brother with a slow meaningful grin. "Well, well," he murmured.

Tyler grinned. "Didn't I tell you?"

"Yeah, but I didn't believe you. I figured she'd look like one of those computer women, with a plastic body and a keyboard panel where her face should be."

"So did I. The day I went to meet her plane in Austin, I was just dreading this week. But, Cal, she's not only beautiful, she's so . . . nice. And when she relaxes and forgets to be all cautious and reserved, she's really fun to be with."

"Yeah? How much fun?" Cal asked with a brotherly leer.

Tyler glared at his brother. "C'mon, Cal. This isn't the kind of girl you can joke about like that. She's special."

Cal fell silent, looking at his older brother with warm interest and shaking his head. "Ty, you better watch out," he said finally.

"Why?"

"You're fallin', brother. This looks serious. And you know what McKinney men are like. Falling in love is a terminal illness for us."

"Yeah, sure," Tyler said scornfully. "Look who's talking, with a girl in every rodeo town."

"I've never been in love," Cal said quietly. "I've never talked about somebody the way you're talking about this woman, Tyler. When it happens, it hits us hard, the men in this family. You're gonna be struck down in the prime of life if you don't watch out."

Tyler shifted awkwardly on his feet, gazing in startled silence at his brother's face. But in his mind's eye he was seeing Ruth's face, her wide dark eyes and sweet lopsided smile.

"THERE'S NO ROOM for this collar piece," Ruth said, squinting at the folded length of fabric on the floor. "It says you need to cut four of them, and there's hardly room for two, Virginia."

"I know," Virginia said placidly. "But I only need one of this back piece, you see? So I can fit the collars on the other side after that's been cut, if I put two of them upside down."

"Oh," Ruth breathed, watching in fascination while Virginia's capable hands arranged the flimsy pattern pieces on the fabric. "That's so neat, Virginia, the way it works out."

Virginia set aside her scissors and smiled at the young woman kneeling opposite her on the round braided rug. "Yes, Miss Ruth, it's really neat."

Ruth waved her hand in an abrupt gesture. "Call me Ruth, all right, Virginia? I can't get used to this Southern mode of address. Especially when you and I are friends."

Virginia shrugged cheerfully. "If you like. I never think of it, really. It's just a habit."

"What do the big arrows mean?" Ruth asked, returning to her study of the pattern pieces.

"That's the grain of the fabric. You have to cut with the grain, or your garment will hang crooked."

Ruth grimaced. "I hate when clothes don't hang right."

"Did you call your daddy?" Virginia asked, her voice somewhat muffled by a mouthful of straight pins that she was inserting, one by one, into the neatly arranged pattern pieces.

"Yes, I did. He's fine."

"Did you tell him you're staying longer?"

"Yes," Ruth repeated. "What are all those little notches?"

"You have to cut them out real carefully," Virginia explained, frowning as she began to cut a long firm line with her pinking shears. "They show you exactly where to match the back and front pieces when you sew them together."

"I see. I should have taken some home economics courses in high school. I was always busy taking extra chemistry classes, and now I feel so stupid, not knowing anything about cooking or sewing."

"Most girls learn those things at home, but you didn't have a mama there to teach you. It's not your fault."

Ruth smiled gratefully at the older woman. "You know, I think that's why I like it here so much," she commented shyly. "This is the first time in my life that I've ever felt like part of a family, Virginia. I know I'm just kidding myself, that I'm only a visitor and I'll be going home in a few days. But sitting at the table and laughing with everybody, or kidding with old Hank, or visiting with Lynn and Cynthia and you and Lettie Mae . . . it feels so good."

Virginia paused and knelt erect, smiling at the earnest young woman across from her. "You're going to miss us when you leave, Ruth."

"I know," Ruth said wistfully. "Especially when you and Lettie Mae actually let me into the kitchen and teach me to do things. I really love that. Besides, my father's..." she paused, flushing, and fell abruptly silent.

"Your father's doing what? Ruth, could you hand me that chalk, dear?"

"My father's apparently found himself a girlfriend. Can you imagine? Virginia, he's almost sixty!"

Virginia smiled dryly and made a careful chalk mark on the bodice of the dress. "Incredible as it may seem, people of sixty can sometimes still be interested in relationships."

Ruth's flush deepened. "Oh, Virginia, I didn't mean..."

"I know what you meant," Virginia said mildly. "I imagine it's a real shock when your daddy gets involved with somebody after years of being on his own. It surely was for the young people in this house. But it's not so strange, after all."

Something in the older woman's voice made Ruth pause and look at her with sudden interest. "Virginia? Is there by any chance somebody in *your* life?"

Virginia looked up and Ruth noted that her plump face was a little pink. "Maybe," she said, then began to pick up the cut pieces of fabric and paper pattern.

"Maybe?" Ruth echoed, scrambling to her feet and following Virginia as she crossed the room to the ironing board. "What do you mean, maybe? Either there is or there isn't, right?"

"Well, not exactly," Virginia said mysteriously. "There might be if I choose to have somebody, that's all."

Ruth continued to gaze at the older woman in silence while Virginia carefully unpinned the pattern and stacked the paper pieces on one end of the ironing board.

"Now, the first step," she began, "is to deal with the darts in the bodice. We find the chalk mark here—"

"Forget the sewing lesson," Ruth interrupted briskly. "No more instruction until you tell me about this man."

Virginia hesitated, looking over at the younger woman with sparkling blue eyes. "You won't tell anybody?" she asked finally. "I'd die if the family knew what I was doing."

Ruth nodded solemnly. "Cross my heart."

Virginia paused a moment longer, then pulled a bundle of ragged papers from the bottom drawer of her dresser and handed them over with an awkward little smile.

Ruth sank into the padded rocker and paged through the letters, her eyes widening in amazement. "Virginia, these are..."

"I know," Virginia said calmly. "I put an ad in a lonely-hearts column, just to see what I'd get back. And you know what? There were so many letters they almost flooded my box at the post office."

"But why?" Ruth asked shyly. "Are you unhappy here, Virginia?"

Virginia turned her silvery head away so Ruth couldn't see her face. "Of course not. I've always been happy here, Ruth. But things are changing so much."

Ruth looked in concern at the older woman and dropped her voice to a whisper. "Don't you get along well with Cynthia? Is that it?"

Virginia shook her head. "It was hard to get used to her at first, but nobody could dislike her, Ruth. She's such a good person, and she's fair and nice and considerate of all of us. It's just that everything's so *different,*" she finished helplessly.

Ruth nodded her understanding. "It's hard to adjust to a new way of doing things," she said.

Virginia gave her a mirthless smile. "Wait till you're sixty," she said, "and see how hard it is then."

"So what do you want?" Ruth asked, watching as Virginia toyed nervously with the bodice piece in her hands. "Do you want to retire?"

Virginia shook her head. "Not just yet. They still need me, and I feel I'm doing a good enough job. What I want is to know that there's a future for me when I *do* retire, that's all. I hate not knowing what lies ahead. I'm just so scared, Ruth."

Ruth nodded, feeling awkward and troubled. "Tyler said..." she began, and paused to clear her throat, then continued. "He said you and Lettie Mae were completely secure, Virginia. I asked him just today, as a matter of fact, and he said he'd checked your accounts for you and made sure you had enough for a comfortable retirement."

"So he did, bless his soul," Virginia said with a fond smile. "Tyler's such a good boy, always has been. But," she added, her expression suddenly bleak, "that was more than five years ago, Ruth. Things have changed some since then."

"Changed? How?"

"Well, for one thing," Virginia began, wetting her finger to test the iron and pressing darts into the piece of fabric, "I've had to help out my nieces and nephews quite a bit."

Ruth looked up at Virginia, trying to conceal her alarm. "Help them out? You mean financially?"

Virginia nodded, concentrating on her ironing. "Their parents all have other kids and debts and problems, while I just had myself to look after and all that money sitting in the bank. It seemed so selfish not to help out when they needed it. And then when I saw my balance starting to dwindle, I did something real foolish."

She set the iron down and met Ruth's eyes directly, telling her in a halting voice about the prospectus for Vanguard Mines and her brief fling at high-stakes investment.

"J.T. warned me," she concluded miserably. "He said I'd lose my shirt, and I did. Lost my knickers besides," she added, trying to smile at her own folly. "If I have to depend on my own bank account, Ruth, I'm going to end my life as one of those bag ladies, sleeping in an alley somewhere."

"But wouldn't J.T.—"

"I'm not taking charity from the family," Virginia said firmly. "J.T.'s been real generous over the years, but things aren't all that prosperous around here these days, Ruth. I can't stand the thought of being a drain on them when I'm old, just because I've been so stupid."

"But, Virginia . . ."

"I'll stay here till I can't do the job anymore," Virginia said. "Then I'll leave. I'm going to try to find someone to marry," she added in a matter-of-fact voice. "I've given it a lot of thought, Ruth, and decided that's the best thing for me to do. I know how to manage a house. I can make a nice life for some man my own age. It's what I'm trained to do. If he gives me a home and security, I'll give him a damn good housekeeper in return."

"So you wrote to this column," Ruth said, indicating the ragged pile of letters.

"It's not so awful, Ruth. Don't look like that. Some of them are just a scream, but a few sound real nice. Look at those two on top."

Ruth paged through the letters, quickly scanning the two that Virginia indicated.

"'...and I've always had a real good sense of humor,'" she read aloud. "I believe life should be fun even if you're on the shady side of fifty. If you think the same way, then maybe we could team up for some laughs and possibly...' This one sounds nice," Ruth ventured. "After all, who wants a man without any sense of humor?"

She had a sudden burning image of Tyler's dark eyes and warm teasing grin, and felt herself growing uncomfortably warm all over. Quickly she turned away to read the second letter.

Virginia glanced shrewdly at the younger woman for a moment. "That's what I think, too," she said finally, continuing with her careful pressing. "I decided I'd answer two of them, just to see what they're like. But that second man is the first one I'm checking out. I'm meeting him in town for supper on Tuesday, and the one with the sense of humor is taking me to the benefit dance next week in Crystal Creek."

Ruth nodded absently, studying the second letter, which was neatly written on sparkling-white bond paper.

"I am a widowed gentleman of sixty-two," she read, "who is well educated and financially secure. I am also very clean and tidy, and appreciate a clean and well-groomed lady. I believe that quality of life is very important, and I sure don't like sloppy or dirty people."

Ruth glanced up at Virginia's soft pink face. "I can see why you'd pick him first, Virginia," she said slowly.

Virginia nodded, giving Ruth a wry grin. "Who wants a dirty old man, right? And there's a few of 'em in that bunch, believe me," she added darkly, waving a hand at the pile of letters.

Ruth smiled back and returned to her fascinated study of the letters, chuckling occasionally while Virginia threaded her sewing machine and the winter twilight deepened beyond the windows.

CHAPTER SEVEN

CAL MCKINNEY rode up the winding rocky trail, stoically ignoring the dull pain in his back. He was still brooding over the look on J.T.'s dark troubled face a couple of hours earlier as he'd watched his younger son riding out of the ranch yard.

Cal had only been home a couple of days and the whole family was horrified that he was on horseback already. Especially since Nate Purdy, hastily summoned to the ranch by J.T., had announced that Cal needed at least a month's rest and gentle exercise before he returned to the rodeo circuit.

"A *month!*" Cal exploded. "My God! Does Doc Purdy have any idea how many points I'd lose in a month away from the circuit? It's just a sore back. I've had hundreds of 'em. A little riding and some stretching and it'll be good as new by the weekend."

But none of them was convinced. They didn't understand the fascination of the rodeo world, the thrill of winning, the warm brotherhood of cowboys, the carefree life-style.

Cal lounged casually on the big placid mare he'd chosen for her easy gait. His body was relaxed and loose, but his handsome face was drawn with concern.

What did his father expect him to do with his life? Should he come back and live here on the ranch, tagging around behind his older brother and doing chores like one of the hired hands?

There were lots of chores on the ranch, no doubt of that, but certainly not enough management positions to keep three grown men occupied. And his father and brother already had the administrative duties pretty well evenly divided between them.

Cal thought about Tyler, who had always seemed slightly cool, hard-edged and ambitious, even though he could certainly be generous and loving with his family. But Tyler was strangely different these days. Maybe it was because he'd fallen so passionately in love with the idea of this winery.

"On second thought, maybe it's not the winery he's in love with, Janey," Cal said to his mount, who perked her ears cheerfully at the sound of her name. Lynn had named this heavy plodding mare Plain Jane, for obvious reasons, but the whole family loved the mare for her sweet disposition.

He patted the horse's neck and grinned, thinking about Tyler and his pretty California scientist. Cal wondered whether his brother even knew how his eyes flared with emotion when he looked at Ruth, how his face softened and even his voice took on a gentle husky tone.

"Poor ol' Ty," Cal mused aloud, squinting at the lacy drift of clouds behind the little cabin. "My brother's fallen like a ton of bricks and he doesn't even know it. What a shock he's gonna get when he finds out that he's hooked."

Not that you could blame him, Cal thought. Ruth Holden was a sweet woman, intelligent and thoughtful and gentle, a perfect partner for Tyler with her quick insights and her well-ordered thoughts. Mind you, the two of them seemed to spend most of their time arguing.

"Love is just a mystery," Cal said philosophically to Janey. "Thank God I'm not—"

He fell abruptly silent. Just ahead was the isolated little cabin where he and Tyler had passed so many happy boyhood hours. Cal shivered, though the afternoon sun was warm on his back, and pulled his jacket collar closer up around his ears. He could have sworn he'd seen something flit past the cabin window, something that resembled a shadowy human form.

Cowboys were always a superstitious lot, and Cal knew there were ranch hands on the Double C who claimed the old cabin was haunted. They whispered stories of seeing lights flickering in the window late at night, and occasionally wondered aloud if the old horse wrangler's ghost came around on moonless nights to mourn his lost love.

"Damn stupid nonsense. There's no such thing as ghosts, right, Janey?" Cal said to his horse, who jerked her head and clanked the bit noisily against her teeth in agreement. Cal reined abruptly off the path and gave the mare her head, letting her pick her way up the hillside toward the cabin.

Grimacing with pain, he swung his long body out of the saddle, looped the reins over a crumbling post and moved cautiously to the heavy plank door.

Cal eased the door open and peered into the cabin's interior, a shadowy space in which dust motes danced in the pale beam of sunlight from the little window.

Suddenly he gripped the door frame and stared, his jaw slack with disbelief.

A girl stood in the center of the cabin, behind the old sagging table set with dishes and food as if ready for a sort of picnic. The girl was tall and solidly built, with a tense white face and a cloud of dark hair. She gripped a long, sharp hunting knife in her fist and stared defiantly at Cal, her pale eyes glittering.

Cal drew back involuntarily, still rigid with shock, shivers chilling up and down his spine at the look in those strange transparent eyes. The girl moved silently away from the table, still brandishing the knife, and backed up toward the window so her dark hair rayed all around her head. Cal's shock deepened when he saw that she wore a maternity smock over her jeans.

"Who..." he began in an unsteady voice, and paused to compose himself. "Who the hell are *you?*"

Tyler drove his pickup truck rapidly along the tree-lined country highway, looking down with concern at a big, yellow plastic pet carrier on the seat beside him.

Finally, unable to stand the silence any longer, he pulled onto an approach and bent to peer through the open door of the container. Ruth's cat stared fixedly back at him from the shadows, a pair of sad, terrified green eyes glowing piteously amid the warm inert mass of orange fur.

Tyler took a deep breath and reached his hand inside, trying gently to withdraw the cat from its cage. But Hagar resisted in silent panic, turning from heavy fluff to a solid mass of bone and muscle, backing up and plastering himself tightly against the rear wall of the carrier.

"*C'mon,* cat," Tyler pleaded. "Don't be like this. You don't know how much trouble it was, making all those secret calls to her father and all the arrangements to get you shipped out here, and then a special trip all the way to the city to pick you up. Show some appreciation, can't you? Come out here and breathe some nice fresh air."

Hagar opened his jaws in a faint hiss and flattened himself even more stubbornly against the inner wall of his enclosure, exuding an aura of fear so intense that it was almost palpable.

"Okay," Tyler said, defeated. "Stay in there if you want. Suffocate, and make her hate me for life. Stupid cat."

Hagar hissed again from the musty shadows, even more weakly this time. Tyler pulled back onto the highway, his face tense. How often, he wondered, did animals die from the shock of air travel?

This had seemed like such a good idea at the time, the impulsive urge to call Don Holden and arrange to have Ruth's cat shipped to Texas.

Tyler couldn't bear the thought of parting with Ruth. At least, he told himself, not until they made some decisions about the winery. But she loved this cat, and she obviously wasn't going to relax and enjoy her stay at the Double C as long as she was worried about Hagar's safety.

Shipping the cat to the ranch had seemed like a sensible thing to do, so Ruth would stay around a few weeks and help with the planning of the winery. Tyler had almost convinced himself that his only motivation was concern for the future of his business, and a desire to take full advantage of Ruth's technical expertise. He was reluctant to acknowledge even to himself how much he simply wanted to please her, and how it was beginning to distress him when she was upset about anything.

Tyler couldn't deny, though, that part of his motivation in bringing Hagar to Texas was his concern about the upcoming trip to Lubbock. He had high hopes for that trip, and not just on a business level. But for his dreams to materialize, it was important that Ruth feel relaxed and at ease.

He grinned wanly, thinking how he'd enjoyed planning this surprise, how frequently he'd imagined Ruth walking into the guest house and finding her cat fast asleep on the bed. She'd be so happy and relieved . . . maybe she'd even be moved to hug and kiss Tyler again as an expression of gratitude.

Tyler shifted restlessly on the woven Navaho blanket that covered the truck seat, his body suddenly weak and shivery with longing.

Ruth had carefully avoided any further intimacy since that day by the cabin, but Tyler still couldn't seem to banish the memory of their embrace. He'd never felt this way about a woman, so vulnerable and full of yearning, devastated by a simple kiss.

He shook his head in sudden weariness and glared at the winding hilly road ahead, addressing himself to the yellow plastic case.

"Not that it matters," he said bitterly, "since you won't cooperate anyhow, and you'll probably get so upset that you'll die on me, and then she'll hate me forever. Can't you just come out of there and be a nice, happy cheerful cat? Cynthia's got a nice cat called Tiffany," he added in a wheedling voice. "You two will likely be real good friends."

Tyler shook the case lightly and tipped it a little with his free hand. Hagar clung to the back, his claws hooked painfully through the wire mesh.

"Goddammit, you'd think I was torturing you, when all I did was give you a nice holiday. How many cats get to travel halfway across the country on an airplane?''

The only response was another series of faint muffled hisses. Tyler slapped a hand on the wheel in frustration and drove silently toward the ranch.

CAL LIMPED past the triple garage, leading the horse he'd just unsaddled and gazing curiously at the bulky plastic case covered with airline stickers that Tyler hefted from the front seat of the truck.

"What's that, Ty?"

"Ruth's cat," Tyler said briefly, his face grim.

"Her *cat?*" Cal stared at his brother. "From *California?*"

"Where else would her cat live?" Tyler asked with some irritation.

Cal grinned mildly. "Having some trouble with the cat, are we?" he inquired, his voice solemn. "Kitty's not cooperating?"

"Shut up, Cal." Tyler lifted the carrier and peered through the wire grate.

"So," Cal inquired, falling into step beside his brother while the big mare plodded amiably behind them. "What's Ruth's cat doing here? Is he a frequent flier, Ty? Just slipped down to the big T for a little holiday, did he? Maybe wanted to get away from home and do a bit of tomcatting?"

Cal chuckled at his own humor, then winced as his brother glared at him.

"Ruth's worried about the damn cat," Tyler said wearily. He paused, then went on to describe the formidable Mrs. Ward and her inventive ways of dealing with unwanted cats.

Cal howled with laughter and gazed at the plastic carrier. "No *wonder* he wanted a holiday. Who wouldn't, stuck with a woman like that?"

"Ruth doesn't know I sent for him," Tyler said, crouching in the shadow of the stables and peering cautiously out into the ranch yard. "I asked Don to ship him down here so she'd relax and stay a while, because I really need her help with this winery. That's all," he added defensively, seeing his brother's grin.

"Sure it is," Cal said in a gentle soothing voice. "That's the only reason in the world you want her to stay around, Ty. Any old scientist would do, but she just happens to be the one who's handy, right?"

"Right," Tyler said, avoiding his brother's sparkling gaze. "Look, Cal, I need to get the damn cat inside the guest house and see if I can coax him to come out of this case. He won't budge, and Ruth's probably going to be real upset, seeing him like this."

Cal bent his long body stiffly and peered in at the cat. "It looks dead," he reported, "but its eyes are open."

"It's not dead. The goddamn thing keeps hissing. Just listen."

Cal bent over again, then nodded. "I don't know if it's hissing," he said cheerfully. "But it sure as hell ain't purring."

"Do you know where Ruth is right now?"

"In the kitchen. Lettie Mae's teaching her and Cynthia how to make the secret chili recipe."

Tyler looked at his brother in surprise. "No kidding?"

Cal shook his head solemnly. "No kidding. I stopped in there for a drink when I got back from my ride, and you never heard so much giggling and cackling. A real old hen party, except that Grandpa's in there, too, egging them on."

Tyler grinned briefly. He began to edge away from the stable, clutching the handle of the pet carrier. "That's good, then. I'll just slip over to the guest house and—"

"Wait a minute, Ty." Cal drew his brother back into the shadows, then paused awkwardly.

"What is it? Cal, I've got to get this damn cat into—"

"In a minute. Tyler, do you know a girl called Jodie Hiltz?"

Tyler frowned, his handsome face drawn with concentration. "Hiltz? Jodie Hiltz, you say? I don't think so. Who is she?"

Cal looked intently at his brother. "The name doesn't ring a bell of any kind? Never heard of her?"

Tyler shifted nervously on his feet, glancing toward the guest house. "Look, Ruth could come out here any minute. I don't have time for one of your jokes right now, okay?"

"Remember old Joe Hiltz? Lived in Crystal Creek in a tumbledown shack by the river, with a whole houseful of kids?"

Tyler nodded impatiently, still clutching the cat carrier. "Of course I do. He got killed on the road a few years back, and his wife moved to Lampasas."

"That's right. Well, Jodie is the oldest kid. She's about nineteen now, I'd guess."

Tyler frowned, his tanned face deep in thought. "I remember. She came back to town, right? I heard she's working for Ralph over at the drugstore. You know," he added with a brief grin, "I feel like I've had this exact conversation with someone else just recently. Do you ever get that feeling?"

"Sometimes I do," Cal said gently. He paused, squinting at a distant hilltop where a small herd of cows were silhouetted against the deep blue sweep of winter sky. "I just saw that girl about an hour ago. Right here on our land," he added casually, shifting his gaze to look directly at his brother.

Tyler forgot his impatience and stared back, his dark eyes puzzled. "On our land? What do you mean, Cal? Did she come to the house, or what?"

"She was in the old horse wrangler's cabin."

"*What?*"

"Up on the hill, you know, where we used to play when we were kids?"

"I know where the cabin is. As a matter of fact, that's probably where I'm going to—" Tyler broke off abruptly and turned to look at his brother. "What was she doing up there?"

Cal shifted awkwardly under his brother's dark penetrating gaze. "I got the impression she was waiting for you, Ty."

"For me?" Tyler asked blankly. "Up in that old cabin? What the hell for?"

Cal shrugged. "She wasn't all that coherent. She was as shocked as I was when I walked in, and she was holding this damned big knife like she meant to use it any second. I wasn't real anxious to get into a conversation with her."

"Well, you must have asked why she was trespassing."

"Sure I did. And she said I should ask you. She had a picnic lunch up there, with that old table all set for two. Flowers and candles, stuff like that."

Tyler shook his head, still gazing at his brother with a bemused expression. "I see," he said at last. "You went into this isolated cabin miles from anywhere, that nobody's used for ages, and there was a girl in there having a picnic. Also clutching a knife and waiting for me. Right, Cal?"

"Right," Cal said calmly. "And another thing . . ."

"Yeah?"

"She's pregnant, Ty."

"I know she is."

Cal gave his brother a quick startled glance. "You do? I thought you didn't even remember her."

"Ruth told me. Matter of fact, that's where I had this conversation before. Ruth saw that girl in the restaurant one day, and pointed her out to me for some reason."

Cal hesitated, shifting uneasily on his booted feet. "Ty, this Jodie, she seemed to be kind of—"

"Look," Tyler interrupted his brother. "I don't know anything about this girl. Either this is your idea of a joke, or else you must have misunderstood, swallowed some kind of line or something. Maybe she's got a boyfriend on the ranch that she meets up there, and she told you I knew about it just to throw you off."

"But that's not what she said. She said she was waiting for you."

Tyler shook his head, his eyes beginning to darken with anger. "Well, she wasn't. And we damn sure don't want strangers trespassing up there, not after all the trouble we've had with cattle rustlers. I hope you told her so, and sent her packing. I sure will if I ever catch her on our land."

He moved away and strode across the yard toward the guest house with the plastic pet carrier swinging in his hand.

Cal, watching his brother's wide strong shoulders and lithe springing gait, was unable to shake a sense of impending trouble.

"SO THERE WE WAS," old Hank said, pausing to munch on a buttery slice of freshly baked bread, "runnin' our horses hell-for-leather up this little draw, with that band of vicious outlaws just a-yellin' and a-whoopin' behind us. We run right up into the end of that canyon, and we was trapped. Murderers behind us, horse thieves up on the cliffs all around us. Dozens of 'em, screamin' like coyotes an' throwin' their lynchin' ropes over the nearest trees. Guns everywhere, pointin' at us."

He paused, reached for a toothpick and foraged thoughtfully among his back molars. Ruth gazed at him, wide-eyed and fascinated, while the others exchanged small knowing grins.

"So?" she breathed.

"So what?" Hank swiveled in his chair and looked stiffly over his shoulder, waving his coffee mug. Lettie Mae came over to fill the mug, smiling and dropping a hand on the old man's bony shoulder.

"What happened?" Ruth asked in an agony of suspense.

"With them outlaws? Well, girl, I'll tell you. Them outlaws killed ever' damn one of us."

General laughter erupted in the kitchen, and Ruth joined in, hesitantly at first, then with rising merriment. She beamed at the others in the big room, loving the warm rich aroma of hot chili and fresh bread, a smell that seemed part of the comfortable family atmosphere.

Cynthia sat opposite in jeans and sweatshirt, busily writing down the chili recipe from memory. Lettie Mae hummed and brushed butter on the rounded golden tops of her fresh loaves while Virginia sat nearby, knitting placidly.

"This is heaven. Just heaven," Ruth said in a soft dreamy voice, a little embarrassed when she realized that she'd spoken her thoughts aloud.

But the others just smiled at her and went on with their own pursuits.

"Ruth? Can you come with me a minute? I want to show you something."

Ruth shifted in her chair and saw Tyler standing inside the doorway, looking as bright-eyed and nervous as a little boy with a surprise.

He nodded casually at the others in the kitchen, declined the offer of a slice of fresh bread and waited with visible impatience while Ruth took her sweater from a peg near the door and joined him.

"I'll be right back," she said to Virginia. "I want to see how you turn the heel on that sock."

"Better hurry," Virginia advised calmly. "I'm leaving for town soon."

She and Ruth exchanged a significant glance, and Ruth smiled to herself as she left the kitchen. Virginia had a date tonight with the "clean and tidy gentleman."

Ruth strolled across the yard beside Tyler, wishing she could confide in him about what Virginia was doing. Now that she was getting used to his forceful personality, Ruth found more and more that she liked to talk about things with Tyler. He had an uncanny knack for understanding her, and an offbeat sparkling sense of humor that made fun out of the most ordinary happenings.

"Look, Ruthie," he said earnestly, interrupting her wandering thoughts. "I want you to remember that sometimes people do things for the best of motives but they don't always . . . they don't always work out just right. But you still shouldn't hold it against them because they . . ."

Ruth abruptly stopped walking in the middle of this rambling monologue and gazed up at the somewhat desperate-looking man. "Tyler McKinney, what on earth are you trying to say?"

"Nothing," he said, avoiding her eyes and looking guilty. "Nothing at all, Ruth."

She glanced at him again, puzzled by his behavior, and hesitated on the threshold while he opened the door of the guest house. "Tyler," she began, "are you sure there isn't—"

But she got no farther. As soon as the door opened a furry streak of orange hurtled across the room and bounced against Ruth, then began to rub frantically against her legs with rumbling purrs of ecstasy.

Ruth gasped in shock and wonder. "*Hagar?*" she whispered in a choked voice. "Sweetie, is that you?"

Hagar continued to arch and purr like a small rusty dynamo. Ruth scooped him up and hugged him, her eyes streaming tears.

"God," Tyler said in awe as he witnessed this reunion. "He's more like a puppy than a cat. I never saw a cat display so much emotion."

"Poor thing," Ruth crooned, burying her face in the quivering mass of rusty fur. "Poor baby, he must have been so scared. Weren't you, sweetie? Weren't you scared? Yes, you were...."

Tyler shifted on his feet, waiting for Ruth to finish cuddling her cat and turn the full force of her indignation on him.

But when she raised her face to gaze at him, there was no anger in her wide brown eyes. Tears still sparkled on her lashes, but she was smiling, her face soft with gratitude.

"Oh, Tyler," she whispered. "This was so sweet of you."

He stared at her in astonishment, then gave an abashed grin while she moved into the room, still cuddling her cat, and motioned for him to follow.

"Actually," he began, "it wasn't all that much. I just called your daddy and asked him if..."

"There, there, sweetie," Ruth was murmuring to her shivering cat, rocking him like a baby. "It's all right now. You're safe at the ranch with me, and you're really going to like it here. You just curl up on the bed and have a rest now. See how nice and soft it is."

While Tyler watched she tipped the big cat onto the bed and stroked him gently. Hagar lay with eyes closed for a moment, then got up and dug his claws feebly into the bedspread.

"He's starting to look quite a lot better," Tyler ventured, looking hopefully at the big cat. "Isn't he, Ruthie?"

At the sound of the man's voice, Hagar opened his eyes and fixed Tyler with a baleful green glare. He tumbled heavily from the bed and disappeared beneath the armoire, his bushy orange tail quivering.

Ruth smiled. "He'll probably spend a few days under there while he gets used to things," she said cheerfully. "He likes the security of being under furniture. But he'll cheer up soon and start liking you, Tyler. I know he will. He's really a very friendly warmhearted cat."

Tyler wisely refrained from expressing an opinion on Hagar's friendliness and warmth. But he was greatly cheered by Ruth's words, and the indication that she believed Hagar was going to be around long enough to get used to things.

"I hope he'll be happy," Tyler said briefly. "But mostly I was concerned with you, Ruthie. I knew how much you missed him."

Ruth knelt to peer lovingly under the armoire, then straightened and smiled at Tyler. "How did you do it? You must have called my dad when I wasn't around."

Tyler nodded. "He thought it was a great idea. You should have heard him laugh."

"I know," Ruth said. "He laughs all the time these days. Falling in love seems to agree with him."

Tyler leaned against the mantel and gazed at her. "Falling in love agrees with most people, Ruth," he said softly.

"Oh, Tyler..." Ruth came toward him, smiling and holding out her hands. "Tyler, this was just so sweet of you. I can't tell you what a relief it is to have him here. Even if I only stay another week, I'll enjoy it so much more when I know Hagar's safe and happy."

"I hope you'll stay a lot more than a—"

But Tyler wasn't able to finish his thought because Ruth was in his arms, nestling against his chest, laughing and kissing him.

He wrapped his arms around her, enjoying the delicious feel of her body. She was so slender and fine-boned, so softly curving and warm, and her lips were cool and soft against his.

Tyler shuddered deeply and strained her close to him, burying his face in the fragrance of her hair, moving his lips over the silky softness of her face and throat, lost in pleasure while his body grew hard and urgent with need.

She moved against his body with a gentle unconscious invitation that made his blood race, made his arms tighten around her and his kisses grow bolder and more questing.

"Tyler," she sighed, her lips moving under his. "Oh, Tyler, that feels so—"

"Ruth?" a voice called. "Ruth, I'm almost ready to leave. Where are you?"

Ruth pulled out of his arms, laughing breathlessly, her face pink and her eyes shining like stars. "That's Virginia," she murmured. "I need to tell her something before she leaves."

"Ruth . . ." he groaned, reaching for her.

"Wait, Tyler," she whispered, turning back to kiss him again and give him a warm meaningful smile that made his knees go weak. "Wait till we get to Lubbock."

And with that promise Tyler had to be content. He followed Ruth across the room and leaned in the doorway, watching as she stood by Virginia's car with her hair blowing in the wind. Both women were talking and gesturing happily, and Virginia waved at Tyler as she turned her car and headed down the road toward Crystal Creek.

Beneath the armoire, Hagar glared with slitted eyes at the tall man and hissed in a weary perfunctory fashion.

"Go on, be nasty, but I won, you mangy fur ball," Tyler told him with a joyous grin. "Complain all you want, but *I'm* the one who got the last kiss, cowboy."

VIRGINIA SAT in the padded booth at the Longhorn Coffee Shop, gazing across the table in covert fascination at the little man opposite her.

Clyde Kane was indeed a clean tidy gentleman. He had pale blue eyes, a shining pink face and a gleaming pink-domed head surrounded by a drift of snow-white hair. His shirt was also snow-white, and so were his fingernails and the handkerchief that was folded nattily in his jacket pocket.

He smiled at Virginia and reached for the salt shaker, trapping it carefully between the sides of his index and middle fingers as if he were unable to grip with his fingertips.

He glanced up, intercepting Virginia's startled glance, and gave her a bright smile. "I always hold the salt shaker this way in restaurants," he said cheerfully. "Or other people's houses."

Virginia nodded uncertainly.

"Germs," Clyde told her. "See, there's germs everywhere, resting on every surface, just waiting to get us. We can't be too careful."

Virginia nodded. She and Clyde had met only a half hour earlier, but they had already had an extensive discussion about germs. Listening to Clyde talk, Virginia could almost see the germs he spoke of, marshaled like a little army with tanks and artillery, waiting patiently in their tiny bunkers to spring on the enemy and mow them down.

In fact, Clyde seemed to view all of life as a battle between people and germs. What was more, Clyde believed the germs were winning this war hands down, so only a few of the smartest and most careful people would survive.

Virginia frowned, watching as her companion repeated his strange, stiff-fingered maneuver with the pepper shaker, apparently as a demonstration. "I don't understand, Clyde," she said finally. "How does holding something that way protect you from germs?"

"Well, think about it," Clyde said equably. "If you hold the salt shaker between your fingertips, like most people do..." He held up his fingertips and gripped an imaginary salt shaker, giving Virginia an alert questioning glance.

"Yes, that's the way most people do," she agreed dryly, but her tone was lost on Clyde, who was deep into his lecture.

"Well, then you get germs from the salt shaker onto your fingertips, see? Then you touch something else, like your garlic toast, for instance, and the germs get transferred onto it, and then you eat them."

He settled back, fixing his watery blue eyes on Virginia with an expression of triumph, then turned his attention to his cutlery. He removed the handkerchief from his pocket and polished each implement with great energy, rummaging through the napkin holder for fresh napkins and laying his knife and fork out on them as he finished his housekeeping tasks.

"You can't be too careful," he confided to Virginia. "Restaurant kitchens are just terrible places. They sneeze on these things and everything. Thousands of germs, crawling all over them."

Virginia shuddered and leaned back in the booth, feeling hot and foolish in her best silk blouse and the blue linen suit she'd donned so hopefully for this date.

Why hadn't she realized, when the man stressed cleanliness so often in his letter, that he was a fanatic on the subject? But then, as she and Ruth had noticed, the cleanliness part sounded nice on paper. Nobody wanted a dirty old man....

"Ready to order?"

Virginia looked up at Dottie Jones, who stood beside them with her notepad poised. Dottie's cheerful glance flicked casually from Virginia to her escort, but if the coffee-shop owner saw anything unusual about the occasion, she gave no sign of it.

"I'll have the fish and chips, please," Virginia said, blessing the other woman for her tact and discretion, which were famous in Crystal Creek.

Clyde frowned at the menu. "I'll have the steak sandwich, very well done," he announced. "No salad, no vegetables. They never wash the vegetables in these places," he added to Virginia, as if Dottie somehow couldn't hear him unless he was ordering.

Virginia flushed miserably and exchanged an awkward glance with the other woman. "Oh, Clyde," she began, "I don't think that's..."

But he was rummaging busily in a large carryall on the vinyl seat beside him. "Could you serve my meal on this?" he asked, handing over a dinner plate carefully wrapped in clear plastic.

Dottie took the plate and eyed the man placidly. "You gonna wash it afterward?"

"Of course," he said stiffly.

"Sure thing." Dottie took the plate and tucked it under her arm as Clyde watched her closely. Virginia, meanwhile, fervently wished she could sink though the linoleum floor and disappear forever.

"Be careful!" Clyde said. "Keep the plastic wrapped completely around the plate until you're ready to use it, would you? Don't touch it with your fingertips."

"I wouldn't dream of it," Dottie told him. She paused, looking curiously at Clyde's anxious scrubbed face. "What about tools?"

"I beg your pardon?"

"Utensils. Knives an' forks. How come you trust our utensils but not our plates?"

"China is much more porous than metal," Clyde said with dignity. "Germs can penetrate the surface and flourish in restaurant china if it's not very, very carefully washed, at temperatures high enough to kill bacteria. I just don't like to take any chances."

Dottie's bright eyes flicked to Virginia for a moment, but she kept her face impassive. "Well now, that's real interesting," she told the little man. "I never even *knew* that."

Virginia choked and gazed fixedly at the bright gingham curtains, afraid to start laughing in case she slipped into hysteria. She pleated her napkin in trembling fingers and bit her lip, thinking about the next date.

At least she'd learned one lesson from this dreadful experience.

Next time, she'd forget all about cleanliness. She'd pick the man who had a sense of humor.

CHAPTER EIGHT

A WINTRY NORTHER came howling down through Central Texas overnight, carried on bitter winds that swept the hilltops bare and filled the valleys with clammy drifting shrouds of mist in the early light.

Jodie shivered as she hurried along the sidewalk toward the drugstore, with her hands plunged deep in jacket pockets and her shoulders hunched against the wind. Dust and debris swirled along the town's empty main street, cold and dirty and infinitely depressing in the thin pale light.

Jodie grimaced and looked at her surroundings with distaste, thinking how wrong this all was. She didn't belong here.

She belonged out at the McKinney ranch, surrounded by warmth and luxury, with lots of people to wait on her and look after her. And she'd be there, too, just as soon as everybody found out about the precious baby she carried and Tyler McKinney stepped forward to shoulder his responsibilities.

Jodie stopped at the corner to let the mail truck go by and pressed her hand wearily into the small of her back. The day she dreamed of could hardly come soon enough. She was getting so tired of everything, of the effort involved in seeing Tyler regularly, and the clumsy weight of her pregnancy, and the lonely, grinding poverty of her life.

Soon, she thought, her pale eyes glittering. Things had to change soon, or she'd...

Jodie stopped suddenly and gazed at the big midnight-blue Cadillac parked in front of the drugstore. This, she realized with a painful rush of excitement, was one of the McKinney vehicles, and it was usually Tyler who came into town this early in the morning. She glanced wildly up and down the street, finally catching sight of his familiar form as he approached the gold-lettered entry doors of the bank.

Jodie caught her breath and gazed with aching adoration at those beloved shoulders, then leaned over and peered tentatively into the big car. Her heart leaped with excitement when she saw the suitcases in the back. These tan nylon bags belonged to the woman who'd come from California. Jodie had, in fact, seen them a number of times, tucked away against one wall of the guest house at the Double C.

The woman was leaving!

Tyler was taking her back to Austin to catch the plane, and she was going away. Jodie's eyes flared with triumph, and her mouth curved into a rare smile. She hurried into the drugstore, nodded at the pharmacist sitting in his cubicle at the back of the store and hung her jacket on a peg near the cash register. Glancing up, she stiffened with shock as Ruth Holden approached the counter, carrying a plastic-wrapped package of sheer black nylon stockings. Ruth gave the girl a shy smile and rummaged in her handbag for her change purse.

Who are you trying to kid? Jodie thought bitterly, grabbing the package. *Pretending to be so sweet and perfect when you're busy trying to steal somebody else's man, and the father of her baby besides. You're just a cheap slut, that's all. You're...*

"It's really cold today, isn't it?" Ruth said in a soft voice, gazing at Jodie with concern. "Do you have far to walk when you come to work?"

"I live out behind," Jodie said without expression. "But I go over to the Longhorn for breakfast sometimes. I'm pregnant," she added with a meaningful glance at the older woman, "and I need to eat good."

"I see." Ruth hesitated, watching as Jodie counted the change and entered her purchase on the old-fashioned cash register. "I'll bet it's going to be really cold farther west," Ruth ventured, clearly trying to make conversation with the sullen girl. "We're driving over to Lubbock, and the radio said they actually had some snow there overnight."

Jodie's hand paused in the act of folding the sales slip. She fixed her pale eyes sharply on Ruth's face. "Lubbock?"

Ruth nodded. "We're going there to tour some of the wineries," she said with a gentle shining smile that revealed a dimple in her left cheek. "I'm really looking forward to the trip."

Jodie kept her face impassive, but inwardly she was raging. Her mind raced frantically, trying to think what to do.

Lubbock was hundreds of miles away. They'd be gone at least overnight, and she had no way of checking on them. Jodie remembered the suitcases piled in the back seat, and her soul burned with impotent fury.

But her voice was calm when she spoke. "I wouldn't do that if I was you."

Ruth glanced up, puzzled. "I beg your pardon?"

"You heard me. You shouldn't go to Lubbock with Tyler McKinney."

"I don't..." Ruth faltered and glanced nervously around the quiet store, then back at the pregnant girl planted solidly behind the counter. "I don't really understand what you mean."

"I guess you don't," Jodie said calmly, putting the package of stockings in a small paper sack and dropping the sales slip in as well.

"But why would you—"

"Those McKinney men aren't always what they seem, you know," Jodie said, giving Ruth a meaningful look. "There's lots of secrets out at that ranch, things an outsider like you won't ever know. Especially about Tyler McKinney. If you're smart, you'll just go on home and not come back."

Jodie watched with grim satisfaction as the woman's cheeks drained of color and her brown eyes widened in shock. She opened her mouth as if to speak, thought better of it and turned toward the door, her slender back tense beneath her tan cashmere sweater.

Serves you right, Jodie thought furiously. *And you better listen, too. If you don't go back where you belong, I'll kill you, lady. Because you sure as hell don't belong at that ranch with Tyler, and it's high time somebody told you so.*

She took the price-sticker gun and began pasting prices on packages of shampoo in a carton stacked in a corner of the store. Jodie frowned, pretending, as she pulled the little plastic trigger with grim satisfaction, that it was aimed at Ruth Holden's pretty dimpled face.

"THESE VATS are gravity presses," the tour guide said, indicating a row of huge metal cylinders at the back of the winery. "That means that the grapes are loaded in here as soon as they're delivered from the field, and their own weight squeezes out the juice. We extract sixty percent of our juice through gravity. That's the clearest, finest juice, used for our premium wines."

A plump tourist in a velour jogging suit stood on tiptoe, gazing in awe at the vast gleaming cylinders. "What makes white wine?" she asked. "Do they use green grapes to make white wine?"

Ruth caught a flicker in the eyes of the young tour guide. She glanced up at Tyler, who stood beside her at the back of the small crowd of people. "In every tour group," she whispered, "there's somebody who asks that. It never fails."

The guide smiled politely, his white teeth flashing against dark skin. "Actually, no," he said. "All juice is clear when it's first extracted, regardless of the color of the grapes. To make red wine, the juice is moved over to those tall vats behind you and left to soak along with the seeds and skins for a few days. But it has to be very rigidly controlled because the longer it soaks, the richer the color and flavor become."

Everybody turned to stare at the towering steel vats. The young guide uncorked a bottle of red wine while his group of listeners gathered around, holding out their glasses expectantly.

"This is one of our finest wines," he said, "a Cabernet Sauvignon. Be careful not to hold the glass by the bowl, because your body heat will alter the flavor. Now, first swirl the wine around a little and observe the 'legs' on the side of the glass."

The tour group had been taught this technique earlier while they waited in the lobby. They all wiggled their glasses solemnly and tried to look knowledgeable as they squinted at the clear reddish liquid clinging to the glass.

Ruth followed suit, smiling up at Tyler, who was frowning in concentration while he examined and tasted his sample of wine.

"Cabernet is a very sophisticated wine," the tour guide told the visitors. "The Texas wine industry is trying very hard to develop good Cabernets and Chardonnays in order to gain credibility on the national scene, and we're succeeding at an amazing rate.

In fact, one of the largest of our local wineries has increased its production of Cabernet from three hundred cases to more than nine thousand in the span of just four years."

Tyler shifted abruptly and Ruth could see his dark eyes glittering as he absorbed these figures. She smiled privately and gave a rueful shake of her head, thinking that after this trip, Tyler would probably be ready to rush out and start planting his grapes before the cold winter mists had time to lift from the valleys of the Double C.

The guide caught the shake of her head and glanced at her anxiously as she tasted the clear red wine. She smiled to reassure him and tried to draw back out of his line of vision, knowing that her presence among the tourists made him nervous.

In fact Ruth had been surprised and pleased by her warm reception in the Texas wineries, where the Holden name was apparently well-known and respected, and Napa Valley wines were revered for their quality. She and Tyler had been invited into the most select wine-making circles in the High Plains of Texas, including this busy pleasant winery and the luxurious private home where they were expected for dinner later in the evening.

The people were knowledgeable and friendly, and so passionately dedicated to the making of excellent wine that Ruth was embarrassed by her earlier skepticism and her careless dismissal of the state's fledgling industry. She was amazed to discover that she felt completely at home on these bare windswept plains, surrounded by people who shared her love for the business and who showed friendly respect for her expertise.

In fact, the whole day had been intensely enjoyable, except for her disturbing early-morning conversation with the strange dark-haired girl in the drugstore before they left Crystal Creek.

"Tyler..." Ruth began when they were back in the lobby of the winery, sipping the last of their samples.

"Yeah? Ruthie, do you remember how many bottles they can fill and label a minute?"

"Four hundred, I think he said. But this is just a medium-size winery, Tyler. That's why I picked it for an in-depth tour, because it's probably about the size you'll be looking at."

"At first," he said, holding his glass to the light and squinting at the pale Chardonnay.

"At first," she echoed with fond sarcasm. She paused to sniff her wine, impressed by its light pleasant bouquet. "Tyler, you're just hopeless. Do you always want to run before you've even learned to walk?"

"Run?" He put a long arm around her shoulders and looked down at her with a flashing grin. "Hell, sweetheart, I want to *fly*."

Ruth laughed and relaxed beside him. They were sitting in the deep plastered embrasure of one of the tall leaded-glass windows, watching the tourists clatter through the wine boutique and waiting for the winery owner, who had promised Tyler a personal interview.

The sun glistened on a shallow blanket of fresh snow beyond the windows, sparkling like a field of diamonds in the afternoon sun. Prisms of light from the leaded glass threw broken rainbows onto the white walls and heavy dark beams, and the sunshine felt pleasantly warm on their backs.

Ruth sighed in pleasure and moved closer to the man beside her, thinking how enjoyable the day had been. She savored the thought of a fine dinner ahead, good conversation, and the long winter evening that would come afterward, when she and Tyler returned to their hotel rooms....

She shivered a little with anticipation and he looked down at her in quick concern. "Chilly, Ruth? Do you want me to get your jacket from the car?"

"Oh, no," she said hastily, avoiding his eyes. "I was just... thinking."

"Yeah?" He arched a dark eyebrow and gave her a grin. "About what? Winepresses?"

"Not exactly," Ruth said, still unable to meet that warm teasing gaze. "Actually," she began awkwardly, "I was thinking about that girl."

"Which girl? Ruth, is this a real good Chardonnay? World-class, would you say?"

Ruth frowned at the liquid in the bottom of her glass. "Yes, I'd say it is. This wine could fare well at any international competition."

"The guide said they've won lots of prizes."

"I'm sure they have. I'm really impressed by the flavor. The girl I was telling you about back in Crystal Creek," Ruth added, picking up the other thread of their conversation. "The pregnant one in the drugstore."

Tyler lifted his arm from around her shoulders and waved his empty glass with an abrupt, angry gesture. "God, Ruth, I can't tell you how sick I am of hearing about that girl. Let's talk about something else, okay?"

"But, Tyler, she said—"

"I don't care what she said. This whole thing is just getting so damned—"

"Miss Holden? Mr. McKinney? John told me you were waiting out here. It's an honor to have you visit our winery."

Ruth smiled and got to her feet, extending her hand to a tall, sun-browned man in a Western-style suit who looked more like a rancher or cowboy than a winery owner. "Mr. Clark, it's good of you to give us your time."

"To a lady from the Holden vineyards? I'd give you the shirt off my back," their host said with a charming smile. "I'm aiming for your Chardonnay, Miss Holden," he added with a grin. "It's only fair to warn you."

Ruth laughed, delighted by his words. "Well, I'm certainly flattered, but I'm afraid we're training up some competition for you, Mr. Clark. This is Tyler

McKinney. He's planning to open a winery over in Claro County."

Charles Clark shook Tyler's hand and gave him a beaming smile. "Welcome to the brotherhood, Mr. McKinney. It's a wonderful, frustrating, all-absorbing, maddening kind of life you're getting into."

"I know. And I'm going to love it," Tyler said, looking into the other man's cheerful honest face. "I'm just going to love it."

Ruth, holding his arm and gazing up at him with shining eyes, could see that he meant every word.

"WE STARTED with hybrids," John Kennock said, waving his crystal goblet expansively. "People kept telling us we couldn't grow vinifera up here on the plains. Too little rain, too much hail, too short a growing season, too much frost. We believed every word of it."

Ruth glanced over briefly and met Tyler's gaze across the low mass of flowers in the centre of the table. Then she turned back to the man on her left. "Did the hybrids do well?"

"They did all right. But a few of the wineries decided to take a risk and planted vinifera, and they did even better. Now we're moving almost completely toward the traditional vines."

"Really? In this climate?" Ruth looked at her dinner companion in wide-eyed astonishment.

"Vinifera is an amazing plant. It's the most widely cultivated vine in the world. Its cultivation goes back at least six thousand years, and it just keeps adapting to changing conditions."

The winery owner stopped suddenly, turning to his pretty wife with an embarrassed grin. "Good Lord," he muttered. "Look who I'm lecturing about grapevines. Hit me, Joanna."

Ruth smiled at both of them. "Don't worry, Mr. Kennock. I may be a trained enologist, but I'm just beginning to realize how much I don't know about your part of the industry. You people are really teaching me a lot. I can't remember when I've enjoyed myself so much."

Across the table, Tyler smiled and raised his glass to her in a small private salute, thinking that what she said was certainly true. In this atmosphere, among people who understood her dreams and shared her passion, Ruth had certainly blossomed and become warmly animated.

She wore a silky, charcoal-gray evening sweater and matching skirt, borrowed from Cynthia for the occasion, and the rich dark color highlighted her complexion and dark eyes. She laughed frequently, so absorbed in her discussions with the group of winery owners and their wives that she forgot her usual shyness.

She was so beautiful that Tyler was hardly able to look away from her glowing face. Throughout the evening, as they sat laughing and talking around the elegant dinner table with their hosts and the other couples who'd been invited to meet the visitors, he found himself buffeted by surging waves of sexual desire. And it wasn't the urgent, thrusting kind of random masculine impulse that he normally felt. In the short time he'd known her, this woman had wrapped herself so completely around his heartstrings, burrowed into the very center of him.

Tyler was beginning to realize, in fact, that this was the woman he'd always dreamed of, a woman with a gentle sweet manner and a core of steel, designed to be a partner to her man in everything he did. She'd hold his hand, soothe his hurts, warm his bed and raise his children. But she'd also stand beside him against all attackers and fight with wits and courage to protect her home and her man.

She was everything he'd ever wanted, and Tyler McKinney was in love.

This understanding came slowly, dawning on him in the warm glow of the candle flames that flickered between them and was reflected deep in her eyes. Suddenly Tyler could hardly bear the laughing company, the jokes and stories and passionate technical discussions about wine and wine making. He yearned to get Ruth away from there, into a warm secret place where he could hold her and pour out his heart, tell her how he adored her and how wonderful it was that they'd found each other.

He talked and laughed automatically with the other guests, impatient and restless with longing. For once, he wasn't even interested in the fascinating topic of his own winery. He wanted nothing but to seize Ruth and run away with her, out into the frosty night and the waiting darkness.

Occasionally she met his seeking eyes and he caught a look on her face that he'd never seen there before, a sort of bewitching promise coupled with a warm hint of mischief that took his breath away, left him limp and helpless with desire and anticipation. Something was definitely going to happen to Tyler McKinney on this snowy winter evening, something so wonderful he could hardly bear to wait.

At last he was in the car headed for the hotel, with Ruth resting comfortably beside him. Tyler glanced cautiously at her delicate profile, edged with silver in the muted light.

"Did you enjoy the evening, Ruth?"

"Oh, Tyler, it was wonderful! They're the nicest people, aren't they? And they're so excited about what they're doing, all of them."

"The business seems to be good for marriages, doesn't it?" he ventured, keeping his eyes on the road and his voice deliberately casual. "It's not often you spend an evening with four other couples and everybody seems to be happily married."

"I know. I think it comes from sharing something so completely," Ruth said, looking thoughtful. "It's probably really important in a marriage to have something you both care about, some common interest that unites you."

"Besides kids," Tyler said dryly.

Ruth laughed. "That's right. Children don't really seem to hold people together, do they? At least not these days. But something like building a winery, something that you both love and work for and pour your heart into—"

She stopped abruptly, realizing what she was saying, and turned to gaze out the window again, biting her lip in silence.

Tyler smiled to himself, then caught sight of a brief frown on her expressive face.

"Now what are you worried about?"

Ruth smiled awkwardly. "Tyler, would you mind not reading my thoughts every single minute? Can't I hide anything at all from you?"

"I hope not," he said calmly. "Not if something's upsetting you. What is it, Ruth?"

"If you must know, I'm thinking about Hagar."

"*Still?*" Tyler stared at her. "Ruth, I flew that damned cat halfway across the country so you wouldn't have to worry about him. He's eating like a pig and sleeping twenty hours a day. Everybody on the ranch loves him. What's to worry about?"

Ruth shifted uneasily on the leather seat, unable to look at him.

"Ruth? What is it?"

"Hagar's always been my cat," she said finally. "Just mine. He's never really been close to anybody else, ever since he was a tiny kitten."

A light dawned, and Tyler chuckled aloud. "You're *jealous,*" he said in delight. "Ruth Holden, you're jealous of a poor old guy who's almost a hundred years old."

He continued to smile as he gazed at the frosty stretch of highway. Beside him, Ruth looked out the window in troubled silence.

"I'm not jealous," she said finally. "I'm just worried, that's all."

Old Hank, with his usual capriciousness, had decided for some reason that he liked Ruth's cat, and the affection was apparently mutual. Hagar had taken to spending most of the day with the old man, curled up in a huge rusty ball at the foot of his rocker. Sometimes he even lay in Hank's lap, where he purred noisily while Hank stroked him with gentle gnarled hands. Frequently the old man murmured to the big fluffy cat, soft inaudible whispers that appeared to be of deep interest to both of them.

"They seem so happy together," Ruth complained. "Whenever I go near them I feel like an intruder."

"He's a comfort to Grandpa. The old guy's lived a long life and been pretty much a loner," Tyler said gently. "Now he's thinking about the final checkout, and he can't really tell anybody how he feels. I think that's why he likes to talk to your cat."

Ruth's face softened. "Maybe you're right. I don't want to be selfish, Tyler. Do you think Hank's taking good care of him, though?" she added anxiously.

"Will he remember to feed him and brush him every day?"

Because of their obvious affinity, Hagar had been left with Hank during this trip, moving happily over to the little stone house at the edge of the ranch yard. With customary brusqueness Hank had waved off Ruth's list of anxious instructions about the care and feeding of the big cat.

"He'll be just fine," Hank said airily. "If he gets dirty I'll toss him in the horse trough. If he's hungry, he can go down to the barn an' catch rats like any self-respectin' tomcat. Quit yer damned *fussing!*"

Tyler grinned again, remembering. "Of course he'll be all right," he said soothingly. "Virginia's keeping an eye on things, Ruthie. Don't worry, okay? For once in your life, take a little holiday from worrying."

Ruth looked over at him with a smile and placed her hand gently on his knee. "You're right," she said. "It's crazy of me to spoil a lovely holiday like this by fretting about things."

"Damn right." Tyler hesitated, feeling as shy and awkward as a high school boy out for the first time with the girl of his dreams. "Charles gave me a bottle of his best reserve stock," he ventured. "Shall we sample a bit of it before we turn in?"

"That would be nice," Ruth said gravely, avoiding his eyes.

Tyler pulled into the hotel parking lot and grinned over at her, arching one eyebrow suggestively. "Your place or mine?"

She laughed aloud and took his arm as they hurried across the frosty moonlit pavement. The air was crisp and chill, shimmering with ice crystals in the cold neon light.

But in Tyler's heart it was springtime, and warm breezes danced over the wild sweeping plains.

IN ONE CORNER of Ruth's hotel room a single floor lamp, shaped like a tall lily of brass and crystal, cast a muted glow onto the walls and ceiling. Just beyond this soft golden pool of light, Tyler sat in a large velvet armchair with Ruth on his lap.

She snuggled against him, sipping dreamily at the excellent wine they'd poured into a pair of heavy glass tumblers from the hotel bathroom.

Tyler set his glass on a low table nearby and drew her closer, running his hands over her body, kissing her hair and the fragrant hollow of her neck.

"Tyler!" Ruth protested, laughing. "You'll spill my wine."

"I probably will," he muttered, running his tongue around the delicate pink shell of her ear. "Put it down so I can rip your clothes off, okay?"

"Oh, no. I get to undress you first," she said, placing her glass out of harm's way and meeting his eyes solemnly. "It's a rule."

"Really? Who says?"

"It's an ancient wine maker's tradition," Ruth said, slipping the jacket from his shoulders and beginning to unbutton his shirt. "Sort of an unwritten law. The consultant is in charge of all seductions."

"What a great idea," Tyler said, leaning back with a startled grin as she opened his shirt and buried her face in the dark springing hair on his chest. "Are there any other rules I should know about?"

"Oh, lots of them," Ruth assured him soberly, frowning as she studied the fastening on his belt buckle, then opened it and reached for his zipper. "The consultant gets to dictate the pace, the duration and all related activities."

"What about the poor guy who's hired her?" Tyler said, still smiling at her. "Does he have any rights at all?"

Ruth shook her head, opening his jeans and touching him gently. "Not a single one," she whispered. "He's required to lie back, be quiet and enjoy it."

Tyler shivered and arched his back as her hands roamed over him. "Oh, God," he choked, grinning down at her. "That's sure a tough one, Ruthie. How can a man ever be expected to enjoy something like this?"

He lifted her gently onto the other chair, stripped off his shirt and jeans and turned his attention to the sweater she wore, tugging impatiently on the fastening at the back of her neck.

"Be careful," Ruth whispered. "This is one of Cynthia's best sweaters."

"Careful!" he muttered. "Ruthie, I'm on fire here. Let's just rip the damn thing off, okay? I'll give Cynthia the money to buy a new one."

Ruth chuckled, pushing his hands away and reaching behind her to unfasten the sweater. "And tell her it was damaged in the heat of passion?"

"Why not?" Tyler said cheerfully. "I think she and Daddy probably know a little bit about passion. Let's get that skirt off, too, shall we?"

He lifted the loosened sweater gently over her head while she stepped out of the skirt and folded it across the arm of her chair.

"Oh, my," Tyler said, gazing at her in awe. "Look at you!"

She smiled up at him, a little awkward in her silvery-gray bra of fine French lace, and a silky garter belt that topped a wisp of gray panties and sheer black stockings.

"Pretty tarty, isn't it?" she ventured shyly. "I've always loved sexy underclothes."

"Me, too," Tyler said fervently.

"That's clearly evident," Ruth commented, gazing at the alarming bulge in his undershorts.

Tyler chuckled and swept her into his arms. "Ruth Holden," he murmured against her hair, "you are without a doubt the most surprising, incredible, delightful woman I've ever met. Absolutely."

Ruth smiled and nestled close to him, loving the warmth of him, the hairy, hard-muscled strength of his lean body, the jutting maleness that pressed against her with such urgency. "I'll bet you say that to all the girls," she whispered into his chest.

Suddenly her mind filled with a vividly disturbing memory of the pale-eyed girl at the drugstore, uttering her strange chilly warning about the McKinney men and their secrets.

Ruth shivered and tried to draw away.

"Cold, Ruth?" he murmured huskily, misunderstanding the shiver. "Let's just slip under the covers and get warm, shall we?"

He lifted Ruth easily in his arms and carried her to the bed, pulling back the soft covers, then climbing in after her and enfolding her again.

When Ruth felt his warm arms close around her, felt his long hard limbs merge with hers and his lips move hungrily over her face and breasts, all thought and memory fled. She could hardly recall her own name, because there was nothing anywhere in her world but raw sensation, pure pleasure and a rising searing excitement that left her limp and breathless.

He took off her bra and caressed her breasts while she moaned softly, washed over with delight at the feel of his hard seeking mouth, his dark hair brushing her skin, his gentle questing hands.

Ruth lifted her hips and helped him as he fumbled with the fastening on her garter belt. She tugged shamelessly at his shorts, suddenly in a fever to be naked with him, to be free and unfettered with nothing at all between them.

"Tyler," she whispered, needing him to understand. "Tyler, please don't think I'm like this all the time. It's just that I—"

"Ruthie, I know," he murmured, caressing her with long delicious strokes, his hands so loving and gentle that she shuddered and quivered at his touch, completely unable to control her body's reaction to him. "I'm just the same."

"You are?"

She rolled her head on the pillow and gazed into his eyes, running her hands hungrily over his chest, his lean hips, his steel-hard thighs and loins.

"Yes. It has to mean something to me, Ruth. I just can't be casual about this like some other guys. And you mean the whole world to me. I love you, Ruth. You're the woman I've looked for all my life."

Ruth's eyes widened. She gazed at him in startled silence, searching for words to respond to this stunning declaration.

But Tyler wasn't listening anymore. His handsome face was dark with passion and his eyes were concentrated, full of need and fire. He moved closer to her, his hands growing more urgent, his fingers delicate and tantalizing as he fondled her.

"Ruth?" he whispered. "Darling?"

"Yes," she said, smiling at him and opening herself to him. "Yes, Tyler."

A BROWN HAND traced lazy circles on her back, and firm lips kissed the hollow of her throat. Ruth stirred and trembled, still drowning in feeling.

Tyler sprawled beneath her, eyes closed, face soft and boyish with fulfillment as his hands continued to caress her gently.

"Tell me you love me," he demanded, opening his eyes and gazing directly into hers, grasping her in a sudden iron grip.

"Tyler..."

"Say it. Tell me you love me. You know you do, so say it."

Ruth grinned and rolled away to lie on her back beside him. "What gives you so much confidence?"

He turned his head on the pillow and looked at her, his dark eyes dancing. "You may not have noticed, since you seemed a little distracted, but I was in the room during this past half hour, too, you know."

"Were you?"

"Yeah. And there was a girl in here who certainly seemed to be in love. In fact, I believe the word was actually mentioned a couple of times."

"So," Ruth said, keeping her voice light, "why ask for more? Why not be content with that? Tyler, could you hand me my wine, please?"

He leaned up on one elbow, his broad naked chest gleaming in the shaded lamplight, and reached for the heavy tumblers, handing one to her. "Because," he said, "I don't want to be just a sex object for the consultant, that's why."

Ruth smiled lazily and stroked his lean hip where the blanket fell away. "Is this a mole or a birthmark?" she asked, fingering a large irregular dark spot on his hip.

"It's a birthmark. My daddy was thrilled to see it when I was born. He said it was shaped just like the map of Texas."

"You know, it is, sort of," Ruth said, gazing at the inch-wide mark on his hip. "Isn't that fascinating? Look at it. There's the Panhandle, and the—"

"Quit changing the subject, Ruthie."

"Is there a subject?"

"Sure, there is. We're talking about whether you love me."

"Oh, that. Why don't you just relax and enjoy life?" she said in a fair imitation of his warm Texas drawl. "Quit this damned worrying all the time."

Tyler chuckled and gazed down at her, shaking his head. "Who'd have thought you were one of those use-him-and-cast-him-aside girls? Prim little Ruth Holden?"

"I have no intention of casting you aside. Not for a while yet, anyhow."

"Yeah? Why not?"

"Because," Ruth said solemnly, though her eyes were sparkling, "I believe you may still have some limited potential for pleasure. You're not quite wrung out yet."

"Oh, God," he moaned, choking with laughter. "What an incredible woman. Ruthie, wring me out. Go ahead and have your way with me. I'm all yours."

"Drink your wine," Ruth told him with a fond smile. "The night is young."

CHAPTER NINE

TYLER WAS BACK from Lubbock and Jodie was happy. She stepped awkwardly up onto the lumpy couch in her stockinged feet, frowning and twisting her body, trying to see all of herself in the tiny cracked wall mirror beside her pictures of Tyler.

She preened briefly, admiring the new outfit she'd purchased from the mail-order catalog. Her skirt was black and silky, short enough to show off her legs, topped by a perky white maternity top splashed with huge black polka dots and trimmed at the throat with a big red fabric rose.

Jodie smiled at her cloudy reflected image and dabbed a bit of pink lipstick onto her mouth, dreaming about the evening ahead.

Tonight was a benefit dance at Zack's for the Waldens, a local family whose house had burned to the ground just before Christmas. Zack had offered his whole place free of charge for the evening, and a group of local business people had planned the event, selling tickets at ten dollars each and organizing all kinds of raffles and other money-making schemes for the evening.

Everybody in the region would be there, including the McKinney family, and Jodie knew this would be a special evening. Tonight she expected Tyler Mc-Kinney to claim her as his own, to let the world know how much they meant to each other and how excited they were about the baby she carried.

Jodie stepped dreamily down from the couch, put on her high-heeled pumps and her shabby, black rabbit-fur jacket, grabbed her big patchwork handbag and let herself out into the frosty darkness.

She hurried down the lighted main street, awkward on the unaccustomed heels, enjoying the festive atmosphere of traffic crowding the streets and music blaring from the pickup trucks and vans that were all heading toward Zack's.

Party-goers passed her on the street, smiling politely, townspeople and visitors from the neighboring ranches. The women were dressed in their best, primped and perfumed for the occasion. Jodie felt smugly at home among them, knowing she looked nice even though her body was growing more heavy and swollen with every week that passed.

After all, her mama always said that a woman was prettiest when she was pregnant.

Jodie frowned briefly when she thought about her mother, clutching her jacket tighter around her ripe young body. She slipped through the front door of Zack's, where the sudden blast of warmth and music was like hitting a solid wall. The place was brightly lit and throbbing with a country beat, full of smoke and laughter and raucous voices.

A group of cowboys crowded the vestibule, arguing noisily among themselves and ogling the girls who came in. They eyed Jodie with startled appreciation but said nothing, shifting uneasily. The whole town knew that there was something strange about this girl apart from her obvious but mysterious pregnancy. Jodie Hiltz was an enigma, with her pale eyes and cold unsmiling face. She tended to make men nervous, even the most ebullient types like Bubba Gibson.

Jodie hung her jacket on a peg in the vestibule, slipped into the washroom to check her dress and makeup, then edged through the wide swinging doors to the crowded lounge.

Cal McKinney was on the little stage with his arm around a tall striking redhead in tight jeans and white silk shirt. The cowboy laughed aloud, his handsome face glinting blue and green in the colored spotlights, and shouted for the audience to be quiet. Jodie slipped into a corner near the back and craned forward to watch avidly, always fascinated by anything the McKinney family did.

Maybe Cal had finally found a girlfriend and tonight he was introducing her to the townspeople. If so, this beautiful flame-haired woman would soon be Jodie's sister-in-law.

Her pale face grew taut with interest. She edged closer, frowning. There was something vaguely familiar about the woman, and this impression was confirmed when the audience quieted enough for Jodie to hear what Cal was saying.

"You thought she'd left us, folks, but she'd never desert Crystal Creek when one of her friends was in need. Jessica's not that kind of girl. She wants to sing a song for y'all, but you're damn well gonna pay for it. Let's pass the hat, an' remember that every bill you put in helps to buy clothes an' furniture for the little Walden kids. So no small stuff, okay, cowboys?"

The black Stetson circulated rapidly among the crowd, passing so close to Jodie that she could see some twenties and even a couple of fifties among the bills mounded in the upturned crown. The money offering was handed back up to Cal, who squinted at it critically, then leaned close to the microphone again. "Okay, folks, that looks pretty good. I guess you've earned your song. Jessie?"

He glanced at the tall redhead beside him. She nodded and gave the crowd a dazzling smile.

"Ladies an' gentlemen," Cal said with an expansive wave of his long arm, "I give you the best singer in Texas, Miss Jessica Reynolds!"

The woman moved close to the mike and began to sing, eyes closed and lissome body swaying in the smoky room. Her voice soared, incredibly rich and lovely, mesmerizing the crowd so completely that a profound silence fell and tears sparkled on a few tanned cheeks.

Zack Stone stood near the door staring at the singer, his dark face cold and intense, his eyes burning. The handsome young sheriff of Claro County, Wayne Jackson, was also gazing up at Jessica Reynolds with a look of hunger and yearning that made Jodie's breath catch in her throat.

That was just the way she wanted Tyler to look at her. And he would, too, when he...

The minute she thought of Tyler he materialized in the doorway, as if she'd created him by some kind of magic. Jodie held her breath and stared at him, her heart beating crazily, her world spinning.

Tyler was dressed as usual in jeans, boots and sport jacket. He was bareheaded and that same unruly lock of dark hair fell across his forehead as he strolled into the room, giving him an endearing boyish look. He smiled up at Jessica when she finished her song, greeted the people near him and then leaned forward, looking back toward the crowded entry.

Jodie's spirits plummeted and her body turned cold when she saw Ruth Holden enter the room with Lynn and Cynthia McKinney. Ruth wore a simple red jersey dress that fitted her trim figure snugly, and her hair shone under the bright ceiling lights.

Bitch! Jodie thought furiously, staring at the woman. *You rotten bitch, why can't you just...?*

But her furious thoughts were stilled and she watched with painful, tight-lipped intensity as the woman smiled at Tyler and moved over beside him, shyly greeting his friends.

Tyler put his arm around Ruth Holden and drew her close to him with an unmistakable air of proprietary pride, his tanned face shining as he hugged her.

Jodie stared in shocked pounding fury as Tyler whispered something to the woman in red and she turned to smile gently up at him. Tyler bent his dark head and kissed her as if they were the only people in the room, while his friends laughed and slapped his shoulders in delight.

Ruth's face was flushed, her dark eyes starry as Tyler drew her out onto the dance floor and swept her into his arms, circling the floor to the beat of the cheerful cowboy band and the shouts and clapping hands of his friends and neighbors.

Jodie watched them whirl by in a shining blur of red and denim, her mind reeling.

It should be me, she thought. *It should be me, it should be me....*

And it would be, she decided, her face suddenly hardening with grim resolve. This couldn't be allowed to continue. Jodie intended to put a stop to this woman's shameless pursuit of her man, and she was going to do it tonight.

No matter what happened, she was doing it tonight.

"CARE TO DANCE, Ruth? I think I could just manage one of these slow waltzes if you're real gentle with me."

Ruth smiled up at Cal McKinney, who stood in front of her with his brown callused hand extended politely. She got to her feet and moved into his arms, thinking how similar he was to Tyler, and yet how different.

There was a family resemblance in their features, and their bodies were alike. But no man could make her feel the way Tyler did, thrill her to the very depths of her soul and make the whole world shimmer and tremble with passion.

"You're smiling," Cal said, grinning down at her. "What are you thinking about, Ruth?"

"Tyler," she said automatically, then blushed when Cal threw his head back and laughed so heartily that other dancers on the crowded floor turned to smile at them.

"God," he choked, "isn't that just my luck? I'm dancing with the prettiest girl in the room and all the time she's in my arms, what's she thinking about? My goddamn *brother!*"

Ruth smiled up at him. "Oh, I've seen the occasional pretty girl hanging on your arm tonight, Cal," she said. "I don't think you're really all that lonesome."

He returned her gaze, his eyes suddenly serious. "There's different kinds of lonesome, Ruth."

"I know," Ruth said quietly. "I think I've been familiar with all of them through the years."

"God, isn't Tyler a lucky man," the young cowboy murmured softly. "Speaking of lucky," he added after a moment's silence, "who's that funny-looking guy with Virginia? Have you met him, Ruth?"

Ruth shook her head. "Not really. But," she added carefully, "Virginia told me he has a great sense of humor."

She and Cal both glanced at a table near the dance floor where Virginia sat, looking beautiful in a silky pink dress with a ruffled bodice. Various members of her family were at the table with her, along with a big, red-faced laughing man who sported a wild bush of gingery red hair and an impressive paunch.

"Yeah, he seems like a real card, all right," Cal ventured, eyeing the stranger. "Did you hear him a while ago when he was on the stage singing along with the band?"

"I tried not to listen," Ruth confessed. "Some of his lyrics were pretty crude."

"That's a polite way of putting it. And then a few minutes later when he pulled out that pair of panty hose and stuck them on his head . . . what was *that* all about?"

"I think he was telling some kind of joke," Ruth said with her engaging lopsided smile. "He was imitating a bunny rabbit."

"Wow," Cal said with a grin, sweeping his partner stiffly around the floor. "That's a unique concept. The legs hang down like floppy ears, right?"

"I guess that's the general idea," Ruth said dryly. "Virginia didn't seem all that impressed, though," she added in a deliberately casual tone.

"Yeah, I noticed." Cal glanced over Ruth's shoulder at the housekeeper, who was watching in bleak silence as her escort capered merrily around the table, doing an impromptu Irish jig for the benefit of the onlookers. "Poor Virginia, she doesn't look a bit happy, does she?"

"I guess when it comes to a sense of humor, it's possible to have too much of a good thing," Ruth said solemnly.

She found herself bubbling for a moment on the verge of laughter, but repented when she saw how truly miserable poor Virginia was looking.

Cal glanced down at his partner. "Where did she meet this guy, Ruth? Do you know?"

"Yes, but I'm not telling. Cal, are you sure you're all right?" Ruth looked up in concern as they bumped into another dancer and Cal winced in pain.

"Sure. I'm fine. In fact, I'm hitting the road again tomorrow. Entering a couple of smaller rodeos over in New Mexico, then heading up to Mesquite."

Ruth stared at him, aghast. "You're not," she protested finally. "It's only been a week or so. You've hardly had a chance to get better at all."

"I told you, I'm just fine. Rodeo cowboys are always packing some injury or other, Ruth. They can't be taking a month off every time they have some little ache or pain."

"Little ache or pain!" Ruth echoed. "Cal, Dr. Purdy says you have a compressed disk in your back. He told your father that if it ruptures before it has a chance to heal, you could have permanent spinal injury.''

"Oh, hell, doctors are always saying stuff like that,'' Cal said airily. "Nothing's gonna happen to me, Ruth. You can't kill a cowboy.''

Ruth was silent a moment, gazing blindly at the whirling crowd of dancers. "Does your father know you're leaving?''

Cal shrugged, his handsome face sobering. "Not yet. But Daddy knows I can't hang around home doing nothing. He couldn't, either, if it was him.''

"Cal, I wish you'd—''

"Hey, Ruth, see that girl over there? The pregnant one in the black and white top?''

Ruth turned and caught sight of a familiar white face at the edge of the crowd of onlookers. She shivered a little in Cal's warm arms and glanced up at him with a questioning look.

"You know who she is, Ruth?''

"She works at the drugstore,'' Ruth said cautiously. "Doesn't she?''

Cal nodded and hesitated, as if thinking about how much to tell her.

Ruth watched him curiously, wondering if Tyler's handsome brother had some kind of relationship with the strange dark-haired girl. Maybe that was why Jodie Hiltz seemed to take such a passionate interest in the McKinneys, and why she'd said those mysterious, disturbing things to Ruth the day they left for Lubbock.

But this girl was pregnant, and very young.

Ruth frowned, thinking about Cal's sunny face and boyish good humor. Surely Tyler's brother wouldn't be the kind of man to take advantage of someone who was barely more than a child?

As she was wrestling with the problem of Jodie Hiltz and waiting for Cal to speak, Ruth felt a strong hand fall on her shoulder. She smiled, trembling at the sweet familiar touch.

"That's enough, little brother," Tyler said cheerfully. "You've held on to my girl for two whole dances and she's starting to enjoy herself too much. Time for me to cut in."

"Any girl who spends time with me enjoys herself," Cal said with his familiar brash grin. "And then what happens? My brother takes over and puts a stop to all her pleasure."

Ruth laughed and moved into Tyler's arms, smiling up at him and melting into his embrace as the music started again, a slow dreamy ballad that sobbed from the steel guitar and fiddle.

Ruth circled the room with Tyler, their bodies moving together in comfortable rhythm, their cheeks touching as he bent his dark head toward hers.

"Having a good time, sweetheart?" he murmured.

"A wonderful time," she whispered back over the soft haunting cadence of the ballad. "I can't remember when I've had so much fun. Tyler, these people..."

"Yeah? What about them?"

"They're all so warm, Tyler. They seem so happy and friendly with one another. It must be wonderful to live here and be one of them."

"Oh, they have their problems, too," Tyler said, his face darkening briefly as Bubba Gibson circled past them with Billie Jo Dumont in his arms. Bubba was making a bold show, whirling Billie Jo's lush young body and bending her low on the turns while she tossed her hair and preened in his arms.

By now, Ruth knew all about the neighboring rancher's blatant affair with this woman who was younger than his own daughter. She glared at the stocky gray-haired man, shaking her head in contempt.

"There are people like that everywhere," she said dismissively. "But still, this place has such a wonderful feeling of warmth and solidity, Tyler, like one of those little French villages where the same families have lived together and looked after one another for centuries."

Tyler nodded, gathering her more tightly in his arms and kissing her cheek.

"I had the same feeling in those villages," Ruth mused, nestling against him and smiling dreamily. "I always felt like an outsider, wishing so much I could belong."

"Well," Tyler murmured huskily, "you can belong here, Ruth."

"Oh, no." She looked up at him and shook her head. "I think you'd probably have to be born here, Tyler, to really have a sense of belonging."

He gazed down at her steadily, his dark eyes intent and blazing with emotion. "You could marry me, Ruth. Then you'd really belong. You'd be one of the McKinneys."

She laughed and slapped her free hand lightly on his broad shoulder, then glanced up at him, caught by his expression. "Tyler," she whispered. "You're not serious, are you?"

"More serious than I've ever been in my life. Marry me, Ruth. I need you. I can't live without you anymore, and even if I could, I don't want to. If you go away my whole world will just turn to dust, because you'll take the sun away."

Ruth trembled in his arms, speechless with shock, apprehension and dawning happiness. She was silent while he whirled her into a dark corner of the room and bent to kiss her lips tenderly, then looked deep into her eyes with a questioning expression.

"Tyler," Ruth said breathlessly, "we hardly know each other. We just met a couple of weeks ago."

"We've spent every day together since then," he said calmly. "I know all about your life and how you feel about things, and you know the same about me. And I meant it, Ruth, when I told you I've been looking for you all my life. I knew I'd recognize you the minute I found you, and I did."

She gazed at him with parted lips and shining eyes, struggling with her deep fear of commitment, thinking about the wondrous life he was offering.

She'd have the chance to work with him, building a successful winery from the foundations up, incorporating all the most modern technology. She'd live among these delightful people and enjoy the warm family setting she'd craved all her life. And best of all, she'd go to bed with Tyler McKinney every night, wake up with him every morning, share his dreams and laughter, bear his children....

"Ruth? Say yes, darling. Please say yes. I love you so much."

"Tyler...excuse me a minute, all right?" Ruth said, still breathless. "I need...I need a little time to myself. I'll just run into the washroom and..."

She fell silent, feeling awkward and frightened and ridiculously happy as she hurried out into the vestibule. Her heart was beating frantically as she headed for the pair of rough plank doors marked Steers and Heifers, and let herself into the shabby women's washroom.

There was only one other person in the big dingy room. Ruth's soaring spirits were checked abruptly when she recognized Virginia Parks. The housekeeper was leaning against one of the sinks, gazing tragically at herself in the mirror while she struggled to repair the ravages in her makeup caused by a recent storm of weeping.

"Virginia!" Ruth murmured softly, crossing the room and putting her arms around the plump older woman. "What's the matter?"

Virginia turned and gazed at her friend with bleak red-rimmed eyes. "Oh, Ruth," she choked. "This is just so..."

A pair of girls came in, laughing and talking in shrill voices, and headed straight for the bank of mirrors where they stood pursing their lips and making mysterious little adjustments to their huge mops of tortured hair.

"Oh, my *God*," one of them sighed dramatically, leaning forward to gaze fixedly at her reflected image. "This is just *awful*. And Blake's been looking at this mess all evening. I could just *die*."

Her friend murmured cursory words of comfort, turning to examine the plunging neckline of her T-shirt and her lush, blue-jeaned hips.

Virginia tensed and glanced at them miserably, but Ruth moved between Virginia and the newcomers and spoke in a low voice. "Don't worry, Virginia. They're so wrapped up in their own problems we could probably set ourselves on fire and they wouldn't even notice. Now, tell me what's wrong."

"You know what's wrong," Virginia muttered, moving over into a quiet empty corner. She leaned against the wall and gazed unhappily down at her feet. "You've seen him, Ruth. He's just awful. I'm so purely mortified I can hardly stand it."

"So what?" Ruth said cheerfully. "Maybe this guy's a mistake, but you don't ever have to see him again, Virginia. Chalk it up to experience and laugh about it. It's not a tragedy."

"Yes, it is!" Virginia looked up briefly and met Ruth's eyes, her plump face twisted with anguish.

"I don't understand, Virginia," Ruth said, holding her friend's arm gently as women trooped in and out of the washroom. "It's just one evening."

"No it isn't. It's my whole life!"

"Your whole life? What do you mean?"

"Think about it, Ruth," Virginia said wearily. "Those two men, Clyde Kane last week and then this idiot... they were the best of the bunch, Ruth! They were my first choices. And they're both so awful."

Ruth began to understand. "So now you feel..."

"What's going to happen to me, Ruth? This was just a stupid pipe dream, thinking I could find a man to marry and have a place to live. It's not going to happen. Not ever."

Ruth hesitated, searching for words. "But Virginia," she ventured finally, "maybe you were just unlucky with these two. Maybe one of the others would be..."

Virginia shook her head so violently that her silver hair swung around her face. "No, Ruth. It was crazy. You know what I'm finally beginning to realize? I don't *want* to get married, not even if I found the nicest man in the world. I don't want to adapt my whole life to somebody else, and learn to live with another person again. I want to be free and independent.''

Ruth gazed at her friend's flushed unhappy face, not knowing how to comfort her. "Virginia...what are you going to do?''

"I don't know,'' Virginia wailed softly. "I've gone and given all my money away, and now it's impossible to have a free independent life when I leave the ranch. God knows what's going to happen to me. I'll have to go into a home for impoverished old ladies, or some such thing. Ruth, I just want to die.''

Ruth felt a sudden flood of anger as she witnessed the suffering Virginia's family had inflicted on someone whose only fault had been an excess of kindness and generosity. "Does it ever occur to anyone,'' she asked dryly, "that your family could repay those loans you made to all of them? Has anybody ever thought of that?''

Virginia shook her head wearily. "They'd never be able to manage it. That kind of money doesn't come back, Ruth,'' she said. "Not inside a family. That money is just gone with the wind.''

Ruth nodded, recognizing the truth of this bleak statement.

Virginia looked at the younger woman, trying to smile. "Now I feel bad about you, too.''

"Me? Why?''

"When you came in here, you were shining like a candle,'' Virginia said gently. "Now you look about as miserable as I do. Ruth, don't let anything take your happiness away. Not even me.''

Ruth stared at the other woman's sweet blue eyes, thinking about all the richness of her own life and the dreary future that lay ahead for Virginia.

Something had to be done, she decided. They had to think of something. Maybe she and Tyler could find a way to help Virginia, if she...

"Hey, listen up! Everybody out, girls! They're fixin' to make the big draw any minute now!''

Squeals of excitement echoed through the crowded washroom, while women tossed lipsticks and combs into handbags and headed for the door.

"What draw?'' Ruth asked Virginia, who was moving to join the general exodus.

"An all-expense-paid trip to Dallas to see a George Strait concert,'' Virginia told her. "Lettie Mae and I bought six tickets each.''

"You did? Why?''

"Because,'' Virginia said with a ghost of a smile, "the winner gets to have dinner with George Strait.''

"Who's George Strait?''

Virginia rolled her eyes in disbelief. "Oh, my. You'd better be sure Lettie Mae doesn't ever hear you say that. He's a famous country singer, Ruth,'' she added gently. "*And* he's just about the cutest guy in America. Maybe in the whole world.''

"I see.''

"Maybe I'll win," Virginia said, trying to smile, "and George will fall in love with me over dinner and want to marry me."

Ruth smiled back, cheered by Virginia's sense of humor, and more determined than ever to do something for the poor woman.

She watched as the washroom emptied and sighed in relief at the sudden peace and quiet. Now maybe she could have a few minutes to herself, some time to think about the terrifying, wonderful thing that Tyler had just said to her.

JODIE STOOD in the vestibule, staring coldly at the washroom door where Ruth Holden had disappeared a little while earlier.

In a minute, Jodie thought, her pale face tight with anger, the bitch would be coming out again, and Jodie intended to find some way of getting her alone and telling her the truth about Tyler McKinney.

But, as it happened, luck was on her side. The upcoming draw was announced from the stage, and the washroom emptied almost immediately as a flood of screaming women gathered in the lounge, jostling one another and waiting in an agony of suspense for the winner to be announced.

Jodie lingered a few minutes until she was fairly certain everybody was out of the washroom... everybody but Ruth Holden.

At last she drew a deep breath and marched toward the heavy door. She pushed on the rough planks and stepped inside, pausing to glare with burning eyes at the woman who stood quietly near the long bank of mirrors.

The woman turned abruptly to meet her gaze. Jodie was intensely gratified by the way her smile faded and her face went pale with alarm.

"Yeah, that's right. You *should* be scared," Jodie told her in a shaking voice, a little surprised to find that she was actually speaking these words aloud after her long angry silence. "You're right to be scared of me, you little slut, because I'll sure kill you if I ever get the chance."

The woman from California backed up against the sink, reaching behind her and gripping the cold enamel for support while she kept her eyes fixed on Jodie's face. Then she swallowed and looked around wildly.

But there was no escape, Jodie noted with satisfaction, except for the door that she deliberately blocked with her solid young body.

"Why...why would you want to kill me?" Ruth ventured at last, speaking in a low frightened voice. "What have I done to upset you, Jodie? It's Jodie, isn't it? That's your name?"

"Yeah, it is," Jodie hissed, taking a couple of threatening steps forward. "And don't try that phony sweet stuff on *me,* you sneaky little cheat. Maybe you can fool everybody else, but I know what you're like. I know lots of things about you."

She grinned, feeling a vicious surge of power when she looked at the woman in front of her. It was almost comical the way Ruth Holden's face was white with terror and confusion, her eyes darting anxiously around the empty washroom.

"What do you know about me? What are you talking about?"

"You know damn well what I'm talking about!"

Jodie's resolve faltered slightly when she saw how puzzled the woman looked. But then she remembered that slim curving body swaying in Tyler's arms while Ruth Holden kissed his lips, laughing up into his face, and his dark eyes shone with happiness....

Jodie set her jaw and glared. "You know what I'm talking about," she repeated doggedly.

"I'm afraid I don't," Ruth said, beginning to regain her composure. Her chin went up and her dark eyes gazed steadily into Jodie's. "I think you're either very rude or very disturbed, and I'd like you to move aside now, please, so I can leave this room."

Jodie, who had been trained all her life to respect her elders, was briefly taken aback by this abrupt shift in the balance of power. She swayed uncertainly on her high spike heels, then thought of Tyler and felt her strength and anger come rushing back.

"I'm not moving till you promise me you'll leave him alone," she said in a low belligerent voice.

"Leave who alone? I don't know what you're talking about." The woman's eyes widened in sudden understanding. "Is it Cal? Are you upset that he danced with me? Because, Jodie, I really don't think he—"

"No, it's not Cal," Jodie hissed in a furious mocking voice. "It's *Tyler,* and you goddamn well know it!"

"Tyler!" Ruth's mouth dropped open. She stared at her young tormentor, slack-jawed with astonishment.

"Yeah," Jodie said, feeling calmer now that the words had finally been spoken. "I know how you've been chasing him, don't think I don't. And it's just the cheapest, awfullest thing anybody ever did."

"Look, I don't know who you are, or why you're saying these things," Ruth began, taking a deep shuddering breath and facing Jodie squarely. Her cheeks were pink, and her wide brown eyes began to flash with anger. "But I think you'd better be careful, Jodie. You're talking about things that are absolutely none of your business."

"Like hell," Jodie said rudely. "Tyler McKinney is my business, all right."

"Really? And what makes you think so?"

"This," Jodie said, thrusting out her swollen abdomen and patting it with a smile of gloating triumph. "This makes me think so, lady. Because *this*—" she caressed the thrusting polka-dotted silk again "—this is Tyler McKinney's baby."

Ruth Holden gasped and sagged against the sink, her face white with shock, her eyes wide and staring.

"What . . . what did you say?"

"I said this is Tyler McKinney's baby," Jodie repeated calmly. "I've been keeping his secret long enough. I'd never in this world do anything to hurt Tyler, but I can't stand the way you keep throwing yourself at him. It's time you knew the truth, Miss Ruth Holden."

Ruth drew herself up with an attempt at dignity, and shook her head. "I don't believe you," she said finally. "This is absolutely ridiculous. You're just making it up."

"Yeah?" Jodie asked softly. "And why would I do that?"

The other woman shook her head helplessly. "How would I know? Probably you got pregnant and now you're alone and scared, and you think this is a way to get some money from the McKinneys. But, Jodie, you have to realize that it's a terrible thing, what you're doing. There are other ways to get help, you know. You could get into really serious trouble by making this kind of false accusation."

Jodie ignored her, staring dreamily at her wavy reflection in one of the cheap mirrors. "Tyler's just the most wonderful man, isn't he?" she murmured softly, almost talking to herself. "Especially when he's naked. There's not another man in the whole world who looks as good as Tyler with his clothes off."

Ruth stared at her in horrified silence.

"And that funny little birthmark on his hip," Jodie went on with a sly secretive smile. "Did you know that, Ruth? Did you know that he's got a birthmark on his left hip shaped just like a map of Texas?''

The silence in the big shabby room was so profound that it was a breathing, palpable thing, while Ruth held herself stiffly erect and gazed at Jodie's face.

''We like to play little games with that birthmark when we're in bed,'' Jodie said dreamily, lost in her memories. ''He gets me to point out Dallas, and Houston, and Amarillo, and he laughs because I'm tickling him. Then he takes his . . .''

Her voice went on and on in that sly confiding tone, recounting the most intimate details of Tyler McKinney's body and his lovemaking, until at last the woman from California couldn't bear it any longer. She gave a low choked moan of anguish and rushed past Jodie, pushing her way out of the washroom, her eyes streaming tears.

Jodie gazed in satisfaction at the closed door. Slowly she moved over to stand in front of one of the mirrors, twisting a strand of hair thoughtfully around one finger as she smiled at her pale reflection.

CHAPTER TEN

TYLER STOOD restlessly at the outer edges of the noisy group crowded around the stage, gazing over the masses of people and watching the closed door to the ladies' washroom. He was waiting in an agony of suspense for Ruth to come back, a little surprised by the turmoil of his emotions.

He'd known for a long time that he was falling in love with Ruth Holden. In fact, during their short stay in Lubbock, he'd actually told her so. He'd tried to let her see how she was moving closer and closer to the center of his heart and making everything else seem small and unimportant.

But Tyler hadn't realized until tonight when he actually spoke the words aloud, just how indispensable she'd become to him. Now he understood that he'd told her the simple truth. If she left him and went back to California, she'd take his heart away with her.

Without Ruth, Tyler's life wouldn't even be worth living anymore.

And his feelings no longer had anything to do with the winery or any of his other business plans. She was simply the other half of himself, the woman he'd dreamed of through all these lonely hardworking years. Ruth was the air he breathed and the stars in the sky. She was his life, and if she refused to marry him, he didn't know how to go on living.

Tyler shifted restlessly, his face tense and still as he peered into the vestibule again.

"Hey, brother," a cheerful voice said at his side. "C'mon, get a load off your feet."

Tyler smiled automatically and followed Cal to an empty table near the back of the room, watching as his brother folded his long body into the chair with a grimace of pain.

"You're still hurting, aren't you, Cal?"

"Some," Cal admitted. "But it's not near as bad as it was at first." He was silent a moment, toying with a pile of cocktail napkins on the scarred leather table-top. "I'm leaving in the morning, Ty."

Tyler nodded. "I figured you would. I've seen you getting more restless every day."

Cal grinned. "Yeah, well, it's not easy to sit around and watch you running everything. Matter of fact, it never was."

"Come on, Cal," Tyler said. "You'd hate my job, and you know it. There's just not enough glamour and excitement for you in the day-to-day operation of a ranch."

"Gawd, ain't that the truth?" Cal sighed, leaning back and extending his legs. "I don't know what's ever gonna be interesting enough to keep me happy. I sure as hell haven't found it yet."

"You will," Tyler said. "It comes to all of us, sooner or later."

"It's come to you, hasn't it, Ty?" Cal said, looking steadily at his brother, his handsome face serious for once. "You love her, don't you?"

"Yeah," Tyler said with a brief shining smile. "I love her. You know, Cal, I just can't believe how—"

"Hello, boys. Mind if a weary old lady joins you for a minute?"

The brothers looked up and greeted Virginia, who stood nearby looking wan and tired.

"Virginia, darlin', you just sit yourself right down here," Cal said, rising gallantly to hold out a chair for their housekeeper and passing her one of the brimming tankards of beer that had just been delivered to their table.

"Well, how's it going, Virginia?" Tyler asked. "Did you win the big draw? Are you heading off for your date with George Strait?"

Virginia sighed and gave them a rueful smile. "I'm sure not. But you know who is?"

Tyler and Cal shook their heads. "Ty was talking, as usual," Cal said. "We never did get to hear the winner's name."

"It's my niece, Jennifer," Virginia told them. "And you know what?" she added with another bleak little smile. "I was the one who gave her the money for the ticket. Doesn't that just kill you?"

"No kidding." Cal leaned back in his chair and gazed at the older woman. "And she's still hogging the whole thing? She won't do the decent thing and give you the trip?''

"Oh, goodness, no," Virginia said calmly. "Jennifer's always been quite a selfish girl," she added impartially.

"Isn't she the one who wanted to be a ballerina?" Tyler asked.

Virginia nodded. "She did. But then when she grew up, she developed a thirty-eight-inch bust. They just couldn't fit her into a tutu anymore."

Cal looked interested. "You know, I should call Jennifer someday," he commented thoughtfully.

Virginia slapped his arm. "Don't you dare, you wild gypsy man. Besides, she's convinced now that she's going to catch herself a star."

"I'm a star," Cal said, looking injured. "I've been a star for years."

"You're a fading star," Tyler said with a brotherly grin. "These young girls, Cal, they're all looking for someone whose star is on the rise."

"Well, if I'm fading," Cal said equably, "then *you're* just about burnt out, cowboy. Which reminds me, where's poor Ruth?"

"She was in the washroom a few minutes ago," Virginia reported. "I spent some time in there crying on her shoulder."

"Yeah? Why?" Cal asked, grinning at a pair of young women who swayed past the table and tossed their hair pointedly, smiling back at him with warm inviting looks.

"Oh, nothing much." Virginia toyed listlessly with the handle of her beer mug while the McKinney brothers gazed at her bent head in concern.

"Who's that guy you were with tonight, Virginia?" Tyler asked after a long awkward silence. "Do we know him?"

Virginia shook her head. "He's just a casual acquaintance. Why?" she added in sudden alarm. "What's he doing now?"

Cal peered across the smoke-filled room. "He's got the panty hose on his head again. And it looks like he's dancing."

"Oh, God," Virginia muttered, and buried her face in her hands.

"What's with the panty hose?" Tyler asked his brother, curiosity momentarily overcoming his concern for Virginia.

"They're bunny ears," Cal said with a delighted grin. "He's being a little bunny rabbit."

Tyler gazed across the room, fascinated. The big red-faced man stumbled around in a small clearing at the edge of the dance floor, nylon-stocking legs flopping onto his shoulders while he was cheered on by a rowdy crew of onlookers.

"Who told you that?" he asked, turning back to Cal and trying to hide his laughter. "About the bunny, I mean?"

"Ruth did. Apparently she caught part of his act earlier tonight."

"I want to go home," Virginia said faintly. "Right this minute."

Tyler's handsome face creased with alarm. "Right away? You came with Daddy and Cynthia, didn't you? Virginia, I don't know if they're ready to—"

"Well, I am," Cal announced, levering himself stiffly from the chair. "That's enough dancing for this cowboy. Come on, Virginia, I'll take you home."

Virginia smiled at the tall young man with gratitude and relief, taking his arm and hurrying along beside him to the crowded exit doors.

Tyler watched them go, then glanced at his watch and got up to wander anxiously out into the vestibule again. His nervousness increased as he stood gazing at the closed washroom door with its jaunty grinning heifer painted on the front. Tyler hesitated, feeling awkward and worried, and smiled with relief when Beverly and Lynn emerged.

The two young women were laughing, their heads close together. They looked up at Tyler with bright teasing smiles.

"Hi, Tyler," Lynn said casually, punching her brother in the arm. "How come you're hanging around outside the heifer pen?"

"I'm looking for Ruth. Is she in there?"

Beverly and Lynn exchanged a questioning glance, then shook their heads. "We didn't see her," Beverly said.

Tyler frowned, feeling another cold stirring of uneasiness. "She's not in the bar, either. I just came from there."

"Maybe she stepped outside for a bit of fresh air," Lynn suggested. "I think all that smoke was starting to get to her."

"But it's strange that she didn't—" Tyler fell abruptly silent, then smiled easily at his sister and his cousin. "It's nothing, girls," he said, waving them away. "Just thinking out loud. You two have fun, and try to be good for a change, okay?"

He waited while the two young women vanished in a blur of color and music. When they were gone he strolled outside, breathing deeply of the starry frosted night.

Tyler looked up and down the crowded street, where pale moonlight washed over the pavement and poured deep pools of darkness into the alleys. A few feet down, a bench was set back beneath the overhanging branches of a tree, and a pale figure sat huddled alone in the darkness.

Tyler edged closer and recognized Ruth, wrapped in her woolen jacket, sitting absolutely still and gazing fixedly at the opposite street.

"Ruth?" he ventured, his heart beating crazily with an unnamed dread. "Ruthie, what's the matter, sweetheart? Aren't you feeling well?"

He sat and took her cold hands in both his own, but she shuddered and snatched them away with a little choking sob.

"Ruth! What is it?" Tyler put his arm around her slender shoulders and bent to peer into her face.

"Don't touch me, Tyler," she said in a level, expressionless tone. "Please don't touch me."

Tyler stared at her in stunned amazement, but her face was withdrawn and cold. He shook his head helplessly and removed his arm from her shoulders. "I don't understand, Ruth. I just don't understand what you're so upset about."

"Oh, I think you do," she said quietly. "I'm sure you do, Tyler."

"How could I understand? Ten minutes ago, last time I saw you, we were dancing and I asked you to marry me. You didn't seem upset then, Ruth. In fact, I got the definite impression that you were going away to think about it. Now you're sitting here in the dark and acting like you hate me."

She shrugged and turned her head away, so taut and rigid with misery that Tyler was afraid she would break apart if he touched her again.

"Ruth," he said in anguish, "you have to tell me! You can't just sit there and not tell me!"

"Oh, Tyler." Ruth shook her head wearily. "What is there to tell?"

"You can tell me why you're so upset. You can answer the question I asked you before. For God's sake, Ruth, say something."

"Answer what question?"

"Will you marry me, Ruth?"

"I wouldn't marry you," she said with a bitter edge to her voice, "if you were the last man on earth."

"Ruth, what is it?" Fear coiled within him, turning slowly to anger. "Look, I don't know what you think you're doing, but this is no joke, Ruth. It's not a bit funny. Why don't you just—"

"No, Tyler, it's not a bit funny!" Ruth turned to face him, her eyes wide and black in the moonlight, her face a pale blur of agony. "It's not funny at all. It's just terrible."

Tyler leaned back against the hard plank bench, staring at her.

"I talked to somebody in the washroom just a few minutes ago, Tyler. I learned about something so awful that I..."

Ruth's voice broke and she fell silent, staring down at the slim cold hands twisted together in her lap.

"Who did you talk to?" Tyler's mind raced, trying to imagine who had spoken to her, what she could have said, what on earth could possibly have happened to distress Ruth so much.

"Jodie," Ruth said tonelessly. "I talked to Jodie Hiltz."

"Jodie *Hiltz?*" Tyler gaped down at her in openmouthed astonishment.

"That's right, Tyler. Jodie Hiltz. And she told me all about you, and her, and the baby."

"Baby!" he echoed blankly, his mind reeling.

"Yes, the baby. Oh, Tyler," Ruth moaned, hugging herself and rocking in agony on the bench. "How could you? How could you do such a thing? She's just a *child,* Tyler. She's probably still a teenager.''

"She probably is," he said, struggling to recover his composure. "So what?"

"So *what?*" Ruth stared at him, aghast. "How can you sit there and say such a thing?"

"Ruth," Tyler began patiently, "I have no idea what you're talking about. I don't know what that girl could possibly have told you that would upset you so much. What did she tell you, Ruth?"

Ruth drew a deep breath and gazed up at him, her eyes cold and still. "She told me you're the father of her baby."

THE LONGHORN COFFEE SHOP rocked with laughter and merriment. Couples and groups from the party kept drifting in and out, joking with Dottie and Nora, ordering soft drinks and huge platters of greasy fries while they danced to the rowdy tunes that blasted from the jukebox.

Clearly the whole town was in a festive mood tonight. Long after the doors were locked and the carpets rolled up at Zack's, the celebration would continue, motivated by high spirits and warmhearted generosity. The local merchants, entering into the mood of the occasion, had agreed to stay open late and donate ten percent of all money taken in during the evening to the Walden family.

Ruth sat across the table from Tyler, still unable to look into his face. She was so battered by misery that her body felt physically sore, as if she'd been the victim of some kind of terrible accident.

And, of course, she had.

Like so many women, she'd fallen in love with the wrong man and her trust had been betrayed. Just the same old story, Ruth thought, but there was still nothing more painful, more agonizing and brutally damaging to a woman's soul.

With all her heart Ruth longed for home, for her father and the winery and the rugged sheltering cliffs around their house. Stunned with unhappiness, she watched as a young cowboy swung his girl in the little space near the jukebox.

"Ruth, I don't know where all this is coming from," Tyler was saying, his handsome face tight and pale with emotion. "I truly don't. Did Cal tell you something about—"

"Cal?" Ruth raised her face and gazed directly at him. "What's Cal got to do with anything?"

Suddenly she remembered dancing with Cal earlier in the evening, recalled the strange cautious way he'd pointed out Jodie Hiltz and seemed on the verge of saying something.

"Oh, God," Ruth said slowly. "Cal knows, too, doesn't he? He was going to tell me earlier and then changed his mind. Who else knows, Tyler? Is everybody in the family laughing at me?"

Tyler stared at her across the table. "Ruth, I don't—"

"You know what I hate about it?" Ruth said, forcing her tone to sound casual and conversational. "I was just thinking about this, Tyler. I hate the whole attitude it represents. In fact, I think that's what bothers me the most."

"What attitude?"

"This arrogant, Texas feudal-male complex. It's so disgusting."

"I don't know what you're talking about," Tyler repeated, grim and tight-lipped, clearly struggling to maintain control of his emotions.

"Of course you don't. You never think about it, do you? It's just accepted that the big landowners like you are masters of all you survey. A little girl like that, she's no more than part of the scenery, is she, Tyler? The feudal lord can pleasure himself with the local maidens and then just toss them aside anytime he likes. It goes with the territory."

"For God's sake, Ruth!"

She shook her head, hating the venomous spirit that had seized control of her, the cold furious voice that didn't sound like hers, the haze of hurt and anger that clouded her eyes and obscured everything.

"The reason I mentioned Cal," Tyler said in a level, measured tone, "was because he told me something about that girl a while ago. The day I brought your cat home, as a matter of fact. He said he'd seen her up in that little cabin where the vineyard's going to be."

Ruth looked up sharply. "Oh, I see. Is that where you go to meet with her, Tyler?" she murmured bitterly. "After all, you'd want to find someplace that's far away from prying eyes for all your little trysts, wouldn't you?"

She was silent a moment, and then her face turned even paler with shock.

"My God," she breathed, looking up at him in horror. "That cabin...that was where you kissed me the very first time! Tyler, I can't believe...I just can't believe..."

Her voice broke suddenly and she looked down at the checked tablecloth, forcing a ghastly little smile when Dottie came around with the coffeepot to fill their mugs.

"Look, Ruth," Tyler began, his voice cold and level. "I told you before, I don't know where all this crap is coming from. I'm sick and tired of people telling me about Jodie Hiltz. I never touched the girl. I'd hardly know her if I saw her on the street. And I'm sure as hell not the father of her baby!"

Ruth glanced up at him, aching to believe him, longing for the evening to stop spinning so crazily and set itself right again. She wanted more than anything in the world to go back to that shining moment when he'd asked her to marry him, and her heart had started dancing in response, and she'd slipped into the washroom to be alone with her happiness and her fear.

His face shimmered and faded before her eyes, replaced by Jodie's pale features and transparent dreamy eyes. "He's so handsome without his clothes...he has a birthmark on his left hip shaped just like a map of Texas...."

Ruth moaned softly and dropped her face into her hands, buffeted by waves of searing agony that threatened to consume her.

She remembered the rich pleasure of the hours just last night when Tyler had come silently through the darkness and into the guest house, into her bed, and they'd made love and laughed and teased by firelight until after the moon was gone.

"Show me Amarillo," he'd whispered. "Good girl. You're learning your Texas geography real good, aren't you, little Ruth? Now Houston...let's see if you can find Houston. Now all the way over to El Paso... Oh, God, Ruthie, that feels so good...."

Remembering the silly playful intimacy, the warmth and childlike sweetness of it, made Ruth shudder with a hot jealous anguish that she'd never known before in all her life.

Because he'd obviously played the same game with another woman. Not even a woman, but a child so young that she was an innocent victim of his power and position. And now that girl was pregnant, and clearly expected her seducer to take care of her and the child she carried.

"Ruth!" Tyler said in a low forceful tone.

"What?" she asked wearily. "What do you want, Tyler?"

"I want you to answer my question. Why do you believe this... this little girl instead of me? You don't even know her. Why do you automatically assume that she's telling the truth and I'm lying? She's just some vicious little teenager, Ruth, playing some kind of crazy game. Why are you allowing this to happen?''

Ruth looked into his dark burning eyes. She couldn't tell him the damning things Jodie had said about him, simply because speaking those words aloud would tear her apart altogether and cause her to lose the last fragile semblance of control.

''I know she's telling the truth, Tyler,'' Ruth said tonelessly. ''Don't press me for details because they won't be pleasant for either of us. I'd like you to take me home now, please. I have to start packing if I'm going to catch a plane tomorrow.''

She gripped the edge of the table and started to rise, then sank back onto the vinyl chair, her eyes widening in alarm.

Jodie Hiltz had just entered the coffee shop, alone as usual, and was looking around with a calm inquiring gaze. When she caught sight of Ruth and Tyler near the back she hesitated, then approached them, walking with studied negligence in her cheap high heels and shabby fur jacket.

''Hi, Tyler,'' she said with a bold meaningful smile, looking directly at the dark-haired man as she passed his chair. She pulled her jacket aside with slow deliberation to display her protruding silk-covered abdomen and paused significantly by their table, smiling her sly dreamy smile while the two gazed up at her in shocked silence.

"Well, so long. See you later," Jodie said finally, licking her lips and giving Tyler a seductive little glance before she moved on.

He reached out and caught her arm, holding her in a fierce grip. "Look, kid, just what the hell do you think you're doing?" he asked, leaning forward to speak in low furious tones. Jodie's pale eyes widened in shock. She glanced around at the others who crowded the restaurant, oblivious to the tense little drama being played out at the back.

"Never mind them," Tyler said through gritted teeth. "Just answer my question."

"You're hurting me," Jodie said in a tone of child-like surprise.

"Tyler, stop it!" Ruth whispered urgently. "Please don't do this."

Tyler loosened his grip slightly but continued to hold the girl near their table, fixing her with his penetrating dark gaze. "Answer my question," he repeated in a cold voice. "Right now, or you'll be sorry."

"Tyler, honey," Jodie protested.

"Don't call me that!" he snapped. "I don't even *know* you, dammit! Why are you telling all these ridiculous lies?"

"Lies?" Jodie gazed full at him, her eyes clear and steady. "They're not lies, Tyler. I told Ruth about our baby because I thought she had a right to know, that's all."

"Our baby!" he exploded, then glanced around cautiously at the noisy group by the door and dropped his voice. "Look, you little...look, Jodie or whatever your name is, I don't know why you're doing this. I don't know what's in it for you, or what the hell you hope to accomplish. But I want you to apologize to Miss Holden right now and tell her you're lying, or I'll break your goddamn little neck."

"Tyler!" Ruth said, stunned by his angry harshness.

"Be quiet, Ruth," Tyler said, keeping his eyes fixed on Jodie's transparent frightened eyes. "Tell her, Jodie."

"Tell her what?" Jodie asked sullenly.

"Tell her you're lying. Tell her I've never touched you in my life, and I'm not the father of your goddamn baby!"

Tears began to stream silently down Jodie's pale cheeks. "How could you say that?" she whispered, staring into Tyler's dark angry face. "After all our times together, and all the promises you made to me? How could you say such a terrible thing about your very own baby, just because *she's* sitting here, and you want her to..."

Jodie waved her hand in Ruth's direction and began to cry in earnest, wrenching her arm away from Tyler and stumbling toward a table near the windows.

Ruth looked around in concern at the girl's huddled body, then turned back to Tyler, her face grim.

"You make me sick," she said coldly. "That was just unforgivable, Tyler."

Tyler stared back at her, breathing hard, his face flushed with helpless fury. For a long moment their glances locked. Then he got up silently to follow Ruth as she grabbed her handbag and marched out of the crowded restaurant.

CHAPTER ELEVEN

THE COLD WEATHER vanished as abruptly as it had arrived, carried off by balmy breezes from the west that blew the heavy dark clouds away and sprinkled drifts of sunshine across the rolling hills. The earth warmed and stirred with a shy promise of early spring, and the skies were calm and blue and endless.

In the guest house, Ruth was packing clothes into suitcases. Every now and then she glanced through the window, frowning at the idyllic scene. Even the weather appeared to be conspiring against her. On the eve of her departure, Texas seemed to be going out of its way to be sweet and enticing, to make her regret the richness she was leaving behind.

"I don't care," Ruth said to Hagar, who lay on the bed watching in lazy green-eyed silence. "I hate it here. I can't wait to get home, can you, sweetie?"

But she knew the words weren't really true. Homesick as she still felt at times, Ruth wasn't at all anxious to go home, back into a world that was beginning to seem so far removed. She didn't relish the thought of making a threesome with her father and his new girlfriend, or returning to the grim regime that Mrs. Ward imposed on her household.

Hagar yawned glumly as if echoing these thoughts and rested his furry chin on his front paws.

"Well, I don't care what you think," Ruth told him. "I certainly can't stay here any longer. Not after all the..."

Her delicate face crumpled in agony and she returned to her task, slamming clothes into suitcases with fierce determination.

"Hagar, what did I do with that little book of poems and quotations? I was sure it was on the...oh, yes," Ruth said after a moment's thought. "I loaned it to Virginia last week. I'd better go get it while I'm thinking about it."

She moved toward the door and Hagar leaped lightly from the bed to follow her. He rubbed briefly against her legs, then headed off toward the big house, his bushy orange tail stiffly erect, his tread light and alert as he padded in front of her.

Ruth smiled when they climbed the verandah. Cynthia's cat, Tiffany, lay contentedly nearby, blinking in the sunlight but Hagar ignored her and headed straight for Hank's rocker. Hagar sat calmly and raised his head in benign kingly fashion while the gnarled hands caressed him, then he settled in a huge rusty ball at the old man's feet.

"He really loves you, Hank," Ruth said.

"Why not? He's a smart cat," Hank said serenely. He looked up at Ruth, shading his ancient eyes against the dazzle of the sun. "Set down an' talk to me a bit, girl."

Ruth hesitated. "I'm sorry, Hank. I really have to—"

"Set," Hank repeated with a touch of iron in his voice.

Ruth obeyed and sank into one of the padded wicker chairs next to him.

After capturing her, Hank seemed disinclined to continue the conversation. He rocked and gazed into the distance, his chin on his chest, silvery head nodding in the straw cowboy hat. But when Ruth braced her hands on the chair arms and made a quiet move to rise, he looked over at her sharply.

"I hear you're leavin'," he said.

"Yes," Ruth said, uncomfortable under that ancient dark gaze. "I'm going the day after tomorrow. That was the first flight I could get Hagar on, and I didn't want him traveling alone anymore."

"I don't s'pose he could stay behind," Hank suggested wistfully, poking the fluffy lump gently with the toe of his riding boot. "I'm partial to this cat. He's a real good cat."

"No, Hank," Ruth said with a sad little smile. "I'm afraid he can't."

They sat together in reflective silence, Hank rocking placidly and Ruth gazing at the distant hills, as the pale afternoon sun washed over them.

"What was it made you so unhappy?" the old man asked, startling Ruth with the suddenness of the question. "Was it that woman?"

"What woman?" she asked, looking blankly into his seamed, leathery face.

"That crazy woman from town. I see her slippin' around when she thinks I'm not watchin', but none of 'em will ever believe me."

Ruth was silent. Was Hank talking about Jodie Hiltz? Where had he "seen her slippin' around"? On one of her secret nighttime visits to Tyler?

Ruth shuddered and gazed ahead blindly while the landscape trembled and blurred before her eyes.

"They both caused you a lot of pain," the old man spoke again.

"Yes. They both did," Ruth said automatically, fighting off the mental image of Tyler lying with that ripely curving young body.

"No, I mean them women. The young one and the old one."

Ruth gazed at him curiously, feeling a cold shiver of uneasiness as she remembered the McKinney family stories about the old man's uncanny ability to perceive things that were hidden from others.

"What do you mean?" she'd asked Tyler back in those far-off happy days when they were still warm and open with each other. "Does he have something like second sight? Clairvoyance?"

"Not really." Tyler had shaken his head, frowning thoughtfully. "More like a special kind of understanding. It's like Grandpa's so old that all the barriers have melted away, the things that keep the rest of us from seeing clearly. He knows stuff that's just amazing, and nobody knows how he does it.''

The memory of Tyler's voice faded. Ruth shook herself a little and glanced over at Hank's hawklike profile.

"Two women?" she echoed. "What women are you talking about, Hank?"

"The young one an' the old one," he repeated drowsily. "You got all caught up in their damn problems, an' it was just too much for you."

The young one and the old one. Jodie and... Virginia?

Ruth thought about Jodie Hiltz with her lush pregnancy and her childlike trust in Tyler to look after her.

There wasn't much she could do for Jodie, except pressure Tyler into taking care of his responsibilities, and that was going to be difficult since he and Ruth were barely speaking to each other anymore.

But, Ruth decided, there might still be something she could do for poor Virginia before she flew back to California. She could talk to J.T., tell him about Virginia's plight and ask if...

Her bleak thoughts were interrupted by the appearance of J.T. himself, strolling around the corner of the house with Tyler and Ken Slattery. All three men were deep in conversation, and the afternoon breeze carried drifting scraps of what they were saying. Apparently they were concerned over a shipment of feed that had arrived in poor condition.

Ruth waited, dry-mouthed and trembling, but Ken and Tyler mounted the veranda steps with no more than polite nods to the woman and the old man sitting there, and vanished inside the house. Despite her best efforts, Ruth couldn't help turning to gaze after Tyler, her throat constricting at the sight of that familiar lean body, those long denim-clad legs and the broad shoulders beneath the faded work shirt.

Oh, God, she thought, shivering. *I want to leave this place! I want to leave right now.*

"Afternoon, Ruth. Hi, Grandpa," J.T. said, pausing beside Hank's rocker and smiling down at both of them. "Nice day, isn't it? Feels a lot like spring."

Ruth smiled automatically, looking up at his handsome weathered face and kindly eyes. She squinted against the sun, thinking with a fresh burst of pain that Tyler would look exactly like this in twenty years or so. For some reason the picture of Tyler at fifty made her feel even more melancholy. She found herself fighting another treacherous flood of tears.

For many years Ruth had maintained a harsh opinion of J.T. McKinney, a wholly unreasonable dislike based simply on the fact that his bold Western masculinity seemed to eclipse her father's quieter personality. But during her stay at the ranch she'd come to like and respect J.T. He was a good man, she thought, strong and responsible, loving with his family and fair to everyone in his employ.

She wondered what he'd think if he knew about Tyler's careless brutal treatment of that poor little girl.

Ruth swallowed hard and sat straighter in her chair. "J.T.," she began, struggling to keep her voice even, "could I...could I talk to you for a minute?"

"CARE FOR A SHERRY or something, Ruth?"

J.T. McKinney moved over to the small sideboard behind his desk and mixed himself a very weak whisky and soda.

"I don't think so," she said, trying to smile. "It's still a little early in the day for me."

"Even for wine?" he asked with a teasing grin.

She smiled back at him. "It's never too early for wine."

"Well, I'm afraid I don't have any of the good stuff out here. Would you like—"

"No, no," she said hastily. "I'm fine, J.T. I just wanted to talk to you about something. I won't keep you long."

The rancher leaned back in his chair and looked at her thoughtfully. In the weeks that Ruth Holden had been visiting the Double C, he'd grown very fond of this quiet young woman.

J.T. remembered his friend's daughter as a withdrawn awkward child, then a delicately pretty but shy adolescent. She'd blossomed into a poised and lovely woman, and he wasn't the only one who'd noticed her appeal.

Poor Tyler, J.T. thought with wrenching pain, looking into the wide brown eyes of the woman opposite. *She's turned him down, and I truly don't know how he's going to live with that.*

J.T. knew his elder son well, and loved him deeply in his own quiet and undemonstrative fashion. He'd always known that Tyler was a man like himself, with a lifetime of deep intense love to give to the right woman. But lately J.T. had begun to wonder if Tyler would ever find that woman, especially since his son was so absorbed in his wine-making project and the affairs of the ranch that he had little time to attend social functions and meet new people.

And then, miraculously, the woman of Tyler's dreams had literally dropped from the skies, landed on the Austin airstrip one bright January afternoon and filled his world with happiness.

J.T. had noted and approved the change in his eldest child, the spring in Tyler's step, the glow in his eyes, the new gentle tone and depths of tenderness in his voice.

The love of a good woman was essential to bring out the very best in a man. Nobody knew that better than J.T. McKinney.

J.T. had even allowed himself to daydream a little, delighted privately at the thought of himself and Don being linked through their children. He'd imagined Tyler and Ruth founding a successful business, having a happy marriage and a few grandbabies for the ranch, maybe building a new house somewhere on Double C property and adding to the rich fabric of family life.

His optimism had soared to new heights when Ruth and Tyler returned from their research expedition to Lubbock with stars in their eyes, and seemed incapable of keeping their hands off each other.

"Easy to see," the grinning J.T. told his wife in the privacy of their bedroom, "that those two were tasting something more than wine on *that* little trip."

Tyler and Ruth seemed to have everything going for them, and J.T. had been moved almost to tears by his happiness for his son.

And then, with dreadful suddenness, it had all gone sour.

J.T. had no idea what had caused the obvious painful rift between Ruth and Tyler, and his tactful questions had elicited no information from his son. Tyler went about his day's work in grim silence, his face cold and withdrawn, his misery so evident that J.T. ached with helpless sympathy.

Remembering Tyler's dark unhappy face, J.T. sipped his drink and rubbed automatically at his left arm, trying to soothe the numb ache of rheumatism that seemed to be throbbing harder every day.

Ruth looked at him in concern. "Did you hurt your arm, J.T.?"

He waved his hand dismissively. "Just an old man's aches and pains. When you're fifty-five, Ruth, you start paying for all those crazy things you did at twenty."

She smiled and looked down at her hands, apparently searching for words.

J.T. waited, his eyes watchful, hoping she might be going to confide in him about whatever had happened between her and Tyler. It was hard because if they didn't confide in him he couldn't do anything to help. Respect for their privacy kept him from prying, and as a result he felt powerless and ineffectual.

Cal might know something about the mysterious problems in his brother's romance, but Cal was already gone, swallowed up once more in the bright dangerous whirl of his rodeo life. J.T. frowned again, stabbed by a fresh surge of worry about the welfare of his beloved second son, the happy-go-lucky boy who had been such a cheery ray of sunshine ever since his birth.

He rubbed at his sore arm again and listened to Ruth's halting voice as she began to speak.

"It's... J.T., it's Virginia," Ruth began, startling him. Of all the topics she might have broached, this was probably the last thing he expected.

"Virginia? What about her, Ruth?"

"J.T., she's so unhappy and frightened. I promised I wouldn't say anything to you." Ruth glanced up at him with a look of childlike appeal on her gentle face.

"I have a real bad memory, Ruth," J.T. said quietly. "Just terrible. Anything you tell me, I'm likely going to forget right away where it came from."

Ruth gave him a small grateful smile. "I hope so. I know she trusts me, and I hate to betray her but I just can't go away without trying to do something about her situation."

"What situation is that, Ruth?"

Awkwardly at first but gaining confidence as she spoke, Ruth told the rancher all about Virginia's financial troubles including the housekeeper's rash speculation in mining stock that had ended so disastrously.

J.T. sat straighter in his chair, his dark eyes kindling. "You're not telling me she invested in that damned mine!"

"Just about everything she had left in her savings account, J.T. Thousands of dollars."

"Oh, my God." J.T. shook his head angrily, settling back in his chair with a grim look. "That man should be shot," he said levelly. "Taking advantage of a woman like that, his own sister, for God's sake, just to get a few dollars in commissions."

"She doesn't blame him, J.T. She says she was just greedy and foolish, wanting to make her money all back in one investment."

"I warned her not to touch that damned stock. It didn't smell right to me."

"She told me that, too."

J.T. was silent for a moment, toying with a small bronze sculpture on his desk of a mare standing over a sleeping foal. "This problem of hers," he asked, looking up suddenly and fixing Ruth with those brilliant dark eyes, "does it have anything to do with these men she's been going out with lately?"

Ruth's cheeks turned pink. "I thought you didn't know about them. At least, not anybody except the man at the dance, with the—"

"Panty hose on his head," J.T. finished, grinning briefly. "Oh, I knew about them, Ruth. This is a real small town. It's hard to do much of anything around here without getting caught."

The woman's delicate face registered a brief flash of emotion at these words. J.T. looked at her curiously. Did that expression of distress and anger have something to do with Tyler?

"Actually, those men were connected to this problem," Ruth said in a low voice, collecting herself and carrying on with the conversation. She told him about Virginia's scheme to find a husband so she could be sure of a home in her declining years.

"Oh, hell," J.T. muttered softly, leaning back in his chair and gazing out the window.

Ruth waited, her face drawn and pale with concern.

"I'd always look after her, you know, Ruth," J.T. said finally. "I'd never see her alone or homeless. She was at the Circle T with Pauline before we were married, and she came over here with my wife thirty-five years ago. How could she think I'd abandon her?"

"She doesn't want to be looked after, J.T.," Ruth said firmly. "She wants to pay her own way, but she's got no money to do it, and no real prospects of any. Not at her age."

"But she wouldn't accept handouts from me." It was a statement, not a question.

Ruth nodded agreement. "No, I'm sure she wouldn't."

"Does she want to leave her job right away, Ruth? Is it getting to be too much for her?"

"I don't think so. I think she's content to stay as long as she can give you value for the money you pay her, but she recognizes that it probably won't be that much longer, especially with all the . . . all the changes in the household," Ruth concluded lamely, flushing with embarrassment.

J.T. shot her a keen glance, knowing what both of them were thinking. Up until very recently, a union between Ruth Holden and Tyler McKinney had been considered by everyone as the next likely change in this household.

But he said nothing, just nodded thoughtfully. "So she wants some security for the future, that's all? She wants to know what's going to happen to her?"

Ruth looked up at him, her brown eyes clear and steady. "Yes, J.T., I think that's what she wants. And I know she wouldn't want you to discuss it with anybody else," Ruth added carefully. "She'd hate for Cynthia or Lettie Mae or anyone else to know about her financial state."

"I guess she would." J.T. was silent a moment, running his hand wearily across his forehead. "Well, I'll just have to see what I can do. Thanks for letting me know, Ruth. It was real kind of you."

Ruth gave him a sympathetic smile. "I'm sorry to burden you with this," she said softly. "I know you've got a million other problems on your mind, J.T. I don't even know what you can do to help, but I'm worried about Virginia. She's so miserable."

J.T. smiled back automatically, studying the quiet young woman across his desk. She really was a sweet girl, he thought with growing unhappiness. No wonder Tyler was dying inside at the prospect of losing her. He picked up the little sculpture again and squinted at it, keeping his eyes carefully lowered.

"Anything else, Ruth?" he asked gently.

"I beg your pardon?"

"Anything else you wanted to talk to me about? I'm always here, you know, and I've got big ears and real broad shoulders. If there's ever anything you need to tell me I'll be glad to listen, and I'll sure help if I can."

Tears glistened suddenly in Ruth's beautiful eyes. She pushed her chair back, getting to her feet and moving blindly toward the door.

"There's nothing, J.T.," she murmured in a choked voice. "Nothing that anybody can help me with, anyway. But thank you for..."

Her voice broke and she stumbled through the door and down the hallway while J.T. sat gazing after her in troubled silence.

THE DAY AFTER her talk with J.T., Ruth sat cross-legged in the middle of her bed, sifting aimlessly through piles of books and literature on the wine-making industry. Some she'd brought with her, and the rest had been accumulated during her stay at the ranch, on the visits to the Lubbock wineries and to the grape-growers' association in Austin.

Decisions had to be made about these materials, what should be thrown away and what Tyler could use for his project, what passages were important and should be marked specifically....

Ruth sighed and ran a distracted hand through her hair. This winding-up process was so awkward and difficult, especially since she and Tyler weren't talking anymore except for the bare minimum required to maintain a civil atmosphere at family meals. Still, because of her new respect for J.T. and her growing love of the whole family, Ruth felt a powerful sense of responsibility for the winery project. She wanted to help as much she could before leaving, point out the pitfalls and offer practical money-saving suggestions about equipment and planting methods.

But she shrank from contact with Tyler, finding it unbearably painful even to be in the same room with him. It would be impossible to deal with the business aspects of their relationship in a calm rational manner.

Ruth looked around with an automatic questioning glance, wanting the comfort of Hagar, then remembered that the big cat had been allowed to spend this final evening over in Hank's house because the old man was so saddened by Hagar's imminent departure.

Ruth got up and wandered to the window, drawing the curtain back and looking out at the shimmering starlit night. Her face was bleak, her mind almost numb with sorrow.

This was the last night she'd ever gaze in breathless enchantment at the vast Texas sky, or listen to the peaceful whispering sounds of the ranch animals settling for the night, or the sweetly melancholy notes of the owl in the trees over near the river.

Never again would she see the comforting lighted bulk of the ranch house across the yard, silhouetted like a big ship against a silver-black sea, and watch the shadows of its vigorous laughing occupants moving against the drawn curtains.

And she'd never again have the wondrous heart-stopping feeling that Tyler could appear at any moment, striding around the corner of a building or running lightly up the slope from the barns, his dark head shining in the moonlight, his handsome tanned face and tall body filling her whole world with laughter and yearning.

Ruth turned away miserably, letting the curtain drop from her fingers. Suddenly she stiffened and leaned forward again to peer through a gap in the shrouds of fabric.

Tyler was approaching the guest house. He walked along the darkened path with a purposeful grim look that made Ruth shiver in apprehension. She bit her lip and glanced around nervously, wishing there was some way to fade out of sight and disappear so she could avoid the painful scene that was certain to follow.

But there was only one door to the guest house, and he was almost on the threshold. There was no escape. Ruth took a deep breath and stood facing the closed door, waiting for his knock.

"Come in," she called in a low trembling voice.

Tyler stepped inside, closed the door carefully behind him and stood gazing at her in the soft light. Though the evening was mild, Ruth had built a fire earlier in the evening just for the comfort of it, and the bright leaping flames cast their long shadows onto the walls and glimmered faintly on Tyler's face.

For a long tense moment they stood staring at each other, eyes locked together while the air hummed and throbbed with emotion. Tyler was the first to turn away, moving over to lean an elbow on the mantel, looking down at the litter of books and clothes.

"Packing already?" he asked, trying to sound casual.

Ruth nodded. "I'll need to be in Austin by late tomorrow afternoon to catch my flight, and there are a couple of things I want to do in town first, so I thought I'd better get most of the packing done tonight if I can."

"I see," he said, watching her face intently as she spoke.

Ruth shifted uncomfortably under his silent penetrating gaze and waved her hand at the piled books and papers. "Tyler, there's a lot of stuff here that could be useful to you," she said. "Do you want to go through it with me, or should I just leave it and let you sift through it on your own, or what?"

"Just leave it," he said quietly. "I'll look after it. I wouldn't want to take up any of your time with concerns over my winery, Ruth."

She flushed and raised her head sharply. "That's not fair, Tyler. I've already put a lot of time and effort into your plans, and whether you believe it or not, I really care about the winery. I want it to be a success for your family's sake as well as yours."

"Sure you care," he said bitterly. "That's why you're leaving, right? You're going away at the most crucial stage in planning and development, leaving us all on our own, just because you care so much."

Ruth stared at him, appalled by his words. "How can you say that?" she whispered. "You know perfectly well why I'm leaving, Tyler. It's impossible for me to stay here. Don't you think I'd love to stay and watch the whole business get started? I just can't."

"Why not, Ruth?"

"Oh, for God's sake." Ruth drew a deep shuddering breath and fought to keep her anger under control. "Stop all this nonsense, Tyler, okay? You know why I can't stay. You pretended to love me," she went on in a shaking voice. "You even *proposed* to me, and all the time you were . . ."

"Pretended!" he broke in, outraged by her words. "You think I was pretending, Ruth? You really think I'm that good an actor?"

"I don't know what you are," Ruth said wearily. "I honestly don't. I trusted you, Tyler. I even...even fooled myself into thinking I was in love with you," she added, then went on hastily when she saw his eyes flare with sudden emotion. "But I was kidding myself. How could I love a man who's...who's a liar and a cheat, and so brutal and uncaring that he..."

Ruth fell silent, overcome by her feelings, holding back the bitter tears that burned in her throat and behind her eyes.

Tyler crossed the room in two long strides and gripped her arms, holding her so tightly that she winced and almost cried out with pain. "Look at me, Ruth," he said in a cold voice.

Ruth obeyed, fighting with all her strength to keep her face calm as she looked up and met his dark burning eyes.

"Now, tell me the truth for once," he said. "Tell me why you're doing this. Tell me why you choose to believe that ridiculous child instead of me."

Ruth's courage failed and her eyes wavered. She began to struggle helplessly in his iron grip. "Let me *go*, damn you," she muttered through clenched teeth.

"Not just yet, Ruth. Not till you've answered my question."

"What question?"

"Why do you believe her instead of me?" Tyler repeated. "Ruth, I swear to you that I've never touched that girl. I didn't even remember who she was until you pointed her out to me that day. That's the whole truth, as God is my witness. Why don't you believe me?''

Ruth grew still and tense, so stunned by his words that she forgot to struggle. She stared up at him in horror. "How can you keep on doing this?" she whispered. "How can you just stand there and lie like this?''

"I'm not lying, dammit!"

"Tyler," Ruth said in anguish, "can't you see that I'd like you better if you confessed it? If you told me what happened and why, then we could do something about it, take some responsibility for the poor girl and try to right the terrible wrong you've done to her. Maybe in that case I could even learn to forgive you and we could try to salvage some of what we had. But this ridiculous lying... Tyler, it's just so awful. It makes me despise you.''

"It makes you despise me," he repeated, his voice flat and cold. He released his grip on her arms and stood facing her. "So you despise me, do you, Ruth? Well then, I must have been really wrong about you. What a fool I've been.''

She looked up at him, suddenly wary and defensive. "What do you mean?''

"I had you figured all wrong, Ruth Holden. I thought you were one of those women who's soft on the outside and steel on the inside. I thought you'd stand beside your man when the world turned against him. I thought you'd be loyal and true-blue all the way to the end. But I guess I was wrong.''

The bitter disappointment in his voice was almost more than Ruth could bear. She wanted to scream out at him in her own defense, to tell him how she knew the truth about his shoddy affair with Jodie Hiltz and let him hear the damning evidence that the girl had produced against him.

But it was simply impossible. The thought of Tyler lying naked with that lush innocent girl while she caressed his body and shared intimate playful secrets with him . . . that thought was totally unbearable to Ruth. When she tried to frame the words, or even allowed the mental images into her mind, she was consumed with such intense waves of sexual jealousy and anguish for what she'd lost that she couldn't speak of it. She could hardly even breathe.

Tyler was watching her face, his expression calm and measuring. "Shall I tell you what I think?" he asked in a casual tone.

Ruth stood silently, hugging her arms and gazing with stubborn blankness at the soft licking flames.

"Ruth? Should I tell you why you're behaving like this?"

"Sure," she said without emotion. "Go ahead, Tyler. Tell me."

"Okay. I think you're scared."

"Really? What am I scared of?"

"Life," Tyler said. "You're scared of life, Ruth."

"I see. That's why I don't want to get involved with a man who's a lecher and a liar?"

"No, that's why you won't even consider my side of it, or try to be fair and decent about this. You're glad for an excuse to end this relationship, Ruth. It terrifies you, doesn't it, the thought of leaving home and Daddy and the same room you've slept in all your life. You don't want to share control of your life with anybody, not after thirty years of running things all by yourself, right?"

"Look, Tyler, I really don't think you—"

"Be quiet and let me finish. You don't want to take any risks with your emotions, either, and you sure don't want to get involved with a man who has his own ideas and ways of doing things and might not agree with you about every single thing. It's all just too dangerous for you, isn't it, Ruth? You came real close, but you can't go through with it after all. You're running away, back to Daddy and your cat and the nice safe life you've always known."

Ruth stared at him as he concluded this long impassioned speech, so outraged that she forgot everything else in a hot wave of fury. "So that's what you think, is it, Tyler? What you've done doesn't matter at all. The whole problem is just my fault, right, because I'm such a coward and a baby?"

"Yeah," he said calmly. "That's what I think. That's why you're so quick to believe this lying woman, and why you won't even give me a fair hearing. You almost did it for once in your life, Ruthie," he added. "You almost reached out and grabbed the brass ring. But it was just too scary, wasn't it?"

"Go away, Tyler," she said in a cool expressionless tone. "Please go away. I want to finish packing."

"Ruth," he began. The anger faded and a note of pleading crept into his voice. "Ruth, sweetheart, can't we just talk about it? Isn't there anything I can do to convince you I'm telling the truth?"

"No, there isn't," she said in that same cold dead voice. "After all, you've just made it abundantly clear how you feel, haven't you? Please just go away, Tyler. Virginia says she'll drive me into Austin to the airport tomorrow so there's no need for you to bother yourself with me again. Let me know if you decide to do the decent thing for that poor girl, because I'd really like to hear it. And best of luck with your winery."

She turned her back deliberately and went on with her packing, holding her breath and listening for his departing footsteps. Finally he left, closing the door quietly behind him. Ruth hurried across the room to draw the curtains aside and watch his tall departing figure.

Her face was still and remote, but her eyes were full of shadows and her memory rang with his bitter accusations.

Could it be that he was right?

Was the evidence against him really as overwhelming as she believed, or was it true that she was making unfair judgments just because she feared the kind of change and tumult that this relationship would cause in her orderly life?

Ruth frowned, biting her lips in a helpless agony of confusion and pain while the pent-up tears gathered in her eyes and spilled slowly down her cheeks, glistening like molten silver in the moonlight.

CHAPTER TWELVE

HAGAR CROUCHED in the back of the small van that Lettie Mae and Virginia used for errands and grocery shopping. His green eyes were slitted and miserable as he stared at the yellow pet carrier stacked neatly beside Ruth's suitcases. The big fluffy cat curled himself up as far from this bulky conveyance as he could, whiskers twitching ominously.

Ruth glanced back at him in loving concern, then turned to her companion with a bleak smile. "I don't think Hagar's all that happy about this."

Virginia looked away from her driving to glance at the young woman beside her. "I don't think anybody's happy about this, Ruth," she said quietly.

Ruth nodded and looked away at the gentle Texas countryside rolling past them.

"I'm sure not happy," Virginia went on, "and Miss C. is heartbroken to lose you, and so is J.T., and I know Lettie Mae will miss you, since you were just about her biggest fan. And old Mr. Hank's just plumb broken up about losing this cat. And as for poor Tyler..."

To Ruth's relief, Virginia fell silent without completing her statement. Ruth was already dangerously close to tears when she remembered the group she was leaving behind. All of them, even old Hank, had gathered in the ranch yard to wave sorrowful farewells as she and Virginia drove away.

All except for Tyler, who hadn't put in an appearance at all. He'd left on horseback before dawn without even saying goodbye, and his glaring absence was like a raw and painful wound in the midst of the close-knit family.

Virginia glanced cautiously at Ruth's silent profile. "I don't suppose you want to talk about it, honey?"

"No," Ruth said in a small voice. "I really don't. Thanks, Virginia. I know you're concerned, all of you, but I just can't talk about it."

"That's fine. Things happen," Virginia said philosophically. "Matter of fact," she added with the forced cheerfulness of one determined to change the subject, "something's just happened to me, you know that? I wanted to tell you about it before you leave."

"To you?" Ruth cast a quick glance at her friend, who was smiling as she gazed down the winding, tree-lined road. "You look pretty happy," she ventured. "Is it something good?"

"Oh, yes. Real good."

"You've found another man," Ruth suggested. "A nice one this time."

Virginia chuckled. "Aren't we just the living end, all us silly women? We seem to think it can never be good news unless there's a man involved somewhere."

Ruth smiled back, her heart aching. "I know what you mean. We're all crazy, aren't we?"

"Not me," Virginia said with a firm shake of her head. "Not anymore. My manhunting days are over, Ruth. I know what I want out of life, and at my age it sure isn't marriage."

Ruth hesitated, thinking this over. "I see. Well, then," she began cautiously, "what's your good news, Virginia?"

"Well, it looks like I'm maybe going to have a future after all."

"Really? What do you mean?"

"Ruth, it was the funniest thing. Just when I was at my very lowest point, almost desperate, it's like fate or God or whatever just stepped in with an answer to my prayers."

Ruth's heart began to beat a little faster but she forced herself to keep her face calm and expressionless. "Really? What happened, Virginia?"

"Well, J.T. came to me yesterday and said he had a problem. He asked if I could maybe do something to help him out. It seems his friend Vernon Trent . . . you remember Vern?"

"The heavyset man with the nice face? The one who sells real estate?"

"That's him. Apparently he's talked J.T. into buying a little house in Crystal Creek as an investment property because real estate is just fixing to go right through the roof over the next few years. So J.T. bought this house, which I've known all my life and it's just the sweetest little place, Ruth, a real vine-covered cottage . . . anyhow, he bought the house and the renters have a lease till the end of the year, but after that he doesn't know what to do with the place.''

Understanding began to dawn in Ruth's mind. She gripped her hands together in her lap, awed by J.T.'s clever enterprising spirit.

''It's real hard to find good renters around here,'' Virginia chattered on, her voice rising with a happy inflection as she told her story. ''J.T. wondered if I knew of anybody in my family who might be willing to live in the house and pay a reduced rent in exchange for taking care of the place. He wants to hold on to it for at least fifteen or twenty years, he says, because it's going to be a great tax write-off and a savings plan at the same time.''

Ruth was silent, waiting for Virginia to continue.

''So of course I told him I just might be interested myself, and you should have seen his face, Ruth. He was so surprised you could have knocked him over with a feather.''

Ruth hid a small private smile, thinking that J.T. was not only tactful, wise and generous, but obviously a pretty good actor, too. Virginia wasn't an easy woman to fool.

''But,'' Ruth ventured finally, ''if J.T.'s planning to charge rent, Virginia, how will you be able to manage it if you leave your job?''

''That's the wonderful thing, Ruth. This house has two extra bedrooms with a little sitting room attached. I can take in a couple of boarders, schoolgirls or young working women, and earn enough from that to pay the rent, with money left over to start building up my savings account again. It's just perfect.''

It really was perfect, Ruth thought, stunned with admiration for J.T. Not only would he make a profitable investment, but Virginia would be allowed to live independently and maintain her sense of pride and usefulness. Most amazing of all, he'd accomplished the whole thing in little more than a day.

Ruth contrasted the intelligent compassion of J.T.'s actions with the harsh, uncaring way that Tyler was treating Jodie Hiltz, for whose misery he bore the sole responsibility. Tyler, she thought sadly, might look like his father, but he certainly wasn't the man that J.T. McKinney was, and he never would be.

"I won't leave my job until later in the year, maybe even next spring," Virginia said happily. "They still need me at the ranch, and if I'm going to retire I'll have to train somebody else and keep coming out part-time for a while, but now I know for sure that there's something decent and pleasant waiting for me. Ruth, I'm just so happy.''

"And I'm happy for you," Ruth said, reaching over to pat Virginia's hand on the steering wheel. "I really am. You deserve this, Virginia.''

The older woman gave her a warm misty smile, then turned her attention back to her driving. "You know, I feel so blessed by all this that I want to do something in return," she told Ruth shyly. "I'm going to be real careful when I pick my boarders. If I can, I want to choose people who need help, who've gotten a rough deal out of life and could use a hand.''

This sentiment was so characteristic of Virginia's generous spirit that Ruth felt choked with emotion, unable to speak for a moment.

"Like that young girl working over in the drugstore, the one who's pregnant. Have you ever met her?" Virginia gazed down the highway, oblivious to Ruth's sudden tension. "That poor girl's pregnant, no sign of a man to take responsibility for her, no family to help out because her mama's got all she can handle already. Now, that's the kind of girl I'd like to take in, help her get back on her feet and give her a nice place to live while she has her baby."

Ruth bit her lip and gazed silently out the window while Virginia chattered on, knowing that if she said anything at all she would start crying and never be able to stop.

THEY PARKED in front of the coffee shop in Crystal Creek. Virginia cast an inquiring glance at the woman beside her. "Where should I meet you, Ruth? How much time do you need?"

"Oh...about an hour should be enough. I just have...a few errands to run," Ruth said awkwardly, climbing out of the van. "How about if I meet you back here around two-thirty, okay, Virginia? Is that too long?"

"Not a bit," Virginia said cheerfully, shifting back into gear. "I have a list as long as my arm. See you later, honey. Hagar, you cheer up," Virginia added sternly, catching sight of the glum cat as she glanced in the rearview mirror. "Looking at you, anybody'd think you were going straight to hell. You're just going to California, which is only about half as bad."

Ruth gave a wan smile and watched as Virginia pulled out of her parking spot and headed off down the street. She waited till the little van was out of sight, then turned, squared her shoulders bravely and walked along the quiet sunny avenue toward the antique glass doors of the Crystal Creek drugstore.

Ruth stepped inside the door and paused, breathing deep of the comforting scent of polished hardwood floors, soap and lemon oil, of dust and perfume and sunshine.

This small-town drugstore smelled like some wonderful vanished place from childhood. As usual, Ruth was so diverted by a flood of memories that it took a moment to recall why she'd come here.

With disconcerting abruptness Jodie Hiltz appeared from behind the rows of greeting cards, wearing a pale blue uniform smock over jeans, her wild dark hair caught back at the nape of her neck with a big blue satin bow. Ruth's already low spirits plummeted and her hands began to tremble, but she stepped forward and smiled cautiously at the girl.

When Jodie saw Ruth she stopped short and glared. Her pale face turned even whiter, and her eyes glittered like ice.

"Don't worry, Jodie," Ruth said quietly, walking toward the rack of cards. "This is the last time you're ever going to have to see me. I promise."

She moved nearer the tall girl, who stood with feet firmly planted, making a deliberate show of rearranging the rows of greeting cards and envelopes while she ignored Ruth completely.

"I'm leaving today," Ruth continued, glancing around to make sure there was no one else in the store. "I'm on my way to Austin in an hour or so to catch the evening plane. I just wanted to talk to you for a minute before I go."

"I've got nothing to say to you," Jodie muttered rudely. "Not a thing. Except that I'm glad you're leaving."

"I'm sure you are. But there's still something I want to do for you before I leave, Jodie."

"For me?" Jodie glanced suspiciously at the other woman. "Why would you want to do anything for me?"

"Because I'm concerned about you. You may seem mature and capable but you're still very young and I'm not sure if . . . if anybody's taking care of you."

"I can take care of myself," Jodie said sullenly, turning her face away.

"Maybe." Ruth was silent a moment, gazing at the girl's taut angry profile. "When did you last see a doctor, Jodie?" she asked gently.

Jodie looked up, too startled to maintain her cold indifferent pose. "Not long ago," she said evasively, riffling through the rows of envelopes. "In fact, I went to see Dr. Purdy just a couple of weeks ago. He said everything's fine and the baby's developing perfectly, and there's nothing at all to worry about."

"I don't think you did, Jodie," Ruth said in that same gentle voice.

The girl jerked her head up and stared, her eyes cold and challenging. "Yeah? So what are you saying? Are you calling me a liar?"

"I'm just saying I don't believe you've been to see Dr. Purdy. I called him this morning to ask about you, and he said you've never been to his office at all. He didn't know what doctor was treating you."

"I've been to the doctor," Jodie said, still in a sullen tone. "It's none of your damn business what doctor I go to."

"Jodie, I really don't believe that. About the doctor, I mean. I don't think you're getting any medical care at all. Dr. Purdy has the only practice in town, and I'm sure you wouldn't go all the way into the city for appointments. You don't even have a car."

Jodie glanced over her shoulder at the druggist's cubicle near the back, then leaned forward, her eyes glistening with anger and fear. "Listen, you little bitch," she whispered forcefully, "just *butt out*, okay? Go back to wherever you came from and leave me alone!"

"I will," Ruth said, forcing her voice to remain calm though she was badly shaken by the girl's furious reaction. "But not before you've seen a doctor, Jodie. If you refuse to go to Dr. Purdy, I'll bring him over here. For the baby's sake, Jodie," she added in an urgent pleading voice. "Think of the baby. It's essential that you get proper prenatal care, especially when you're so young."

"Why the hell should *you* care?" Jodie repeated with youthful belligerence.

I care because it's Tyler's baby, Ruth thought silently, her soul twisting in anguish. *Because it might have Tyler's eyes and smile, and his wonderful brilliant mind and funny sense of humor, and I can't bear to think of...*

"Huh?" Jodie said. She smiled boldly and thrust her hard swollen abdomen deliberately toward Ruth. "Why should it matter to you so much?"

"Just out of basic human decency." Ruth paused, struggling to control her tumult of emotion. "Somebody's got to take some responsibility for you and this baby. And if... if nobody else will, then I'm going to. Whether you hate me for it or not, Jodie, I'm going to see that you get some medical care," Ruth concluded firmly, a little surprised by her own courage in the face of the girl's hostility.

Jodie's white face and burning eyes indicated that she did indeed resent this unwelcome interference. She gazed into the older woman's eyes, weighing the strength of Ruth's determination, and obviously decided to take another line of defense.

"Tomorrow, okay?" she said, wetting her lips with her tongue and looking, suddenly, much more like a frightened child. "I'll make an appointment and go tomorrow."

"Today," Ruth said firmly. "I want to go with you and hear what the doctor says. There might be something you need, like vitamins or special treatments or something, and I'm prepared to help you. I just need to know that you're in good hands before I leave."

Jodie stared at Ruth's clear brown eyes, her expression gradually fading from belligerence to a kind of bewilderment. "You really do, don't you?" she asked slowly. "You don't hate me. You're just worried about me."

"Of course I don't hate you. You're not the one to blame in this situation. That responsibility lies somewhere else, Jodie. I honestly can't bear to go back home without knowing that you're going to be all right, and that you'll be taken care of properly."

Jodie's pale eyes flickered. She bit her lips again and glanced around at her employer's cubicle, then turned back to the woman standing in front of her. "But I can't... I can't go now," she said helplessly. "I have to work."

"That's all right," Ruth said in a steady voice. "I called Mr. Wall earlier today and asked if I could take you out for a few minutes this afternoon. He said it was fine with him."

Jodie shifted on her feet and threw her employer another panicky little glance. He smiled from behind the glass and nodded amiably, giving her a casual wave of his hand.

"See?" Ruth said, forcing a smile. "It's fine with everybody. Come on now, Jodie. Dr. Purdy's waiting for you."

She took the girl's arm and began walking with her toward the front door, then gasped in shock and alarm as Jodie clutched her abdomen, gave a ragged moan and crumpled onto the worn hardwood floor in a dead faint.

RUTH SAT TENSELY in a deserted staff lounge at the hospital, trying not to reveal her fear as she fingered an old magazine in her lap and stared fixedly toward the door.

At last, after an eternity of anxious waiting, the doctor appeared in the doorway. Nate Purdy looked as crisp and handsome as always with his silver hair and clipped mustache, though Ruth noticed that he looked tired today.

"Hello, Ruth," he said, sitting heavily across from her and reaching for the coffeepot brewing on a low table nearby. "Sorry to keep you waiting so long. Care for a cup of poison?"

"No thanks," she said automatically. "I've had about a dozen already."

"Oh, my. Probably not a wise thing to do," the doctor said, shaking his head as he lifted his plastic foam cup and sipped the potent black mixture.

Ruth could wait no longer. "Dr. Purdy...how is she? Why did she faint like that?"

"A number of reasons. For one thing, she's mildly anemic. Apparently she had this idea that when you're pregnant you should drink lots of milk, but she didn't want to get fat so she hasn't been eating much of anything else. And there's no iron in milk, Ruth. She's also been under a lot of stress. And," the doctor added with a grim smile that puzzled Ruth, "she doesn't seem to get much sleep at night. It's a wonder she hasn't toppled over before now."

"And the baby?" Ruth asked, her throat tight with fear.

The doctor set down his cup on the low table and fixed Ruth with penetrating steel-gray eyes. He hesitated a long time but his voice was gentle when he spoke. "There's no baby, Ruth."

Ruth's eyes widened in horror. She covered her mouth with a trembling hand, feeling a flood of grief and loss that was almost unbearable.

Tyler's baby...

"Oh, *no,*" she whispered. "You mean she's had... she's had a miscarriage?"

"No, Ruth," Nate Purdy said in that same strangely gentle tone. "I mean that the girl is not pregnant. And," he added, grimacing as he took another sip of the bitter coffee, "she never was."

"She never *was!*" Ruth stared at the doctor's face, struggling to comprehend what he was saying. "You mean she...she made it all up? Dr. Purdy, how can that be true? Her stomach is... she's all swollen...."

"She didn't make it up. In her mind, she really was pregnant. She certainly had all the symptoms."

Ruth shook her head. "I don't understand."

"It's a relatively common medical phenomenon, Ruth. It's called hysterical pregnancy. Through an intensity of desire, the patient literally wills the condition into existence by the force of her subconscious mind. Everything, of course, except for the actual fetus," Dr. Purdy added dryly.

"I've heard of the condition," Ruth said in halting confusion. "I'm sure everyone has. But I always thought...I mean, she's so young that you wouldn't expect her to... And besides, she really *looks* pregnant. Doesn't she?"

"She certainly does. As I said, she's had all the symptoms. Morning sickness, swollen breasts, missed periods, abdominal swelling...she's even begun to feel the baby's movements, right on schedule."

"But you're absolutely positive there's no baby? You couldn't have made a mistake?"

"No, Ruth," the doctor said gently. "I couldn't make that kind of mistake."

"But how could she have all those symptoms? How would she even know what's supposed to happen, and in what sequence?"

"She's the oldest of eight children, Ruth. She's been a close observer of lots of pregnancies. It's not surprising that she knows what happens, and when."

"It all sounds so...so bizarre."

"Oh, it's bizarre, all right. But it's not as uncommon as you might suppose. If the condition isn't detected, these women often carry their 'babies' for the full nine months and then go into actual labor, right on time. There are cases," he added with a brief smile, "when so-called births are passed off to family and friends as stillbirths, when in actual fact there was never a baby at all."

Ruth stared at the doctor, so fascinated that she forgot her misery for a moment. "What makes the swelling, if there's no baby?"

"Well, now, that's another mystery. It seems to be a combination of fatty tissue and fluid retention, but it's certainly an impressive facsimile of a real pregnancy. The mind is such an amazing thing, Ruth. It has powers to affect the body that we're only beginning to be aware of.''

"What will happen to her now?" Ruth whispered. "Does she know that there's not . . . not a baby?"

"Yes, I think she does. We talked about it, and she was pretty upset, even accused me of stealing her baby while she was under anesthetic, but I think she's gradually starting to accept the truth.''

"So what happens to her now?" Ruth repeated.

"Physically or emotionally?"

"Both.''

"Well, her mind will send a message to her body that there's no pregnancy. Almost immediately after that she'll have a menstrual period that's quite heavy and painful, much like a miscarriage. Her abdomen will shrink down to normal size within a couple of weeks, and more than likely she'll return to an absolutely normal physical cycle.''

"The poor girl," Ruth breathed. "How dreadful she must feel.''

The doctor sipped his coffee and watched Ruth's face in silence while she struggled with her emotions.

"But why?" she whispered finally, staring at the kindly man sitting opposite. "Why would she invent such a thing, Dr. Purdy? Is it because Tyler refused to acknowledge her otherwise?''

"Acknowledge her? What do you mean?"

Ruth writhed inwardly, hating to speak of something so abhorrent. But this man was the McKinneys' family doctor, had been for decades. Besides, he was bound to learn the shoddy truth before this whole affair was over.

"They've had a...a sexual relationship. She and Tyler. I know it's appalling, but it really happened. And now he refuses to...take any responsibility for it. I wondered if the pain of that experience might trigger..." Ruth fell silent, unable to continue.

"Well, now, that's entirely another matter. Her relationship with Tyler, I mean."

Nate Purdy settled back in his chair and regarded Ruth steadily, his gray eyes thoughtful. "I've talked to her pretty extensively, but now I'd like to hear from you, Ruth. I gather you and Tyler have suffered considerable pain over this business."

"Yes," Ruth said quietly, meeting his gaze without expression. "Yes, I'm afraid we have."

The doctor cleared his throat tactfully and gave Ruth another questioning glance. "Before all this happened, you and Tyler were..."

"We were very close," Ruth said tonelessly. "I even had myself fooled into imagining that I was in love with him."

"J.T. told me he had a real good feeling about the whole thing," Dr. Purdy said. "He thought you two were just right for each other."

"I thought so, too," Ruth said bitterly, her face twisting with pain. "I really did."

"I see." The doctor took a pen from the pocket of his lab coat and examined it thoughtfully, flicking the point up and down with his thumb. "Now, Ruth, do you recall what this girl told you that made you so certain she was telling the truth?''

"What do you mean?''

"I mean, whatever she said to implicate Tyler so completely that you'd accept her version of things without question.''

"Yes,'' Ruth said quietly. "I remember. I really don't care to discuss it.''

"I see,'' Dr. Purdy repeated, still gazing intently at the slim silver pen. "Ruth, I'm going to tell you something now that's probably confidential doctor-patient information, but in this circumstance I feel you have the right to know.''

Ruth tensed, looking at his sober face.

"Ruth, Jodie Hiltz is a virgin. She's never had sexual intercourse.''

Ruth stared, her mind reeling once again. "You don't mean . . . But, Dr. Purdy, she told me—''

"I think I have a pretty fair idea what she told you, Ruth. She told me some of the same things at first. After we talked a bit, I think she began to realize that none of them are true.''

"But she knows things about . . . about Tyler. . . .'' Ruth's face flamed and she felt her neck growing warm and prickly with heat.

"Anything she knows about Tyler,'' Nate said in that same gentle compassionate tone, "she learned from spying on him, Ruth. Looking through windows in the dark of night.''

That crazy woman from town. Hank's voice echoed inside Ruth's mind. *I see her slippin' around when she thinks I'm not watchin', but none of 'em will ever believe me....*

The hot color drained from Ruth's face as abruptly as it had come. Her memory flared with a sudden blinding image of herself and Tyler lying naked in bed, caressing each other in the glowing firelight, teasing and playing like children, while all the time...

"Are you angry, Ruth?" Nate asked, watching her changing expression with shrewd, thoughtful eyes.

Ruth shook her head slowly. "I suppose I should be, shouldn't I? If what you say is true, it's such a terrible, repulsive thing for her to have done. But I still can't help feeling sorry for her. I just can't imagine what would drive a person to do something like that."

"Actually, it's also a recognized medical condition. It's called erotomania, but nowadays we tend to refer to these people as stalkers."

"You mean like the people who follow movie stars around, sending them love letters and breaking into their houses?"

"Exactly. But it doesn't just happen to movie stars. It happens to everyday, ordinary people like Tyler McKinney, too. When it does it can be a pretty terrible thing, because it's so hard to protect against."

"But...why Tyler? Why not someone closer to her own age, or more...more glamorous?"

Nate pocketed his pen, sighing as he passed a weary hand over his hair. "Two new babies last night," he told Ruth with a brief smile of apology. "This time of year we pay the price for all those balmy romantic spring evenings we had nine months ago."

Ruth smiled automatically, waiting for him to continue.

"The stalking mentality," Nate said, lifting his cup and setting it down with another grimace, "seems to afflict people who have low self-esteem, difficulty relating to the opposite sex and poor prospects generally. They fixate on somebody who's not only attractive to them, but who has prestige in the community and can give them an entré into the world they crave to enter. And they're absolutely relentless. They're also incredibly creative in their methods. You wouldn't believe some of the lengths this girl has gone to in order to maintain her pursuit of Tyler McKinney."

Ruth shivered. "Will she . . . will she get over it, Dr. Purdy? Or will she be following him around for years like some of them do?"

"I don't know. You're right, though. Sometimes this kind of thing carries on for a long time and it's very hard to control, because simply watching somebody isn't against the law. But I'm optimistic that this girl might be a different case."

"Why?"

"Because she's already acknowledged her fantasy. They don't usually do that so easily when they're discovered. I think she's been caught and exposed early enough, and made to feel sufficiently embarrassed that she might be brought back in touch with reality quite easily. Especially if . . ."

Nate hesitated, listening as he was paged from the hospital intercom. He excused himself to answer the telephone in one corner of the lounge.

Ruth waited stiffly in her chair, so torn by conflicting emotions that she could hardly maintain a coherent train of thought. She felt a bewildering mixture of anguish, relief, sorrow, concern and misery. But her overwhelming emotion was shame.

Tyler had been right when he expressed such disappointment in Ruth and accused her of being a coward. Now that she knew the truth and understood that Tyler was an innocent man who'd been falsely accused, Ruth despised herself for being so hasty and unfair in her judgment. She should have stood by him, denied the girl's charges and been loyal to her own instincts.

But she'd been so upset, and so terribly hurt by those dreadful accusations. Tyler was right about her fear of change and commitment, but he couldn't know how sickeningly her world had spun to a halt the moment Jodie Hiltz whispered those terrible incriminating things about the man Ruth loved.

The doctor hung up the phone, paused to exchange a few words with a nurse passing in the hallway, then came back toward Ruth, speaking gently. "Look, Ruth, I don't think—"

"Doc Purdy! Where is she?"

Ruth stiffened at the familiar voice and looked around. Tyler stood in the entry to the lounge, pale and bareheaded in his work clothes. His hair was wildly disarranged and his eyes dark with fear.

"She's right here, Tyler," Nate said mildly, waving a hand toward Ruth. "If you'd given me half a chance when they called up from the desk, I could have told you she was all right."

"Ruth!" Tyler approached her, scanning her face hungrily. "You're really all right?"

"Of course," Ruth said, startled by his intensity. "Why wouldn't I be?"

"Oh, God," he muttered, sinking into the chair opposite hers and passing a shaking hand over his face and hair. "I was so scared. I must have driven into town about a hundred miles an hour."

"But why?" Ruth asked in bewilderment.

"Virginia came back to the ranch and said you were supposed to meet her at the coffee shop but you never showed up. She didn't know where you were. Then Doc Purdy called and said I should come to the hospital right away, and I thought—"

"Sorry, Tyler," Nate said quietly. "I probably should have given a few more details over the phone, but I thought you might want a chance to deal with this privately at first."

Tyler raised his head and cast the other man a quick questioning glance. "Deal with what?"

"Well, son, it's kind of a long sad story. You see..."

Tyler listened, tense and silent, while the doctor began to recount the details of Jodie Hiltz's fantasies, her stalking behavior and her false pregnancy. Tyler cast an appalled glance at Ruth when the doctor repeated his theories about Jodie's spying, and how she'd gained the kind of intimate information that Ruth had found so damning.

"Ruth?" Tyler said urgently. "Ruth, is that true? Is that really what she said to you?"

Ruth nodded but remained miserably silent. She twisted her hands together in her lap, unable to look at the angry young man opposite her.

"And she was watching us through the window the whole time?"

"Yes," the doctor said gently. "I believe she was."

Tyler swore angrily under his breath, still looking with concern at Ruth while Nate went on to describe Jodie's imaginary picnics in the little cabin, her long nighttime bicycle rides and bone-chilling hours of crouching outside lighted windows in the midnight cold.

"Well, I'll be damned," Tyler muttered when Nate finished speaking. "I thought those things only happened in the movies."

"I'm afraid not."

"I tried to talk to her a couple of times. After she...after she caused so much trouble and Ruth was planning to leave because of her, I thought I'd go crazy if I couldn't get that girl to admit she was lying. But she just kept avoiding me. Once she locked herself in the washroom at the Longhorn and wouldn't come out, and yesterday I went right to her house, just about pounded the door in but she wouldn't answer."

"That's consistent with the general pattern. Most stalkers don't really want a confrontation with the object of their quest, because that might destroy the fantasy.''

"But she sought us out," Ruth said in confusion. "Several times, especially the other night at the benefit dance."

"I know. That's one of the things that makes me optimistic. Tyler, want some coffee?"

Tyler grinned faintly. "I've tasted that coffee before, Doc."

"Oh. Well then, probably not. I feel optimistic," the doctor repeated, "simply because she did choose to seek you out. Psychologists would likely interpret that as a cry for help. They'd say she wanted you to reject her and set her free from this fantasy, even though she wouldn't recognize that as her motivation."

"Oh, I'll set her free, all right," Tyler said grimly, his jaw knotted with tension. "Just give me a half hour alone with her."

"Now, that's not going to do any good, son," Nate said gently. "I know you're angry and you have every right to be. But this kind of behavior is motivated by pain and deprivation, and we should feel pity when we see it. The girl is lonely and left out of things, and hopeless about her whole life. She needs your help, not your abuse."

"How can we help?" Ruth asked quietly.

"I was getting to that. Tyler, do you think you could stand to talk with her a bit?"

"Why?"

"Well, because I was telling Ruth that I think Jodie is ready to face reality. I believe a confrontation with you, right now when she's real vulnerable, might go a long way toward clearing out the fantasies and jolting her back into reality. But," the doctor added warningly, "you'd have to be gentle with her. I can't have you shouting and browbeating the poor girl. She's too fragile for that."

Tyler was silent, fixing the doctor with dark unfathomable eyes. "Sure, Doc," he said quietly. "I'll talk to her."

"Tyler . . ."

"It's all right," Ruth said, glancing at the doctor as she got briskly to her feet. "I think Tyler will be fair with her, Dr. Purdy. He's one of the fairest people I've ever met."

Tyler looked at her in surprise but said nothing, while the doctor nodded thoughtfully.

"May I go with him?" Ruth asked. "I feel that I'm involved, too. At least indirectly."

"I agree. Go ahead, and remember that although she needs to be confronted, it should be done gently."

"We'll remember," Ruth promised. She turned and walked out of the lounge beside the doctor. Tyler followed, a grim look on his face.

The three of them paused outside a broad door of polished oak, and Nate looked at them gravely. "Just a few minutes," he murmured. "Be real careful with her, all right?"

Ruth nodded and walked into the hospital room, painfully conscious of Tyler's tall body close behind her.

Jodie Hiltz lay in the narrow bed, her face against the pillows looking young and vulnerable, her pale blue eyes swimming in tears.

Ruth looked at the girl and was startled by the depth of pity she felt for this troubled child. She glanced anxiously at Tyler, dreading his reaction.

But his anger seemed to have vanished, and his face was calm. He approached the bed quietly while Jodie cowered against the pillows and stared up at him with frightened eyes, gripping the covers tight beneath her chin.

"Hello, Jodie," he said in a gentle voice. "Feeling better now?"

"A...a little," she whispered, turning her face away. Her body was limp with humiliation beneath the covers, an embarrassment and shame so obvious that it seemed to fill the whole room with a cold flood of misery.

"I guess you've been pretty unhappy lately," Tyler went on, seating himself casually in one of the vinyl chairs next to the bed and motioning for Ruth to do the same.

Ruth sank into the chair he indicated, hardly daring to breathe, her eyes riveted on his face as he spoke to the girl in the bed.

"I...I guess I have."

"And you've made us pretty unhappy, too," Tyler went on calmly, "with some of the things you said. But they weren't true, were they, Jodie?"

"I...I guess they weren't," the girl whispered in agony. "I guess I was just imagining things. But," she added, looking at Tyler in sudden desperate appeal, "it *seemed* so real. Like it was all really happening. Does that mean I'm crazy?"

"I don't think so." He was silent a moment, looking thoughtfully at the anguished young face on the pillows. "You know what, Jodie?" he said finally.

"What?"

"The same thing happened to me once. You know that? But I wasn't near as young as you are. I was a grown-up man, almost thirty years old."

The girl forgot her discomfort and stared at him in surprise, her eyes widening.

"It was when my mother died," Tyler went on in the same gentle tone. "I knew she was dead. I even went to her funeral and watched them put her in the ground. Then one day a few weeks later I saw a blond woman who looked just like my mother, crossing the street in Dallas. I ran after her but she was gone before I could catch up with her. And you know what I did then?"

The girl shook her head breathlessly, eyes fixed on his face.

"I went home and convinced myself that my mama wasn't dead after all, that she'd just gone away for a holiday without telling anybody and she'd be coming back any day. I really believed it, Jodie. It was one of the realest things that ever happened to me. Every day I'd get up and go downstairs expecting to see her there, laughing and talking with my daddy just like always, home from her little holiday.''

Ruth listened, clenching her hands so tightly in her lap that the nails bit painfully into her palms. Her heart swelled with love for the man beside her, a love so intense and all-consuming that she felt she might die from the rich pulsing strength and sweetness of it.

"What happened?" Jodie asked in a low tense voice.

"Well, one day I just took myself in hand. I guess I knew all the time on some level that it was a just a fantasy, and I knew something had to be done about it or I was going to get real sick. So I made myself learn not to believe it."

Jodie licked her lips and stared at him. "How...how did you do that?" she whispered.

"I started saying the truth out loud. Every morning when I woke up, and every night before I went to bed, I made myself say these words out loud, because there's a lot of power in the spoken word. I said, 'My mama's dead, and she'll never, ever be coming back.'''

Ruth watched his profile as he spoke, aching with love and sympathy. She longed to reach out and take his hand in hers, but forced herself not to touch him.

"And it was just about the hardest thing I ever did," Tyler concluded. "Saying those words out loud and destroying the illusion that had comforted me... Jodie, it was pure hell. But every day it got a little bit easier to say, and then the truth got easier to live with."

Jodie looked from his face to Ruth's. The tears began to flow down her cheeks again. "I've been a real fool, haven't I?" she whispered. "I've been just awful."

"That's all in the past," Ruth said quietly. "We're going to forget all about it, Jodie. But I think Tyler's right. I think for your own sake you should try to say the truth out loud, as soon as we leave."

"No," Jodie said, surprising both of them. "It's better if I do it while you're here." She paused, swallowing hard, then raised her chin to look directly at Tyler. "I made it all up," she said in a small shaking voice. "I never had dates with you or did anything with you. I was... I was never pregnant...."

Her voice broke and she began to sob. Ruth got up and put her arms around the girl, holding her tenderly until the storm of weeping subsided. Jodie mopped her face with a tissue, hiccuped a few times and sipped gratefully at the water Ruth held up for her.

"What will you do now, Jodie?" Tyler asked quietly. "Where will you go?"

"The doctor was just talking about that with me. I don't want to go back home," Jodie said, "but like I told Dr. Purdy, I was thinking that maybe I could go to live with my aunt in Oklahoma. She said once that I could live with them and finish my high school, and they'd give me free room and board in exchange for helping with her kids."

"Do you like your aunt?" Ruth asked.

"Yeah," Jodie said shyly. "She's really neat. She's just like a kid herself, and her husband's nice, too. They both teach school."

"And after you get your diploma?" Ruth asked. "What then?"

"I'd like to look after... look after babies," Jodie said, flushing with embarrassment. "I'd like to get some training so I can work in a hospital or something, helping with the babies."

"That sounds like a wonderful plan, Jodie. And if there's anything I can to do to help..." Ruth hesitated, conscious of Tyler, who was standing beside her with his hand on her arm.

"Both of us, Jodie," he said. "We'll help all we can. Just let us know if you need anything."

The kindness of his tone threatened to elicit another flood of tears. Still, Ruth thought, Jodie looked better already, more composed and less tormented than when they'd entered the room.

The girl summoned an awkward little smile and nodded at them, her eyelids drooping with fatigue.

For a moment Tyler and Ruth stood side by side, gazing silently down at the sleepy childlike face of the young woman who had caused them both such agony.

"Come on, Ruth," Tyler murmured at last. "I'll take you home now."

CHAPTER THIRTEEN

RUTH SAT in the passenger seat of the ranch pickup, biting her lip as she gazed out the window at the afternoon countryside. While she'd been inside the hospital the changeable winter weather had obviously shifted once again. A bank of dark billowing clouds rolled slowly across the sun and the wind freshened, carrying a somber hint of frost.

Beside her Tyler drove silently, his face remote, his handsome profile sharply etched against the hammered silver of the brooding sky. Ruth stole a glance at him, aching with pain, searching for words to express the turmoil of her feelings.

"Tyler..." she began.

"Yeah?" He squinted at a raccoon hurrying across the road and veered slightly to avoid hitting it.

"Tyler, I'm so terribly sorry. I'm so ashamed of myself I can hardly stand it."

"Why?"

Ruth waved her hands helplessly, unable to look at him. "Because you were right. I was a coward. I was so ready to believe those awful things about you, all those lies, and all the time you were..." Ruth choked and fell silent.

"I feel different about it," Tyler said calmly. "Now that I've heard the whole story, I'm not upset with you at all anymore. I think anybody would have believed that girl because, you see, she was actually telling the truth."

Ruth looked at him in confusion, glancing away quickly when his dark eyes met hers.

"In her mind," Tyler went on, "she really believed what she was saying, so her words had the power of truth behind them. She wasn't lying to you at all. She was telling you the truth as she perceived it. No wonder you believed her."

Ruth was silent, thinking about his words, astonished once more by the depth of his understanding.

"I guess you missed your plane," he ventured after a long awkward silence, trying to smile at her. "Sorry about that, Ruth."

"I guess I did. Is Hagar all right?"

"He sure is. When Virginia couldn't find you in town, she brought him back home and he and Grandpa had a real old reunion. Last I saw they were out on the veranda sharing a tin of salmon."

Ruth smiled automatically, then sobered and gazed blindly out the window again, still aching with a sense of loss. She watched in surprise as Tyler pulled off the main road and bumped down a rocky trail, over a barred cattle gate and into a field covered in mesquite and prickly pear.

"Just a little side trip," he told her briefly in response to her questioning glance. "I'll get you back home pretty soon, Ruth. Actually," he went on in a casual conversational tone, "I blame myself for all this mess."

"Why? You didn't do anything wrong, Tyler."

"Sure I did." He parked at the base of a hill and turned to look at Ruth soberly, resting his arm along the back of the truck seat but not touching her. "I was pushy and bullheaded, Ruth, just like I always am, and I drove you away. I have to learn to pull back a bit, listen to the other side of the story and not go forcing my own way all the time. It's a damned hard lesson," he added with a rueful smile that made her heart ache.

"Oh, Tyler," she said, choking back a sob.

He opened his door and stepped out, then strode around to help Ruth from the truck. "Come for a walk with me, okay?" he said. "Are you warm enough?"

Ruth pulled her jacket tighter around her and nodded. "I'm fine. The fresh air feels good."

He put an arm around her and drew her up along a steep rocky path that was suddenly familiar. Ruth recognized the rustling grove of live-oak trees with their perennial dusting of green leaves that survived the harshest winter chill. High on the brow of the cliff was the tumbledown little cabin, wild and isolated against the dark brooding sky.

Ruth shuddered when she looked at the cabin, then glanced cautiously at the man beside her.

He stood gazing up at the little structure with a calm measuring eye. "I think that thing should be torn down, Ruthie. This is where our vineyard's going to be planted, and that would be a great spot for a new house, don't you think?''

Ruth stared at him in stunned amazement.

"Is that okay with you? Could you live up there?''

"Tyler, are you saying...do you really still want me after everything I did? All those awful things I said?''

"*Want* you? Ruth, I'm dying for you. These past few days without you have been the loneliest of my whole life. When I thought you were going away I didn't even know how I was going to keep on living. You're the other half of me, sweetheart. I need you more than anything.''

"Oh, Tyler.'' Ruth burrowed into his arms, wrapped around with his warmth and strength, her heart soaring with happiness. "I love you,'' she murmured haltingly against his chest. "I love you so much.''

"Finally she says it,'' Tyler commented with a teasing grin, bending to give her a long tender kiss. "What a woman. Look what it takes just to get her to say she loves me.''

"I'll say it every single day for the rest of my life,'' Ruth told him, looking solemnly into his laughing eyes.

He smiled and kissed her again, holding her close in his arms on the windy hillside. "Ruth,'' he whispered against her face.

"Yes, dear?''

"Ruth, I said I wasn't going to push for my own way anymore, but there's something I have to ask you.''

She leaned back to look up at him, concerned by the sudden seriousness of his tone. "What is it, Tyler?"

He bent to nuzzle her cheek again, then rested his chin thoughtfully on top of her head, gazing out at the hillside where his vines would soon be growing. "Ruth, through all this horrible time, you know what kept going through my mind?"

Ruth shifted nervously in his arms and shook her head, dreading what he might be about to say, but again he surprised her.

"I kept thinking about a baby," Tyler said.

"A *baby?*"

"Yeah. I knew I never touched that girl and she couldn't be carrying my child. But even when I was so miserable, I couldn't stop thinking about how happy I'd feel if *you* were pregnant with my baby. Ruthie... I want it so bad. A family, I mean. I don't think I can stand to wait very long."

Ruth laughed softly in his arms, overcome with love and a flood of happiness so rich and warm that she could barely speak.

"Ruth? I said I wouldn't be pushy anymore, especially not in something like this. But do you think we could build a winery and have a couple of babies at the same time?"

She looked up at him, smiling through her tears. "I'm pretty certain that we'll soon be producing some very good vintages, Tyler," she whispered. "All kinds of them."

He laughed and hugged her joyously while the wind whipped at their hair and clothes and howled across

the rocky sweep of pasture. Around them the fields lay
sere and barren in the winter chill, but to the man and
woman on the hillside they glowed richly with the
promise of a fruitful life, warm years of sunshine and
bright flowing wine, and a love that would last forever.

If you enjoyed
COWBOYS AND CABERNET

don't miss

AMARILLO BY MORNING
by Bethany Campbell

the third installment of the
Crystal Creek series
coming to you in April

Cal McKinney is a true western cavalier—free, easy
and used to having his way—especially with women.
But bootmaker Serena Davis is different—haunting
and elusive—and terrified of revealing the burden she
has carried all her life. The kind of love the two of
them come to share demands courage and gal-
lantry...and will prove to be the greatest gamble two
people can ever take.

Watch for it next month, wherever Harlequin books
are sold.